No Way, Rosé

POUR DECISIONS

Book 1

Kate Davies

About this title...

Could this be a second chance worth savoring?

Rosa

Don't get me wrong - I'm thrilled that Nonna left her winery to my sisters and me, but I'm terrified, too. With Allegra and Bianca both out of the country, the responsibility falls totally on me - and what if I'm not up to the challenge? Now my ex, Jake Wright, is offering to help out, but that's terrifying in a different way. Working side by side is bringing all those old feelings back to the surface, and I'm falling for him all over again. But does our partnership have a future, or is heartbreak on the horizon?

Jake

I've been away from our hometown for ten long years. Now I'm back, and working with Rosa is both the best and worst thing that's ever happened to me. We're saving her family winery one day at a time - and giving in to the heat between us one night at a time, too. But I'm afraid this pairing has an expiration date...

This book is dedicated to PG Forte and Kelly Jamieson. Thanks so much for inviting me to be part of Oak Creek Canyon with you, for keeping the interest alive over the many years we talked about doing this, and then doing the thing! I had a fabulous time playing in the same sandbox with you. Hope we get to do it again sometime.

Link to Playlist

https://tinyurl.com/NoWayRosePlaylist

Prologue

Rosa

I'm pretty sure that the uncomfortable, too-tall, squeaky leather chairs in Mr. Davenport's office are a deliberate choice.

Don't stick around, don't get too comfortable, let's get this over with and shove all of you out the door as quickly as possible.

I glance down at my iPad, Bianca's face filling the screen. We're still waiting for Allegra to accept the call. Bee is frowning and tapping at her phone. "Are you sure you sent Legs the link?"

"Yes, of course I did," I tell her, surreptitiously checking the invite on my phone to verify. "I just have no idea what time it is over there. Could be middle of the night."

"Nah, closer to eight or nine pm," Bianca says. "Barely dinner time."

I wouldn't know. I've never been out of the Pacific time zone, unlike my globetrotting sisters.

And it's closer to lunch time here at the moment.

Bianca grins as the video chat program pings and the screen splits in two, Allegra joining our three-way call.

"Hey, Bee!" Allegra says, her voice tinny through the iPad's speaker. "And Rosey Posey. Sorry I couldn't make it back. How are you holding up, Rosey?"

"I'm fine," I lie. Across the room, Uncle Geno crosses his arms and frowns. "I'm sorry you two couldn't be here, either."

Bianca has an excuse —she's working on a vineyard in Argentina, and it's almost harvest season there. Allegra, well. She's Allegra.

Allegra shrugs a shoulder. "You know how it is. I'll try to be there for the memorial."

Try. Yeah, Allegra can be trying, in all definitions of the word. I love my sister, but sometimes...

"You've got time," I say, biting my tongue on the lecture that threatens. God knows I don't want to hear Uncle Geno's words come out of my mouth. Ugh. "Yeah, we won't hold it until after harvest season at least. But you really should be here for it, Allegra, after everything Nonna did for us. Pay our respects."

Allegra nods, her face shadowed by the city lights behind her head. "I'll see what I can do."

Uncle Geno coughs, pulling my attention back across the room. He's not happy.

Who am I kidding? He's never happy. The man takes all his emotional cues from Oscar the Grouch.

I shift in my seat, feeling unkind. His mother just died. I should probably cut him a little slack today of all days.

On the other hand, it's not like Bianca, Allegra, and I aren't mourning, too. Nonna raised us herself, after Daddy died and Mama ran off to Italy with Sergio. We owe her so much.

We owe her everything.

Aunt Janet sets down her knitting long enough to place a hand on Uncle Geno's knee. He settles back for a minute.

She's never been one to say much, but a well-placed gesture seems to work for her, at least most of the time.

"Where are you this week, Legs?" Bianca squints, probably looking for locational clues somewhere in the background. "Greece?"

Allegra shakes her head, curls dancing. "Gibraltar." She waves a hand behind her at the gorgeous old buildings. "I might actually get some time to look around before I move on."

"That's so cool," Bianca says, and I can't help it—I frown. Travel-itinerary discussion is not appropriate at a will reading. Especially since Mr. Davenport is just now walking into the room.

Bianca winces apologetically and shushes Allegra with a finger to her lips.

Then I hold up the iPad as Nonna's lawyer takes his seat at the wide, official-looking desk at the front of the room. "Excuse me," I say, pointing at the screen. "I know this is a little unorthodox..."

"But so are we," Allegra adds with a light laugh.

I slant a narrow-eyed glare at the tablet.

"Sorry, sir," I tell Mr. Davenport, deliberately avoiding looking at the other side of the room. I can hear Uncle Geno and our cousins shifting in their seats, giving off waves of irritation, and that's bad enough.

Not Aunt Janet, though. Even without a glance, I know she's sitting quietly, waiting for everyone else to simmer down.

I look up at the lawyer. "You know my sisters, Bianca and Allegra..."

"Quite well," he answers.

Allegra waves. "Hi, Jimmy!"

3

Cousin Gianni snorts, then coughs in a lame attempt to cover his laughter.

I close my eyes briefly. I am patient. I am calm. I am fucking *zen*. "As I was saying, *Mr. Davenport*," I enunciate for Allegra's benefit. And Bianca's, too. The pair of them will be the death of me. "Allegra and Bianca are out of the country but want to participate in the reading as well."

"That's fine," he says, taking his glasses out of their case and putting them on. "As long as you don't disrupt the proceedings," he adds, leaning toward the screen and raising one eyebrow.

We've known James Davenport almost our entire lives—he's been the family lawyer for as long as anyone can remember. And he knows *us*. Sometimes to my embarrassment.

"Yes, sir," Bianca says.

"It'll be just like I'm there in the room," Allegra says.

"That's what I'm afraid of," he says drolly. "Just—be appropriate, please."

Allegra smiles and nods. "Yes, sir." She mimes zipping her lips.

"Thank you." Mr. Davenport looks around the room. "Is anyone else joining us virtually? Your mother, perhaps?"

I shake my head, feeling heat rise in my cheeks. "No, sir."

The waves of Uncle Geno's disapproval from across the room are almost a physical presence.

Well, sorry, Uncle G. It's not like I'm any happier with her decision to miss this. But that's on Mama, not the three of us. No matter how much it feels like we're being held accountable for her choices.

"Thank you all for being here," Mr. Davenport starts, laying a hand on the stack of papers on the desk in front of him. "I know this is a sad and difficult time for the whole family."

He takes off his glasses and rubs his eyes briefly. Sometimes I forget he was Nonna's friend, too.

Clearing his throat, he taps the papers again. "Your mother," he nods at Uncle Geno—"mother-in-law, and grandmother"—he glances around the rest of the room, his gaze encompassing me, Bianca and Allegra via the iPad, Aunt Janet, and our three cousins—"was a remarkable woman. She will be greatly missed. She also lived a full life, loved her family, and had very specific thoughts about her will and what would happen after she passed. Her greatest desire was that you remain a family, supporting each other, regardless of what's in these papers."

I nod. Of course we will. Family is the core of everything, Nonna used to say.

God, I'm going to miss her.

Mr. Davenport starts reading the documents in front of him, and as he goes over details about safe-deposit boxes, life insurance, and bank accounts, my mind starts to wander. I'm not even sure why our generation has been included in this discussion. It's not like any of it will affect us directly.

Uncle Geno has been running the family business since Papa passed away. Much to Nonna's disappointment, Mama was never interested in winemaking, so she was more than happy to leave Belmonte to her brother once she left the country (and her daughters) behind. Our generation? Well, except for Allegra, most of us work for Uncle Geno in some capacity, or will eventually, but it's going to be decades before we actually take the reins.

No, none of that "we" bullshit. Geno and Janet's sons will take the reins. Bianca? Me? Our cousins will probably figure out a spot for us somewhere, but nothing with any authority. And Allegra? By the time she gets that wanderlust out of her system and returns from traveling the world—if she ever does—

I doubt Uncle Geno will trust her with the keys to the winery's second-oldest truck, let alone anything to do with the business. And it's not like Janet was ever given any position of power or influence.

"In regard to Belmonte Winery," Mr. Davenport continues.

My head snaps up, proving to everyone that I wasn't actually paying attention until now. Onscreen, Bianca presses her lips together, probably trying to keep from snickering—the traitor.

"Geno, you have been a faithful steward of the family winery, and I trust you to keep that tradition strong for future generations. All holdings from your father, and his father before him, are passed down to you."

I peek over at Uncle Geno. He's nodding, a pleased but solemn look on his face.

It's a look we're all familiar with. Sometimes it feels like he's older than Nonna ever was.

"I have every hope that your sons, my beloved grandsons, will carry on that tradition on the land bequeathed to your lineage. I love you all."

Oof. Not that it's a surprise, but an actual callout to the cousins in Nonna's will feels like a physical blow, the air sucked out of my lungs at being overlooked. Again.

I grit my teeth and force a closed-lip smile. It is what it is, and no use whining over it, right?

All I know is that I've tried all my life to live up to Nonna and Papa's legacy, and once again, I've failed.

Failed myself, failed my sisters, failed Nonna.

I sigh and look down, trying to see where my purse has slid under my chair. I don't think I can stay here much longer without bursting into tears.

Uncle Geno slaps both palms on his knees, starting to rise. "Thank you, James. I know how hard—"

"We're not finished."

He drops back into his seat, eyebrows raised. "Excuse me? You've gone over everything—the accounts, the financials, the properties..."

"One property." Mr. Davenport sets a paper aside and glances down at the one remaining in his hand. "Belmonte Winery."

My mouth drops open.

"These are the final wishes of Maria Carmela Bianchi Lamberti, in her own words. *My dearest children and grandchildren. I love you all and wish I could have remained with you forever, in our little patch of heaven on earth. I have loved every moment together and wish you all nothing but peace, prosperity, and happiness.*

"*As you know, when I married my sainted Leo, I brought my family birthright, Caparelli Vineyards, with me. It had been passed down to me by my mother, God rest her soul. And though I allowed my husband to run both wineries as one, it has remained my birthright throughout our marriage and beyond. Geno, when you took over for your father, you continued to treat them as one entity, as agreed upon previously. But now, in my twilight years, I wish to rebuild the tradition started by my mother and pass Caparelli Vineyards on to the next generation of winemaking women in our family. My dear daughter, Caprice, has chosen to live and work overseas with her second husband and has shown no interest in Caparelli for many years. Therefore, I leave my vines, my property, and my birthright to my three granddaughters—Rosa, Bianca, and Allegra—to carry on the proud matriarchal tradition of Caparelli.*"

Dimly, I can hear Bianca gasp.

"*I also leave a modest bank account*"—Mr. Davenport holds up a folder—"*to provide some cushion should they choose to bring Caparelli back from disuse. I hope with all my heart that they do. My darlings, my tre sorelle, I wish you all well in your new adventure."*

My pulse pounds in my ears, drowning out everything around me. My breath saws in and out of my lungs as I try to wrap my head around what just happened.

She just—she gave us—she trusted *me...*?

Tears sting the edges of my eyes. I squeeze them shut as I focus on my breathing. Why can't I catch a full breath? Am I suffocating?

Is this what a panic attack feels like? Oh, God.

I open my eyes and focus on breathing in for four, hold for four, out for four.

The silence stretches as Mr. Davenport folds his hands on the desk and looks at each of us in turn. "Any questions?"

Uncle Geno stands, his face thunderous. "What the hell was that?"

"Your mother's last will and testament. It is quite legal, and she was of sound mind and body when she wrote it. There will be no point in challenging it."

"But it makes no sense. Caparelli and Belmonte have been combined for decades! Caparelli can't exist on its own." He turns to me, his hands on his hips. "You agree with me, right, Rosa? You've been working for the family for years. You see how the two are intertwined."

He's waiting for me to nod, to fall in line like the good niece I've worked so hard to be seen as. The practical one, the head-down-work-hard foot soldier.

But I can't.

In my head, I'm hearing the stories Nonna used to tell us, of growing up on Caparelli's grounds, how proud she was when it became hers, how she chose to share it with her husband while still retaining that birthright for her own.

I'm remembering those years after Mama left, when Nonna

8

opened her home to Bianca, Allegra, and me, providing us with a solid foundation of love and belonging after our world had been ripped apart. And now she's leaving us the home, the vineyard, the winery and all?

I'm filled with grief and confusion and a fierce, soul-deep gratitude to Nonna for seeing the three of us as worthy of a gift like this.

Even if a big part of me isn't sure we're up to the challenge.

If *I'm* up to the challenge.

"Besides, there's no way you'll be able to get it up and running on your own in time to save the grapes," Uncle Geno says.

"She's not on her own," Bianca snaps.

We all turn to stare at the screen. To be honest, I'd almost forgotten my sisters were listening in as well.

"Excuse me?" Uncle Geno frowns.

"She's right," Allegra says. "There are three of us. She's not on her own."

My heart clenches with love for my sisters.

He waves a hand dismissively. "Whatever. Not like you'll be doing much from your little European vacation. You're just like your mother."

I suck in a breath. That *bastard.*

"Belmonte needs the grapes. We have plans for them. And if you don't allow us to harvest and use them, they'll rot on the vine."

"Then we'll just turn them into raisins and make a profit that way," my youngest sister says blithely, her *no big deal* attitude obvious even via video call.

"Allegra!"

I fight back a smile. She always cuts right to the chase.

Aunt Janet reaches up and touches Uncle Geno's elbow. He glances at her and shakes his head. Her hand drops back into her lap. With a purse of her lips, she picks up her knitting again.

Uncle Geno turns to me and tries to smile. It looks more like a grimace. "Our arrangement has worked just fine for decades. We've even honored the history of Caparelli vineyards through our Carleo Cabernet."

Oh, right. The Carleo. The romantic, highly fictionalized "tribute" wine that Uncle Geno has been selling for years. The one where Nonna's contribution has been reduced to a side note.

"There's no reason to fix what isn't broken."

Isn't it?

Maybe I'm the only one who's noticed the fault lines over the past decade or so.

Maybe I'm the one who's broken. And this could be a chance to put myself back together again.

I glance at my sisters on the iPad, butterflies in combat boots stomping around in my stomach. For once, I'm not jumping at Uncle Geno's demand.

"I think...I'll have to talk to my sisters about it."

"But—"

I stand up, feeling unsteady on my feet. All these years, plugging away in the shadows, trying to prove my worth and ability to my uncle and cousins. Watching Bianca get shunted away as she tried to build a career as a winemaker. *But Vittorio is our winemaker,* Uncle Geno would say. *Your cousin is just following in the family footsteps. You understand.*

And now, unexpectedly, we might just have an opportunity to build—to re*build*—something of our own.

"Yes, we have to discuss our options." Bianca lifts her chin on-screen, her expression calm. "All of them."

"Girls!" Uncle Geno's face is bright red. I wouldn't be surprised if steam starts billowing out his ears. "I must insist—"

"Nope." Allegra laughs through the video call. "Pretty sure you don't get to insist anything. Andiamo, sorelle mie, let's discuss our options."

Vittorio shakes his head, an incredulous look on his face. Leo is standing in front of Geno, his hand on Geno's shoulder.

Not that any of us think Uncle Geno would resort to violence, but it's probably a good time to beat a hasty retreat.

"We'll be in touch about the financials," I say to Mr. Davenport. Financials? Where the hell did that come from? I sound like a winery owner already.

Winery owner. Something light and fizzy bubbles through me, like a just-poured glass of prosecco. I grab my purse and the iPad and hurry out of the room. Once outside, I stare at the screen, blinking a little in the bright California sunlight.

"I have just one thing to say," Allegra pipes up, her eyes wide.

"What's that?"

"Holy shit."

Chapter 1

Rosa

Two months later...

I stare glumly at the spreadsheet on the computer screen in front of me.

Nope. The numbers haven't changed since the last time I looked at it. Dammit.

It was nice of Nonna to leave us a little nest egg to get started, but there are two problems with it.

One, it was a *little* nest egg when she'd set it aside, and it hasn't gotten any bigger in the intervening years. It just sat there in a neglected bank account, earning next to nothing in interest. We have enough to make it to harvest time, if that.

Two, we need staff. Employees. But employees require payment, and, well...

See issue number one.

Wait, make that three problems. I'm the only sister currently trying to make soup out of this stone, and the broth so far is pretty damn watery.

I can't believe it's the end of June already and I'm still spinning my wheels. I wish one of my sisters was here to help carry the load.

Or someone. Anyone. I managed to hire one guy, and he's already bailed. Argh.

It's not Bianca's fault. She still has another three months to go on this year's contract at Castillo Lorenzo in Argentina, and I refuse to let her bail before the grapes are crushed and pressed at the very least. The work she puts in now will do a world of good for Caparelli at harvest and beyond. She'll be a full-fledged winemaker with the skills and training we need to actually make a go of this winery.

If I can convince her to stay.

I'm so, so glad she was able to get some time off to come home before Nonna passed, to have a chance to say goodbye in person. But I shoved her back on that plane as soon as I could, sending her back to Argentina until the end of the season. I'm not letting either of my sisters make the same mistakes I did—not if I can help it.

They can make their own mistakes, and they probably will. But sacrificing their dreams for the family won't be one of them.

At least I don't have to worry about Allegra doing that. Allegra's off being Allegra, somewhere out in the wide world. Gallivanting around the planet, following in Mama's footsteps, being the footloose youngest child. I don't begrudge her for it.

Much.

Oh well. I already had my rebellious phase—brief though it was—and set it aside years ago to do the right thing.

That's me. "Do the Right Thing" Rosa. Put everything I want aside for the good of—well, everyone else.

I'm still doing the right thing. Maybe. I hope so. Because right now, this entire operation is a cluster. And I'm not talking about grapes.

Three days ago, the guy I hired to look after the vines and grounds—while I did everything else—up and quit. His friend opened a surfboard shop out on the coast, and that apparently sounded like more fun than looking at plants all day long.

And none of Uncle Geno's employees are willing to jump ship to work at Caparelli, even the ones who tended the grounds before we inherited.

Not a chance they'll risk offending one of the top winery owners in the region by choosing the wrong side.

I push away from the desk and stand, stretching in place. My neck's tight after too much time researching vineyard irrigation on the computer. I can't quite tell if there's something wrong with the irrigation schedule or what, but the ground is a little too dry for my liking. I just don't know what I'm missing. I've got more articles to go over, but right now, I need to get outside and check the vines.

I open the front door and cringe, the bright sunlight assaulting my eyeballs. *Good Lord, this is turning me into a vampire.* Shaking my head, I stride across the wide wooden front porch and bound down the stairs, breathing in the glorious scents of almost summer.

The once-pristine front yard is choked with weeds and almost down to dirt in places. After Nonna got sick, Uncle Geno moved her back over to Belmonte where they could "keep an eye on her." The home at Caparelli soon turned into a holding place, somewhere to keep resources that weren't needed on the bigger property. It stopped being a home at all.

He'd already stopped using the winery and wine cave after Papa died...might as well close down the homestead as well. Too much work, too much effort. Why have two tasting rooms when all the wine is being sold under one label? Why hire duplicate staff when you can just combine efforts and do the same work with the same crew? Why develop the product in two locations when it's more efficient to produce all the wines in one place?

Logically, it made a lot of sense. I've always—well, almost always—been a pragmatist. I get what Uncle Geno was trying to do, and he's damn good at it. But logical doesn't always mean it's the *right* thing to do.

Nonna always said she was fine with whatever Geno wanted to do. Just because Papa kept both wineries open and successful didn't mean Geno had to do the same thing.

But I could tell it bothered her, at least a little. The way she got that faraway look in her eyes whenever she'd talk about the old days. How she stopped asking us to take her to walk the vineyards for the day. The way her lips pursed a little when Uncle Geno boasted about how Belmonte's most popular wine was Carleo.

Carleo, using Caparelli's grapes. Carleo, with the fake backstory the public eats up with a spoon.

It's possible I'm more than a little irritated on her behalf over that one.

And the house.

Oh, the house. It was so gorgeous once—I've seen pictures from when Nonna was a kid—and she loved it so much. Even when Nonna's parents passed, Papa put so much time and energy and love into keeping it up, making it a decent winery space, somewhere we all loved to spend time.

I hold up a hand to shade my eyes. The house looms over me, in all its worn-down, dilapidated, turn-of-the-century glory. The beauty it could be, with unlimited time and funds, hovers over the building like a heat vision.

Let's be honest—so many years of neglect is a lot to overcome, especially when it comes to the house and grounds. Sure, the place is still standing, but it hasn't been painted in years, the porch is sagging in sections, the inside smells like something died in one of the walls.

Something probably did.

I don't want to think about that, so I walk around the perimeter, taking mental notes of what needs to be done. A little bit of daydreaming time before tackling the business side again.

One: Dig out the gardens next to the house. Everything is overgrown and weedy and gone to seed. Pull it all out, put down some mulch, plant a couple of rose bushes like Nonna loved.

Two: Spend a little of the start-up money on getting the front porch fixed. It would do no good to get Caparelli up and running again just to lose it all in a lawsuit because someone fell through the rotten wood.

Three: Clean up the rest of the interior, one room at a time. The weather's nice enough to keep the windows open most days, which should help with airing the place out.

Four: Spend a little more of the start-up money on getting whatever dead animal is in the walls *out*.

I frown. *Too much spending of the start-up money. This list sucks.*

And that's just the house. If I can't find someone to replace Surfing Dude, like, yesterday, the vines are going to be in bad, bad shape come harvest time.

I know a little—not much, but a little—about tending the vines. My skill set leans toward organization and planning and management, not trimming and feeding and, God forbid, pruning. I'd kill the damn crops if it was left to me.

Oh, right. It *has* been left to me. Dammit.

That's enough worrying-slash-daydreaming for the day. Squaring my shoulders, I cross to the fence at the front of the yard (new hinges needed for the gate, I add to my invisible-yet-

17

still-expensive list) and step out onto the dirt road that borders the property. Starting at the edge of the yard, the vineyard stretches up the hill and over the rise. I suck in a deep breath. The breeze is full of early summer heat and growing things.

I walk down the road, letting my mind wander over the long rows of grapevines. No matter how stressed I get over the money or the lack of employees or the overall impossibility of the whole thing, it all fades away when I'm walking on Caparelli.

The house is a ways behind me now, and I breathe, letting the worries of the day flow out of me like water.

Across the road, I see the start of Take Flight Winery's vineyard, the mirror image to Caparelli. The Wrights started it around the same time Nonna's parents started ours, and the vineyards—and families—grew up together over time. Two hundred and fifty acres of perfectly manicured vines, tended by a winemaking family that was as well-respected in Oak Creek Canyon as our own.

I used to spend almost as much time at Take Flight as I did at Caparelli, once upon a time. Haven't set foot on that property in ten years, though.

And now it's been sold, according to the Oak Creek Canyon rumor mill, to some athlete with more money than sense, wanting to play winemaker, and all those generations of effort are—gone.

I can't let that happen here.

A part of me is so scared we won't be able to make it work. That *I* won't be able to make it work. I've known the Wright family forever, and they were as good a winemaking family as you'd ever find. But even they gave up and sold out.

For a moment, I feel sorry for Jake and his family. I can only guess how hard it was to sell. Selfishly, though, I'm kind of glad it happened. At least I don't have to worry about running into any of them ever again.

Makes working on Caparelli a little bit easier.

My back pocket buzzes, then buzzes again. I toy with the idea of ignoring it, but it keeps on buzzing, so I finally pull the phone out and click Accept on the call.

"Hey, Bee," I say, squinting into the distance. "How goes the harvest?"

Bianca sighs happily. "Living the dream, Rosey Posey. Living the dream."

I hate that nickname, but you know how family is. Once they land on something, it sticks forever.

"Good to hear it," I say. And I mean it. As much as I hate doing this all alone right now, it would be seven thousand times worse if Bianca felt like she had to give up the opportunity of a lifetime.

"How about you? Things going okay?"

I hesitate. No need to worry her unnecessarily. And it's not like she can do anything about it anyway.

But I wait too long to answer, and her voice sharpens. "Rosa Martinelli. Don't try to hide it from me. What's wrong?"

I keep walking down the road, shoving a hand through my sweat-dampened hair. It's warmer than I expected out here. "It's fine."

"Liar."

"Rude." I kick a rock out of my way, watch it skitter into the scrub grass lining the road. "But you're not wrong."

"Spill."

"You know the guy I hired to take care of the vines?"

"Mm-hmm."

I shrug, even though she can't see me. "Bailed a couple days ago."

"That *bastard*."

As worried as I am about the situation, I still have to smile at that. "Yeah. We need to hire a replacement, like, immediately, but we don't have the money to pay for an actual professional. At least one who won't *also* bail at the first opportunity."

"Yeah, that's not ideal." Bianca pauses for a minute. "I could—"

"Nope."

"It's only a couple months early."

"Are you done with your wines for the season?"

She hesitates, and I pounce.

"No, Bee. Don't even think about it. You're in *Argentina*. It's not like you can split your time between here and there. We'll figure something else out."

"Maybe you could put an ad online?"

I shake my head, then remember Bianca can't see me. "Tried that. How do you think I ended up hiring Damien?"

"What about Will? He's been working on the property for years."

"You know his loyalty is to Uncle Geno." *Already tried that, too.*

Bianca is silent for a long moment. "Well, you'll come up with something. You always save the day."

I bite my lip. If only it were true.

Chapter 2

Jake

I'm drunk.

And yes, it's four thirty in the afternoon and *technically* I'm trespassing.

But lucky for me, the new owner hasn't taken possession yet. And the former Take Flight employees he kept on staff are on the other side of the property today.

I've missed this place, even though I've been avoiding it for the past ten goddamn years. And this will probably be my last chance to say goodbye.

Goodbye to the fields I could walk with my eyes closed. (And right now, drunk as I am, it might be easier to close my eyes and find my way around. Alcohol-induced double vision is no joke, folks.)

Goodbye to the wide, shady oak on the property line, the one that was the best place to nap on the entire estate. And okay, in my later teen years, "nap" was a euphemism for "fool around with the girl next door." Which made it even better, in my then-seventeen-year-old opinion.

It was better. Until it wasn't. And now it's even less better than it ever was before.

Worse? What's the word I'm looking for?

I sigh and look around. I'm not even sure why I'm here, in the place I love most in the entire world, feeling all maudlin and shit. *Get it together, Wright.*

Tomorrow. I'll get it together tomorrow. But today I'm raising a glass—and raising it, and raising it again—to my hopes and dreams and plans. All of them gone at the speed of Take Flight's fire sale.

And the worst part is I can't even be mad about it. The sale of the winery was the last resort. By the time Mom and Dad put it on the market, we all knew there was no other choice.

If I'd been around, if I'd been here to help out, then maybe...

But I wasn't and I hadn't, and by the time I got back, Take Flight was no more.

I can't blame Mom and Dad. They did the best they could with what they had.

But out here, by myself, I can mourn the loss of everything I planned for. Expected. Even fucking complained about once in a while, because the weight of expectations were especially heavy for a fourth-generation Wright raised to take over from the third.

Funny how things work out. All my life, I assumed—along with everyone else around me—that I'd follow in my father's and grandfather's and great-grandfather's footsteps. All that time in school, all those years working in wineries up and down the California coast and in Washington state and Canada and for a brief, shining moment, Italy, preparing for a moment that doesn't exist anymore.

And then—poof. No more winery, no more footsteps to follow. Now they're gone. I feel like—like a dandelion puff, blown on the wind, with nowhere left to land.

Who knew that a six-pack would turn me into a poet? Maybe that's the career change I need right now.

I sit down in the shade, just off the property line. This tree should be enough to hide me from the vineyard crew over the next hill. And if not, I'm close enough to the road to get a head start on bailing.

Behind me, I can feel our—*No, not anymore*—the vineyard, stretched out in straight, wide lines, growing in the late-afternoon sun. It's hot out. I tip my head back and close my eyes.

It's nice here. Quiet. Just me and my thoughts.

And a six-pack. Something poetic about getting drunk on beer while saying goodbye to a winery, don't you think?

I pull the last bottle out of the cardboard carrier and twist off the top. Time to put it all behind me.

I glance over my shoulder. Yep, it's behind me now. Literally.

I crack myself up sometimes.

I take a long pull of the beer, which isn't cold anymore. I've clearly been trespassing long enough, feeling sorry for myself. Time to get the hell out of here, walk down to the edge of town to call a rideshare, and figure out what I'm doing with the rest of my life.

I stand up, dizzy from the heat and the beer, and wipe my palms on my jeans. I'm a little worried because I'm starting to hear voices.

What the hell? I haven't drunk that much.

I look around. There's a person walking down the road, backlit by the sun, talking to themself.

Themselves? Grammar is not my strong suit, especially when I'm ine—ineber—drunk.

No, wait. I squint, lifting the hand not currently holding a beer bottle, and shade my eyes from the sunlight. They're talking on a cell phone.

That's slightly less concerning.

Except now I'm going to get caught trespassing on my family's former property, while drunk, which is not good.

I'm pretty sure it's not the new owner. I hear he's a pro-athlete dude of some sort, and the person walking down the road is clearly a woman.

Too late to run for it, so I sigh, nudge the cardboard carrier filled with empties behind me, and wait for the inevitable embarrassment.

"...I guess I can place another ad online and see what happens," the person says, holding her hair up off the back of her neck. "Not many other options right now."

Oh, God. It's officially worse than I thought.

I shake my head, almost laughing at the shit fate has decided to put me through.

The last time I was under this tree, on this side of the vineyard, was ten years ago. And I was watching this same woman —girl, then, really—walk up the road that day as well.

I was nineteen, heart pounding straight out of my chest, a velvet jewelry box in a gift bag at my feet. Back then, she was looking for me as well, her face lighting up when she saw me waiting for her.

Back then, I would have waited for her forever.

I sigh and clear my throat. "Hey, Rosa."

Her head whips to the side, and I see her rich brown eyes get almost cartoon-character huge the moment she figures out it's me. "I've gotta go," she says into her phone and clicks it off.

Silence stretches out between us, and I wait to see if she's willing to break it first.

"Hey," she finally says, her voice faint.

It's been ten years since we've seen each other, and this is the best we can do.

God.

She slides her phone into her back pocket, and I do my damnedest to not check out her butt in the process.

It's tough. She's got a really nice butt.

"What are you doing here?" She turns toward me and shifts from foot to foot, arms crossed over her chest.

Which I'm also not checking out.

Oh, hell. I'm *totally* checking her out.

Damn, she's grown up.

Rosa pulls her thick brown hair into a high ponytail and wraps an elastic around it to hold it in place. It should make her look ridiculously young, but instead, it works.

Everything about her works. Trim body, curves in all the right places, thick lashes framing wide brown eyes, a sprinkle of freckles on her upper chest that I want to trace with my tongue.

Fuck.

She's also staring at me, head tilted, like she's waiting for something.

Oh, she asked me a question. Right.

"Just, uh, saying goodbye to the old place." I gesture vaguely behind me. "You know. Old times."

Why the hell did I bring that up? I'm an idiot.

Or just really drunk.

Maybe both.

She's nice enough to ignore my drunken stupidity. "Yeah, I heard the sale was finalized last month." Her lips purse. They're full and pouty and look like raspberry ice. "I'm sorry. That sucks."

"Yep." I can hear myself pop the *p* sound, like I'm over-enunciating. Trying to prove I'm sober.

I don't think I'm succeeding.

"I, uh, heard about your grandma. I'm sorry." I'm not just saying that. Her grandma was one of my favorite people when I was younger.

"Thanks." She looks back at Caparelli.

"So, what are you up to?" Which is trite and awkward, but what the hell.

"Oh, you know." She shrugs. "Trying to get Caparelli back off the ground."

Back off the ground? "I thought it was going well," I say. "I mean, according to my folks, the Carleo from your Cabernet vines is a major hit."

Apparently when I find a hole, I keep on digging.

"It is. Or was, I guess." She wrinkles her nose and looks away. "But now that we own the vines...who knows."

"Wait." I shake my head. "*We* own the vines—who's we? Doesn't your family already own them?"

"Uh. Well." She rolls her eyes. "I meant *we* as in Allegra and Bianca and me. Nonna left us her winery. We've separated from Belmonte and are trying to make it on our own."

"That's—wow."

She nods. "Mm-hmm."

We stare at each other for way too long to be comfortable. Then she coughs and scuffs a toe in the dirt road. "Well. I should go."

I shouldn't ask. Seriously, I shouldn't ask.

"Is everything okay?"

I don't even take my *own* advice these days.

She nods, her smile obviously fake. "Of course. It's fine."

Liar.

But I lost the right to call her out on that a long time ago.

"That's, uh, good to hear." I pick up the cardboard container, the tops of the empties clanking together as it swings. "And good luck."

"You, too," she says.

I hook a thumb over my shoulder. "I'd better head out before the new guy's crew catches me on his property."

"I won't tell," she says, and I believe her.

But the other part she said, about being fine? I don't believe that. Not even one little bit.

I try to go, again, but something stops me. I turn back and look at Rosa. Her lower lip is caught between her teeth.

"What's wrong?" My voice is rough, a little sloppy from all the beer, and I can see that it startles her.

"Nothing..." She shoves a hand through her hair, knocking the elastic holding her ponytail in place to the ground.

She doesn't even notice.

Yeah, something's really wrong.

Rosa huffs out a breath. "Okay, fine. Our only employee just quit, Uncle Geno's workers refuse to help us out, I'm completely unable to hire anyone else despite all my efforts, Bianca's finishing out her contract in Argentina and I *will not* let her throw away everything she's worked for by bailing early —although God knows if she's actually going to come back to stay and help out or if she's just going to stay there, Allegra is partying her way up and down the European Union, and if I can't find someone to help me keep the entire place from turning into a smoking crater in the next week, I think I'm going to lose my mind."

Wow. That was...a lot.

"So if you know of anyone who's available and willing to work for, let's face it, ridiculously low wages to start, I would be really grateful if you'd send them my way."

Rosa sucks in a breath and blows it out again, her face pink from what I assume is embarrassment.

I don't know why. She's impressing the hell out of me at the moment.

"So what are you looking for? A groundskeeper? A vine-yard manager? A viticulturist?"

"Um." She closes her eyes. "Yes?"

"Huh." I nod to myself. "Okay. Yeah."

"Yeah, what? You know someone?"

I nod again. Before I can talk myself out of it, I blurt out, "Me."

Her eyes snap open, wide with horror. "Oh. Oh, no. I can't ask you—"

"You didn't ask. I offered." I mean, it's not like I've got a ton of things going for me right now. Diving into an impossible job like this might be just the thing to help me get my head on straight, figure out what I want to do with the rest of my life.

"But Jake..."

I hold up a hand. "Besides, I wouldn't be much of a husband if I didn't help you out in your time of need."

The look on her face is all the payment I require.

Chapter 3

Rosa

What. The. Fuck.

"Ex-husband," I hiss, glancing around to make sure no one heard. Which is stupid because it's not like anyone would be on the private road between our properties. Or, more accurately, my property and his family's former property.

Either way, I know we're alone.

We're alone, for the first time since...well, since he actually *was* my husband.

Which Jake isn't anymore. No matter what his drunk ass says.

"Ex," I say again, taking a step back. "We got an annulment."

"No, we didn't." He shrugs. "Still married."

"We. Got. An. Annulment," I enunciate, my breath sharp and shallow. "I signed the paperwork. The day Uncle Geno found out."

Which was the day we got back with the marriage certificate. We were married for less time than it takes to say *You did what on your high school graduation trip?*

Britney Spears, eat your heart out.

But he's shaking his head, his expression calm and almost—casual, if that makes sense. Like this is no big deal. "Nope, sorry. We're still married."

"You're lying."

He shrugs, empty beer bottles clinking together in the cardboard holder. "Suit yourself."

"We're *not married.*" That has to be true. It has to be.

"According to the state of Nevada, we are. And California doesn't disagree."

Ten years ago, I was supposed to be on my grad trip with a bunch of friends. Instead, Jake and I detoured to Las Vegas and got married in one of those cheesy wedding chapels.

None of our friends—or family—had a clue.

Until we got back and everything went to hell.

"There's no way we're still married."

"There is. If the annulment paperwork was never filed."

"But Uncle Geno..."

"Passed along the paperwork to me—yes, I know." He scratches his neatly trimmed beard. That's new. He barely had facial hair back in the day. "But did I file it? Nope."

"You had to."

"No, I didn't."

"Of course you filed the paperwork," I say, but even to my own ears it sounds shrill, shaky. Like I don't really know if he would or not. "Uncle Geno..."

Jake takes a sip of his beer. "Geno had nothing to do with it. I mean, he *tried.* Told me I had to take care of it. But it wasn't like he could force me."

I whisper, "I signed the papers."

"So did I. But then I just—couldn't go through with it."

"Why didn't you say anything?"

He scoffs. "When? How? You were busy ignoring my phone calls and hiding in your room when I knocked on the door."

I can feel my face flush. "I wasn't hiding," I say weakly. We both know it's a lie.

Jake waves a hand like it's all water under the bridge. "Whatever. My point still stands. I couldn't tell you—because you wouldn't talk to me."

"And you didn't tell anyone else?"

He shrugs. "Wasn't anyone else's business."

My head spins. "We can't be married."

"Are you sure?"

The question hangs there, in the space between us, while my heartbeat speeds up and a bead of sweat trickles down my back.

I can't deal with this right now on top of everything else imploding in my world.

"I didn't want an annulment anyway." He shrugs again. "Went to all that trouble to marry you. Seemed like a stupid idea to give up that quickly."

I hold back a wince because that stiletto slips between my ribs with a twist. In the face of Uncle Geno's rage and threats, eighteen-year-old me gave up almost immediately. Stepped back in line. Head down, mouth shut, like the good little Belmonte soldier I was raised to be.

While my best friend, first love, and apparently not-quite-so-ex-husband fled the scene of the crime.

"But you left," I point out. "Isn't that the *definition* of giving up?"

I can't believe we're having this conversation. Here, now, under a bright California sun. While only one of us is sober.

Jake tilts his head, like he's thinking about it. His features are soft, relaxed. It's probably the alcohol.

I'm a little jealous. No, I'm a lot jealous. With this bombshell, God knows I could use something to drink right about now. He couldn't have saved *one* of that six-pack for me?

He laughs, finally, and squints up at the sky. Have his eyes always been that shade of sapphire blue? "Amazing."

"What's amazing?" I say, even though I'm not totally sure I want to know what he's referring to.

"Nothing." He gestures widely. "Everything."

I shake my head, pulse still hammering in my throat. "I can't do this."

"Yeah, that's a surprise."

The bitterness in his voice stops me in my tracks.

"Look, like it or not, you don't have a lot of options right now. I'm here, I have the skills you need, and I'm willing to do it. So you need to decide if you can set aside your ego and accept my help."

Jesus, he's an arrogant son of a bitch.

He's also right.

"I'll..."

I can't do this. I *can't*.

"I'll think about it."

He nods, walking backward down the road, away from me. "Okay. Fair enough. I'll be at the Orchard Heights Inn until tomorrow night. If I don't hear from you by then, I'll head out."

"Head out where?"

He smiles, slow and lazy. I ignore the spark of heat low in my belly at an expression I haven't seen for ten long, lonely years.

"Wherever the wind takes me, darlin'."

I watch him go, staring at the curve in the road long after he disappears from view.

No Way, Rosé

By THE TIME THE SUN SETS, I'VE DECIDED TO TAKE A PAGE out of Jake's book and get drunk.

On wine, though, not beer. I'm not a *heathen*.

I considered taking a bottle out of the wine rack at Caparelli and enjoying it (aka *freaking out*) in solitude, but I decided this situation called for some company.

So I'm in the back corner of Wine O'Clock, waiting for Sasha to arrive. I haven't sent her an SOS text in ages, so I know I won't be waiting long.

Sure enough, the door opens just as the server sets down the bucket of ice and bottle of Sauvignon Blanc I ordered as soon as I set foot in the place. I wave, and Sasha's face lights up, bright pink curls bouncing as she hurries to join me.

I like the new look; last time we met up, her hair was jet black with gold streaks, an homage to some sports team apparently. I think it was hockey playoff season, but who knows?

Clearly not me.

She tolerates my utter lack of knowledge surrounding any and all things sports related, thankfully.

"Rosa!" Sasha drops onto the bench seat next to me and plants a kiss on my cheek. I can't help but laugh as I return the gesture with a cheek kiss of my own, scooching over to give her some room.

Ever since elementary school, Sasha's infectious cheer has been one of my favorite things. And miracle of miracles, she cherishes our friendship just as much as I do. Even when I get in my head and end up being too busy to really nurture it.

What can I say? She's my people. And I know just how lucky I am to have her.

"So, dish," she says, uncorking the perfectly chilled bottle and pouring us generous glasses. "It's a weeknight. I haven't gotten an SOS on a weeknight for years. It's gotta be something good!"

No beating around the bush for Sasha. I lift my glass in a silent toast and take a sip. It's bright and crisp, and I nod my head approvingly. Bella Vines has another local winner.

"Well." I take a long swallow, chasing it with a bite of cheese from the charcuterie plate I also ordered before she arrived. "Things have gotten...complicated."

"Complicated." She snorts and reaches across me for a cracker and some prosciutto. "You mean more complicated than taking on a neglected winery with exactly zero family support?"

"Hey, Allegra and Bianca are supportive," I protest.

Sasha shakes her head and pops another bite into her mouth. "I don't think you can count it as full support if it's coming from separate time zones," she argues, "but fine, whatever. Yes, you have that support, as limited as it may be."

I drink a little more wine. She's not wrong.

"But you didn't SOS me to talk about your sisters." She taps the table a couple of times with one neatly manicured nail. "Is it something with the winery? Problems with the new employee?"

I pick through the Marcona almonds and grab one so I don't have to say anything for a minute. I chew, swallow, then admit, "He quit a couple days ago. So I'm back to me, myself, and I."

"That bastard!" Sasha lifts her glass in a mocking toast. "To the trash taking itself out."

I clink my glass with hers and shake my head. She's more accurate than she knows.

"So what are you going to do?" She props one elbow on the table and rests her chin in her hand, studying me. Her expression is concerned. And she doesn't even know the half of it yet.

Speaking of which... "Well. I guess I'm not completely on my own," I admit. I cut off a wedge of brie, put it on a cracker, and shove it into my mouth. Anything to avoid this part of the conversation.

Sasha turns sideways in the booth and lifts her knee up onto the big leather bench seat. She's staring me directly in the face. "There's something you're not telling me," she says, eyes narrowed.

Yeah, there is.

I can't avoid this any longer. It's the reason I sent her an SOS, after all. "Jake offered to help," I mumble.

"What?"

"Jake," I say a little louder. "Jake Wright. He offered to help."

I'm fairly certain the rest of the bar can hear her gasp even over the jukebox. A couple heads turn, and I want to sink down under the booth. But when nothing happens immediately, people go back to their own conversations and ignore us. Thank goodness.

"Jake." She sets her glass down on the table. "*Jake* Jake? As in your ex—"

I surge forward and place my hand over her mouth to stop her from finishing that sentence.

"Boyfriend?" I say, baring my teeth in the world's fakest smile. *Please, God, go with me on this,* I think, eyes pleading for her to understand. "Yes, my ex-*boyfriend* Jake from next door is in town, and he offered to help me run the winery for now."

I remove my hand from Sasha's mouth and sit back in the

booth, feeling drained. And I haven't even gotten to the best part yet. *Best? Worst? Whatever.*

Sasha grabs the bottle and tops off our glasses. She shoves mine into my hand and orders, "Details. Now."

So I fill her in—on the surfer jerk bailing, on how I feel so over my head with everything, on how lonely it is at Caparelli by myself.

And how I stumbled across my ex on a walk this afternoon between the vineyards.

Full disclosure—Sasha is one of only two people who know Jake wasn't just my boyfriend. I never said a word to my sisters or cousins or even Nonna. When we got back from Vegas, Nonna was in the hospital and the family was in an uproar over my "disappearance." Geno was furious that he hadn't been able to get in touch with me and heavily implied that my reckless choices were a big part of the reason Nonna was sick. If I'd been there, if I hadn't turned off my phone, none of this would have happened.

Sasha told me from the start it was all bullshit, but I never fully believed it. I let my family down, and I've been making it up to them for the past ten years. And now the centerpiece of my worst mistake is back in town.

I do my best to change the subject, and after a while we move on to local gossip and the new show she keeps trying to get me to watch. But eventually we circle back, because Sasha isn't one to let me drop the subject that easily.

It's both my favorite and most frustrating thing about her.

"So you're telling me"—Sasha gestures with her wineglass, and the golden liquid sloshes dangerously close to the rim— "Jake was just, what? Sitting there at Take Flight, waiting for you?"

"Oh, no." I shake my head firmly. Or at least as firmly as I can at the moment. At some point, we moved on to our second bottle of wine and I'm feeling a little fuzzy. But not as fuzzy as Jake was this afternoon.

"Fuzzy?" Sasha stares at me. "What does that even mean?"

Did I say that out loud? Damn.

"Never mind. Jake...he wasn't waiting for me. It was a pity party for one." I feel a little bitchy for saying that, so I wrinkle my nose and start over. "He was saying goodbye to the family vineyard. And I don't blame him. But, well, he was pretty drunk when I showed up. Which probably explains why he said what he said." I scrape up the last of the brie with a cracker and pop it into my mouth.

"And what did he say, Clarice?" Sasha's classic serial-killer imitation is truly awful, but we both crack up anyway.

When I finally catch my breath, I glance around. Nobody's sitting near us, and the music is loud. This is what I sent the SOS for...might as well spill.

"He said we're still married," I grumble.

"He said *what?*" Sasha stares at me, wide-eyed. "No. No way."

"That's what I said!" I'm indignant all over again. "He's lying to me, Sasha. And I can't figure out why."

She pours the rest of the bottle into my glass, gesturing at me to drink up.

I don't have to be asked twice. I know my way around a rideshare app.

"I mean, we got an annulment. I signed the paperwork and everything," I say.

"I remember." For a minute, we're both lost in the memories of me sobbing into her comforter, hiding my broken heart in her bedroom so my family wouldn't catch on. "And Geno gave them to Jake, right?"

"Yep." I take another long swallow of wine. "And then Jake skipped town."

Sasha leans back against the bench seat and tilts her head. "Did you ever get proof that the annulment went through?"

"I—" My mouth snaps shut for a minute. "I honestly have no idea."

I don't remember much about that summer, to be fair. Nonna was sick, my sisters were panicking, my uncle was expecting me to pick up the slack, and my boyfriend-slash-husband-slash-nothing had fucked off to parts unknown.

Not that I should have expected him to stick around after I let Geno tell him that I agreed our marriage was a mistake and we needed to get an annulment.

But.

It still hurt.

"What exactly did he say today?" Sasha's eyes are way too sharp for someone who's drunk as much wine as we have. "How did he explain it?"

I think back. "He said he wouldn't be much of a husband if he didn't help me out in my 'time of need,'" I say, drawing air quotes with my fingers. "And that he never really wanted the annulment anyway, so he didn't turn in the paperwork."

"Damn." She nods slowly. "Boy's got game."

"Sasha!" I smack her arm with the back of my hand. "You're supposed to be on my side. Get it together."

She laughs and takes another drink. Someone on the other side of the bar chooses a slow, romantic song on the jukebox, and the soft strains pick at something sensitive in me. It's like when you've got a sore tooth and you just can't keep from worrying at it with your tongue. You know it's going to hurt, but you do it anyway.

Seeing him today, under the oak tree—*our* oak tree—was like that. Tugging at something painful that I'd thought was left in the past.

The last time I was under that tree, it had been with Jake. Ten years earlier, the morning I turned eighteen.

He'd stood there, shifting from foot to foot, nerves clear on his face. Then he'd handed me a velvet box in a birthday gift bag—and dropped to one knee.

My breath had caught in my throat, every atom of my being screaming *yes* before he'd even had a chance to get the question out.

It hadn't been an engagement ring. No, that would have caused too many questions, too much suspicion. Instead, he'd given me a thin gold necklace, with a rose pendant on it. A pretty, romantic gift that I could wear every day without anyone questioning it.

Only the two of us knew we'd made a promise that day, one that we fulfilled only a few months later in Vegas.

And when I'd handed the necklace and my wedding band to Sasha and begged her to take them back to Jake, I'd sent a good portion of my heart with her that day as well.

Even today, ten years later, I still catch myself reaching for the rose pendant that hasn't been around my neck for years.

I sigh and drink some more wine.

Sasha is watching me, and I can tell she's going to hit me with some hard truths. It's what I love about her, as much as I hate it, too.

"Look, Rosa, I'm gonna be real with you. This may actually be a good thing."

"A good thing." I go over our conversation in my head. "Which part?"

"All of it. So you have a husband. Maybe it's time you deal with it head on."

"I do *not* have a husband."

"The last person to have the annulment papers seems to

think so." She shrugs and wraps an arm around my shoulders. "Come on, Rosa, what's the worst that can happen?"

I can think of a dozen different outcomes—none of them good. "Accepting Jake's offer is the absolute last thing I should do," I say. "We've got too much history between us."

"Maybe that's why it could work," she muses. "He knows you, Rosa. And he knows his shit."

I narrow my eyes at her. "How do you even know that? He's been gone since high school."

"Well." She finishes the last of her wine. "One of us needed to keep tabs on him. Just in case."

I'm reminded again of why she's my best friend. And why she drives me crazy, just a little bit.

"I've spent the last ten years trying to forget him," I admit softly.

Sasha rolls her eyes. "And that's worked so well," she mocks. "Besides, what else are you going to do? Go back to Geno and admit defeat?"

I can't do that. But without Jake's help, there's no way I can keep this vineyard alive long enough to fulfill Nonna's final wishes—or prove that I'm not a terminal screwup.

There's no one else I can turn to right now. Yeah, I know, family sticks together and helps out and all those clichés. But Bianca is in Argentina and Allegra is in Europe somewhere, and God knows we haven't been able to depend on Mama in years. And if Geno gets his hands on Caparelli, even if it's technically just to "help out," it'll be absorbed back into Belmonte so fast my head will spin. His version of teamwork only extends in one direction.

And I can't let that happen.

Caparelli *meant* something to Nonna. She left it to me—to us—for a reason. If I give up now, I'll be giving up Nonna's dream.

She believed in me. I owe it to her to believe in myself, too.

Even if it's going to be the hardest thing I've ever done.

And that's before my current conundrum raised his far-too-attractive head.

"Jake's probably my only option," I admit grudgingly.

"That's the spirit," she crows, planting a kiss on my forehead. "Now, give me the good stuff."

I wrinkle my nose. "What good stuff? A potential husband appearing out of the mists of time isn't enough for you?"

She waves a hand in front of her dismissively. "Whatever. Is he still hot?"

"Sasha!"

"Seriously. If you're gonna work with your estranged husband"—she ignores my strangled yelp—"he'd better be at least a seven on a scale of one to ten."

I hang my head. "Nine," I mutter.

"Damn, girl. Give me the deets!"

I sigh. "He's grown up—that's for sure."

"Is he taller? I bet he's taller. And has he filled out a little? He was kinda scrawny in high school."

"Sasha!"

She throws back the last of her wine. "Sorry not sorry," she says. "But he was."

Okay, she's not wrong about that, either.

"Yeah. He's"—I gesture with my hands—"broader. In the shoulders."

Sasha nods, hums a little appreciatively.

"And."

"And?"

"He has a beard." I squeeze my eyes shut as she gasps.

"Wait. Wait, wait, wait. What kind of beard? Is he all scruffy mountain man? Artful stubble? Please tell me he's not a no-mustache beardy."

I shake my head. "Nope, neatly trimmed beard and mustache. It looks...good." That's an understatement. He looks hot.

Which is yet another reason I shouldn't be doing this.

I ask her the question I still haven't answered for myself. "Should I accept Jake's offer?"

Sasha smiles gently at me, switching from gossip to emotional support in a heartbeat. "Yeah, Rosa, I think you should. It's the right thing to do. For Caparelli, for your sisters, and most of all, for yourself."

Later, when she's poured me into the Uber and I'm leaning sideways in the back seat, I wonder what she means by that.

But it's probably safer not to think about it too much.

Chapter 4

Jake

Hangovers are a bitch.

I squint at the window, wishing I'd had the foresight to close the blackout shades before falling into bed last night.

Instead, bright beams of sunlight stream in through the gauzy white curtains, lighting up every corner of my room.

I should probably haul my ass out of bed and get downstairs before they stop serving.

I'm not very hungry at the moment, but I paid for breakfast and I hate to waste money.

Plus, there's a high likelihood there will be bacon. Bacon makes everything better.

I stumble through my morning routine, still half-asleep, mind focused on yesterday's conversation with Rosa.

I don't know if she's going to take me up on my offer. Part of me kind of hopes she doesn't. Being around the woman who rejected me so thoroughly after our wedding—tacky and rushed though it may have been—would be a kind of masochism I'm not sure sober me is ready to sign up for.

On the other hand, the chance to stick it to her pompous, asshole uncle is an opportunity I'd be a fool to pass up.

And on the *other* other hand, there's possibly some tiny part of me that wants to see the regret in her eyes when she realizes she could have had me at her side this whole time.

I hadn't been exaggerating when I told her I couldn't turn in the annulment paperwork. It's the honest-to-God truth. I was laid out for days, heartbroken and hurting, and Rosa had ghosted me completely. By the time I came out of my cave I just wasn't able to force myself to do it.

And now? Do I really think spending the entire summer working with-slash-for her is going to make her feel bad for breaking my heart ten years ago?

Whatever. It's a pretty pathetic revenge fantasy in the light of day. Better to set all that aside and just do the damn job.

There is bacon on the breakfast buffet and light, fluffy scrambled eggs and a potato-and-pepper dish that makes my taste buds sing. I'm feeling significantly more human by the time I pour my second cup of coffee into a to-go cup and head out the door.

I don't want to push too hard on Rosa. I know damn well if I do, she'll get stubborn and push back. But in the wine business, time is precious, and I don't know how long those vines have been on their own. If Geno pulled his staff back after the will was read, we don't have a lot of time before the grapes will be useless this year.

I head up into the hills, this time driving the beater truck my folks loaned me while I'm in town, very determinedly *not* focusing on how easily I landed on the side of *we*.

There's still a bite in the air when I arrive at the outskirts of

Caparelli, the ground not yet heated by the sun. I breathe in deeply, enjoying the scent of growing things and dirt and *home*.

No matter how many vineyards I've been on in my life, this particular stretch of land, the space that holds Caparelli and what used to be Take Flight, has a grasp on my soul that nothing else can replace.

I walk through the rows of vines, checking the canopy, the shoots growing from early spring's pruning, the tight, BB-sized baby grapes clustered on the very tips of the rubbery, light green stalks. I bend down to check the soil, absently noting the weeds taking hold around the base of the vines.

"Hey."

I straighten, letting the dirt sift through my fingers as I stand. "And good morning to you," I say, smirking a little.

She's wearing sunglasses—which, yes, it's California and the sun is out, but it's not really that bright at this time of the morning. She sucks in a slow breath and lets it out. "I thought you were going to wait for me to call."

"Changed my mind. Vines wait for no one, darlin'. No time like the present to get to work."

I gesture at the vines in front of me. "I figured it would be a good idea to see what I'm getting into if I start working for you."

"I don't think I ever actually agreed to your proposal."

My mind flashes back ten years. She agreed to my proposal then.

Nope. If this is going to work I've got to bury that topic forty meters below the wine caves, if not further.

"Well, in that case, you've got less than a week before you lose these vines for the season. Good luck." I shake my head and walk around her, heading toward the road.

"Wait." She grabs my elbow as I walk by, stopping my forward movement.

I grit my teeth and ignore the spark of heat that travels up my arm at her touch.

This is going to be harder than I thought.

"What do you mean, less than a week?" I can hear the desperation in her voice, and I steel myself against it. Or at least try to.

I've always been a sucker for Rosa. Always and, apparently, still.

"When was the last time the vines were watered?"

A frown line appears between her eyebrows. "According to the watering schedule Damian and I set up, three days ago. I even double-checked the schedule and verified it against the recommendations I found online. But when I checked the ground yesterday, it seemed overly dry to me. Is it the soil? There's something wrong with the soil, isn't there?"

Oh, man. This is worse than I thought.

"The soil is fine. But there's no way it was watered three days ago," I tell her. "This ground is dry as dust, and the leaves are starting to curl. My guess is that your former employee turned it off when he left, or even before that, and didn't bother telling you."

"Oh my God."

"You need me. Or, at least, you need someone *like* me to start working on this vineyard *yesterday*, because whatever that guy was doing before he quit, it wasn't even close to enough."

Rosa swears under her breath.

I shouldn't find that as hot as I do.

"So in addition to being a quitter, he was shit at the job as well?"

I shrug. "Pretty much."

She turns away and shoves her hands into her hair. "I can't believe this."

Nudging her with my elbow, I say, "Look. I get it—this sucks. You're stuck with the guy you've been avoiding."

"Who's avoiding who? I've been in the same place for the last decade. You're the one who's been all over the world since then." She glares at me over her shoulder.

She's not wrong, but I barrel on. "I hate to tell you this, but at this point you don't have a choice. Or, I guess, your choices are work with me or get ready to rip these vines out."

"Rip them out? Are you crazy?"

"They'll be dead in a week. Useless. Might as well plow the whole property under and start over."

"That would take years."

I look her straight in the eye. "Exactly."

I can see the moment she gives in. Her shoulders lower and her chin drops, her gaze fixed on her shoes. "Okay. I'm in."

A wave of—what is that, relief?—washes over me. I ignore it and stick out my hand, right into her line of sight.

Even with her sunglasses on, I can see that she's narrowing her eyes.

"Come on, shake. I won't bite." *Not unless you ask.*

She hesitates a moment longer, then grasps my hand and shakes it once, dropping the grip immediately.

I wonder if she felt the same spark of heat I did the moment we touched. Again.

Perversely, I hope so. Even though this is going to make us working together a bitch to get through.

If one of us has to suffer, both of us should. And maybe I wish she could suffer a little more than I do. It's a crappy thing to think, but that's how it is. Heartbreak isn't always tidy and nice.

"Okay. I'll go ahead and check out from the bed-and-breakfast. I should be back in an hour or so."

"Check out?" She pushes her sunglasses up her nose and stares at me. "Where are you going to stay, then?"

I shrug. "Here, of course."

Rosa takes a step back, almost tripping over a rock in the path between the vines. I stretch out a hand to steady her, but she twitches out of my reach. "No, you're not."

I raise a brow. "Where else would I stay? My parents sold their house along with the vineyard, and I'm not commuting from their condo in San Luis Obispo. I'm only here for a few months, so no point in signing a long-term lease. And I know you can't pay me enough to cover the cost of a short-term rental or a hotel stay."

"But...what about privacy?"

I'm tempted to ask her how much privacy a wife needs from her husband, but I decide not to be a *total* dick.

"I'll stay out of your way. I just need a place to crash at the end of the day. Put me at the opposite end of the house—we'll barely see each other." I hesitate, then add, "Look, I know getting a vineyard and winery back in shape is expensive. How about we consider the housing part of my compensation, and you can add just a little extra. Cover food and shit."

"That wouldn't be fair," she insists, which is so typical. I'm giving her an out, and she's arguing against her own best interest.

"Fuck *fair*. You're trying to keep this place afloat on a bag of chips and the change you found under the couch cushions. I have free time, the knowledge you need, and apparently I'm nice enough to do it for room and board. Take the goddamn offer and be grateful."

"Why?"

"Why what?"

She leans forward. "Why are you willing to work for room and board?"

"I have my reasons."

Rosa shakes her head. "No, sorry—that's not good enough."

"Why?"

"Because I don't know you! Not anymore. It's been ten years, Jake. I have the right to know your motivation for being here."

I can't tell her everything, but I can tell her something. "Because I want you to win. I couldn't save my parents' vineyard, but maybe I can help save yours."

And it's not a lie. It's not the whole truth, but it's true just the same.

There's a long, silent pause, and then she nods. "Okay."

"Good." I clap my hands together and look around. "Okay, I'm gonna turn on the irrigation system. It's in the shed, right?"

She nods.

I add, "Then I'll head over to the bed-and-breakfast and grab my stuff. I'll be back in an hour or two. Meet you at the house?"

"Meet you at the house," she agrees. Then she turns and walks away, her shoulders straight and her head held high.

She's a goddamn warrior, and right now I'm glad we're on the same side.

Chapter 5

Rosa

I'm screwed.

I'm standing in the hallway upstairs, head swiveling back and forth, eyeing each bedroom doorway in turn. I can't put him in the one next to mine. That would be a disaster. But it's also closest to the only working bathroom. Which I'm using these days, too, and I can just see us barging in on each other in the middle of the night.

Does he wear pajamas? Boxers and a T-shirt? Nothing? God, I hope he covers up before leaving his room. I don't think I could handle a naked ex—

Ex-what? Ex-boyfriend? Ex-husband? Not according to him. Hell, if the annulment went through, like it was supposed to, he was technically never my husband at all. I still think he's wrong, but God, what if he's not?

Shouldn't a wife know what her husband wears—or doesn't wear—to bed?

This is ridiculous. I haven't been this impulsive since...

Nope. Not going there.

This isn't impulsive. It's practical. Jake's saving me money and, most likely, saving the winery as well. Providing him a place to stay is the least I can do.

I push the spark of reckless, impetuous energy swirling around inside me back into the box I've kept it in since that day ten years ago when we drove home from Las Vegas. I couldn't afford to be impulsive then. I can't afford to be impulsive now. Too much is riding on it.

I'll be professional and organized and polite. I'll ignore the spark of heat low in my belly every time Jake looks at me. I'll stay out of his way.

And hope he stays out of mine.

The farthest room will do for Jake. He can make the trek down the hall to the bathroom. It's not like he's paying for the privilege of living here.

I ignore the fact that *I'm* not paying for any of it, either, and stomp down to the room he'll be using so I can open the windows and let some air in.

It's dusty in here, and the bare mattress on its metal frame looks sad and disused. I make a mental note to find some sheets and bedding that fits. And to wash it before he needs to bunk down for the night.

I struggle with the window a little until it opens with a squeak, letting in fresh air to get rid of the musty smell of a room that's sat empty for so many years. Years ago, when the three of us lived here with Nonna after Mama left, this was Allegra's room. There are still holes in the walls from the tacks she used to hang pictures. Not musicians or actors—no, Allegra put up pages ripped out of travel magazines, gorgeous beaches and ancient cities and majestic mountain ranges, all circling the world map that sat in the middle of it all.

They're all gone now, just like Allegra is, visiting as many of the places in those photos as she can while she circles the globe, taking on temporary jobs and backpacking her way from country to country.

I miss both the photos and my sister.

I sigh and head downstairs again, hoping against hope the linen closet has something that will fit the bed.

A load of laundry later, I'm back in the main floor office looking at irrigation options on my computer when an email notification pops up.

I click on it, wincing when I see it's from Uncle Geno. This is the fourth time he's emailed asking for the Cab grapes.

No, not asking. *Telling* me that I need to do the right thing and hand the grapes over to Belmonte. That it's too late in the season to change plans like this, I owe it to the family, blah blah blah.

Even his emails sound pompous.

The first couple of times, I wrote back, trying to placate him.

Now? I just delete the shit out of them.

I lean back, a tiny smile of bitter satisfaction on my face, when the doorbell rings from across the hall.

Shit. Jake's here. And he'll *be* here for the duration.

I suck in a deep breath and walk over to open the front door.

He stands there, early-afternoon sunshine behind him, turning him dark and mysterious on my front porch. A battered suitcase and a duffel bag stitched back together with lime-green thread are at his feet.

"Fancy luggage," I say, not sure if I'm teasing or being rude or, God forbid, flirting. I'm off-kilter and off my game, seeing him here, at my door, for the first time in forever.

I tell the *Frozen* soundtrack in my head to fuck off and wave him inside.

"Your room is upstairs—take a right, end of the hall. The bedding is in the dryer; I'll bring it up when it's done."

"No need." He hefts the duffel strap onto his shoulder and grabs the suitcase. "I can get it later."

I close the door as he takes the stairs two at a time, full of way more energy than I would have anticipated from someone who was pretty drunk the day before.

No hangover? So unfair. I'm still nursing mine.

He takes a right and disappears down the hall. I stand there for a minute, uncertain, then decide I really don't want to look like I'm waiting for him or something. If we're going to be... living together...I have to figure out a way to make it normal. Casual. Just ships passing in the night.

I huff out a breath and head back to the office, glaring at the computer. I'm starting to hate the damn thing.

I'm deep in yet another article on watering schedules for California vineyards when he pokes his head around the doorframe. "I'm gonna walk the fields for a while, take some notes. What are you doing for dinner?"

"Oh. I, uh..." I shrug. "I have no idea. Probably a protein bowl out of the freezer."

"Sounds...edible."

He's judging me.

Fair. I'm judging myself. I've had way too many frozen dinners since taking on this monster of a project.

Belatedly, I remember him saying something about room and board. Shit, is he expecting me to cook for him?

"We could go grab a bite in town when I'm done."

Oh. Oh no. That's even worse.

Be seen in public with my secret possibly-not-totally-ex-husband? The boyfriend I'd stopped speaking to after high school? Oh, God.

"Okay, looks like dinner out is a no."

My face must have given me away. I'd feel bad about it, but he has to know it would be a bad idea.

Doesn't he?

"What do you have in the kitchen? We can throw something together here."

I clear my throat. "I, uh, haven't made it to the grocery store in a while," I say. "Been kinda busy."

He raises one eyebrow. I've always been jealous of that. Can't do it to save my life. "Food is an essential purchase, Rosa," he says. "You need to eat."

"I eat," I protest.

"Protein bars and frozen dinners?"

How does he know me so well when we haven't spoken in a decade?

Jake claps his hands together. "Okay. Do you have a grill?"

I blink at him. "Um. I think so? Maybe in the shed behind the house?"

He nods. "Perfect. Do you want to go to the store, or should I?"

"I'll hit the store, you make sure the grill still works?"

"Sounds good. I'll do a walk-around as well. Until I can see how much work needs to be done and how many people we'll need to hire to do it, we're dealing in speculation. I need to go check out the irrigation system and evaluate the rest of the vines. So go buy something we can throw on the grill, and I'll see you around seven for dinner. Then we can hit the ground running in the morning."

Before I can say anything else, he's gone, striding out the door with those long, loping steps that I remember chasing after when we were kids.

Even now, I can barely keep up.

"HUNGRY, ROSEY POSEY?"

I look up from the meat counter, where I'm debating between hamburger patties and sausages, to see my cousin Vittorio standing next to my cart.

"Hey, V," I say, biting back a sigh. He's caught me. There's no way to hide the fact that I have two of everything in the basket—two ears of corn, two slices of chocolate cake from the bakery, a couple different premade salads from the deli that should be good for lunches. I might as well be wearing a neon sign saying *I have a date tonight!*

Which I don't. But even I can tell what this looks like.

"So who's the lucky guy?" When I don't answer right away, he adds, "Or girl. Don't want to assume."

I shrug. "No lucky guy. Or girl. Just having a business dinner with my new vineyard manager."

He tries—and fails—to hide the surprise on his face. "New vineyard manager, huh? What happened to the last guy?"

I don't remember telling him about the last guy, but I guess gossip makes its rounds in Oak Creek Canyon as fast as the river flows in the springtime.

I don't feel like adding anything new to the rumor mill, so I just wave a hand dismissively. "Didn't work out."

"Huh." He tilts his head, considering. "Where'd you find someone this late in the season?"

No way in hell I'm telling him the truth. "Just lucky, I guess. How are you doing? How's Belmonte?"

"Fine."

He clearly doesn't want to share anything, either. It's not

like we were ever super close, but after knowing him my whole life, the almost total lack of communication once my sisters and I decided to take on Nonna's legacy after the will reading still hurts.

I tried texting the cousins after I left Belmonte, just to say hi, but the radio silence on the other end was too painful, so I stopped.

Family first, unless said family decides to go against Uncle Geno's wishes.

"I'd better get going," I say, gesturing at the shopping cart. I notice there's a shrink-wrapped tray of chicken skewers in my hand and abruptly pull back before smacking Vittorio in the face with it.

He nods slowly and takes a step away. "Hang in there."

"I will," I say. "I'll be fine."

He opens his mouth, like he's about to say something, then snaps it shut.

This is so damn awkward.

"Well, say hi to everyone," I chirp.

"Rosa." He places a hand on my shoulder. "You should really reconsider letting Dad have the Cab grapes."

I shrug, not willing to give a solid yes or no.

"At least this year," he says as I find a two-pack of steaks on sale for less than the hamburger patties and toss it into the cart. "It would make life so much easier for you."

Wait. Is this a setup or something? Maybe running into each other here wasn't an accident.

"Bye, Vittorio." I turn and make my way down the aisle, not bothering to look back.

I hate to admit it, but his comments sting.

It would be nice to have someone on my side, especially after working with my cousins and uncle for the past decade.

Yeah, selling the Cab grapes to Uncle Geno would be easier. Not that he'd actually agree to pay us for them—we're family, after all. And having the grapes would make everything easier for Belmonte as well, but Vittorio didn't say that part out loud.

He means well, but I'm not looking for easy.

And I'm not looking to make life easier for Uncle Geno, either.

TRUE TO HIS WORD, JAKE'S IN THE BACKYARD BY SEVEN, brushing down the grill and getting it ready for the steaks. After my conversation with Vittorio, I ended up buying way more food at the store than just for tonight, so I've been putting things away in the fridge and cupboards, chopping up fruits and veggies so they're ready to eat, making sure there's stuff for breakfast and quick lunches during the day.

I didn't deliberately stock the kitchen with Jake in mind, but deep down I know this is more food than I'd be able to eat in a month.

Well, whatever. He bargained for room and board. The least I can do is make sure there's actual quote, unquote board available when needed.

Also, maybe this way I can avoid the whole *Do I have to make him breakfast every day?* conundrum.

Cereal and milk and a banana. Have at it, cowboy.

I pull down a couple of Nonna's bowls and plates and add cutlery. They're old and should look out of style, but the solid lines and heft make me smile a little wistfully.

These were built to last. Just like the vineyard and winery.

And with a little elbow grease and love, I can bring those back into use again as well.

I carry an armful out and set the picnic table, using cheery woven yellow placemats and a citronella candle to brighten it up. Another trip to the kitchen and there's a plate of watermelon slices and a green salad tossed with poppyseed red-wine dressing.

"Smells great," I tell Jake, who's leaning over the grill like he's competing for first place in a barbecue competition.

He's always been competitive, even with just himself.

I'm not lying. The steaks smell divine, sizzling over the coals in a way that makes my stomach growl.

He tosses a carefree smile over his shoulder. "Patience, Bigfoot," he says, gesturing at my midsection with his tongs. "A few more minutes and they'll be perfect."

I nod and step around him, putting the finishing touches on the table, opening the wine, sneaking a crouton from the salad bowl. I head back to the grill and move the corn on the cob with a pair of tongs so they're not in the direct line of flame. They're charred to perfection, and I'm so tempted to just sit down and dig in.

It's not like this is a date, right? I can eat whenever I want.

But I look over at Jake, who's frowning at the meat thermometer like he's personally offended by it, and decide that would be rude.

And since when have I worried about being rude to Jake Wright?

Ugh, this is impossible.

"Would you like a glass of red? Or I might have some beer in the fridge." I'm lying. I know there's beer in the fridge—because I bought a six-pack today at the store.

What is wrong with me?

He looks up and smiles. "I'm working on a winery again. You think I'd dare drink beer?"

"Fair enough." I pour two generous glasses and take a long sip of mine, trying to get my conflicting emotions under control. "It's not Caparelli wine, but I'm interested in getting your opinion."

I'm hiding the truth a little. Not Caparelli wine, but Caparelli grapes—the ones Uncle Geno is so determined to continue using. I'm not very fond of Belmonte's Carleo, but people seem to like it. Deep down I wonder if I'm just bitter about the fake story my uncle is using to sell it. And the fact that he's using those grapes as leverage, making it as hard as possible to make this work for my sisters and me. At least I know Jake will be honest.

He's never been less than honest with me.

That pulls me up short, because it's true. And if it's still true, it means we're actually still married. Which is something I still haven't come to terms with, and right now, I just don't have the capacity to deal with it.

Dinner first, then wine, then an honest conversation about whether this vineyard and winery can be saved.

Jake lifts one steak with the long-handled tongs and nods approvingly. "Perfect," he says in a low, smoky voice, and I grit my teeth.

I can be a goddamn professional. I *can*.

The steaks are thick and juicy and heavy as he transfers them from the grill to the platter I'm holding for him, followed by the grilled corn. My mouth waters, mostly because of the food in front of me.

Partly because of the man who cooked it.

I place the platter on the picnic table and sit, grabbing my wine again for another long sip. I may not love the Carleo, but it's red and it's here and I need a drink.

Jake takes the seat across from me and plates an ear of corn and the larger of the two steaks for himself. "Better get it while it's hot," he says, reaching past me for the watermelon. "It's always best right off the grill."

He's not wrong. I fill my plate and cut off a bite of the steak, moaning just a little as the flavor bursts on my tongue. It's perfectly cooked and basted with just the right combination of spices. "You're hired," I say as soon as I swallow.

"I thought we established that earlier today," he says, taking a bite of his watermelon. His lips are full and shiny with watermelon juice. I bite the inside of my lip.

"Yeah, I, uh, guess we did," I stutter, then stuff half a dinner roll into my mouth so I'll shut up.

"Hungry?" He grins and swipes the drop of juice off his bottom lip with his thumb. "Don't blame you. Nothing better than a great meal at the end of a hard workday."

He lifts his thumb to his mouth and sucks the juice off of it, and I almost melt onto the bench seat.

"Yeah," I say faintly. "Hard day."

It hasn't been, though. Well, I guess if you count the emotional stress, which is a constant. But overall, knowing there's someone else around to help me carry the load has been —nice. Comforting. Like I'm not completely fucking this thing up.

At least, I don't think so. I haven't gotten his official report yet. "How did everything look?"

Jake shakes his head and lifts a bite of steak to his mouth. "No shop talk until after dinner," he admonishes, then slides the fork in.

Okay, fine. I focus on the food, shoving down the dread that's taken up permanent residence in my stomach ever since Nonna left us Caparelli.

The corn is crisp and juicy, the steak perfectly cooked, the salad and fruit a nice counterpart to the grilled items. By the time I finish my meal, Jake has pushed his plate away and is leaning back, sipping his glass of Carleo.

I clear my throat. "Does getting your opinion on tonight's wine count as shop talk?"

He squints at the glass, swirling the remainder of the wine as he ponders. "Nah, that's fine."

I wait for him to continue, but he just sits there, expression placid.

"And?"

"It's fine. The wine is fine. Nothing exciting, not bad, just... fine."

I let out a breath and nod vigorously. "Exactly! Thank you. I thought I was going crazy."

"Going crazy—over a middling red wine?" He shakes his head. "I don't get it."

I wave a hand at his half-full glass. "That's the Carleo. Uncle Geno's flagship Cabernet—the one he shills like it's the best wine ever made. I've never gotten the appeal. It's not bad, just...okay. But everyone else acts like it's the most amazing thing ever."

"Huh." Jake tilts his head and looks appraisingly at it again. "Mom and Dad told me about it—the Carleo. How it was really popular. I guess you can't account for taste."

"I thought I was just bitter."

The words spill out before I can bite them back. I really have to work on not saying every single thing I'm thinking out loud.

It isn't a problem around anyone else.

"Why bitter?" He sounds interested, curious, not judgmental.

I hesitate, then plunk my glass down and lean forward. "Uncle Geno has been using the Cab grapes from this vineyard to make the Carleo for years now. And he spun this whole story about how he saved Nonna's family vineyard from ruin, making it viable again, to pay homage to Nonna and Papa's great love story. But it's all bullshit. The vineyard was in great shape when Nonna and Papa combined their properties. It wasn't until Geno took over, when Papa died, that Caparelli was abandoned and left to fall apart. He just takes the grapes to build up Belmonte's yield and uses a fake story to sell it."

"That sucks." Jake sets down his glass. "So what's he going to do now?"

I shrug. "Wear me down until I give him the grapes, I guess."

"That doesn't seem like a solid business plan," he says wryly, and I smother a burst of laughter.

"He was not happy when we decided to go out on our own," I confess. "And when he couldn't convince me to keep Caparelli in the family business, he pulled all his workers."

Jake scowls. "That's such a dick move."

"Yeah, well, he'd say keeping the grapes to myself is a dick move, too." I take another swallow of the Carleo. He's totally right—it's fine.

I want Caparelli wines to be better than fine. I want them to be exceptional.

But I don't know how in hell I'm going to make that happen.

"They're your grapes. Yours and your sisters'. And it would be a crime to hand them over just to be turned into—this." His nose wrinkles as he glares at the half inch in the bottom of his glass. "Those vines deserve better. You deserve better."

My heartbeat speeds up a little at his declaration. I know he's talking about the vineyard and the winery, but for just a minute, I let the idea settle into my bones and blood, soften the tension in my shoulders.

I can't remember the last time someone else cared even a little about what I deserved.

"So." I shake off the tenderness, bury it in practicality. "About those vines."

He sighs and pushes back from the table. "Well, there's good news and bad news."

I've been expecting nothing but bad, so I suppose that's something positive to hold on to. "Give me the worst of it first."

"Well, like I thought, the irrigation system was turned off. I estimate the crops haven't been watered in about a week."

"A *week?* Damien only left four days ago." I huff out a breath. "That surf-obsessed *fucker.*"

Jake snorts. "Sounds like a winner."

"How can you tell it's been a week?"

"It's not hard if you know what you're looking for. The leaves were turning and curling, and you were probably another thirty-six hours from losing the canopy altogether. But the irrigation is running now, and some extra water today and tomorrow should bring it back from the brink. Shouldn't be a problem down the road. The quality will still be up to Caparelli standards. "

"Okay. That's good." My knees are shaking a little under the table. How could I have missed this? What was Nonna thinking, leaving the vineyard to me? I clearly have no idea what I'm doing.

Not for the first time, I realize how glad I am that Jake is here—and on my side.

I wouldn't have expected that, after...everything.

He scratches behind his ear, looking out into the darkness beyond the backyard. "I'm not super impressed with the pruning. It looks—pretty basic, to be honest. I don't know how much care and effort your uncle put into these acres."

I bite back a scathing reply. "Not much. The bare minimum, I'd guess."

Jake nods. "Looks like it. There's a lot of potential if done right next spring. But you lost a lot of early grapes in the shattering, which isn't always a bad thing, though it could have been set up better for success. Nothing to be done now, but something to think about next year."

I add it to my mental list of things to do. Luckily I won't have to deal with that one until things settle down and Bianca is home. Maybe Allegra, too.

Not that any of us are equipped to deal with pruning and vineyard management, but hopefully together we can find someone trustworthy by then.

A little voice whispers that Jake is someone trustworthy. Or was ten years ago. But he'll be long gone by then.

Something pings in the back of my head, and I squint at Jake. "I thought shattering was a normal part of the growing process."

"Well, yeah. It can function as a natural thinning." He waves a hand at the acreage behind the house, even though we can't see the vines right now. "But if the vines are over-pruned, they're not protected enough from environmental factors like too much rain or cold weather early in the season. From what I can see, there was a little more shattering than I'd like, which will mean fewer crops at the end of the season."

I rub my forehead, trying to stave off the headache that's brewing.

"And, uh, that's not all."

"Jake." My voice is flat. "I told you to start with the worst part."

"Yeah, I know. It's all kind of bad, though."

"You said there was good news as well."

"I was trying to be positive."

I squeeze my eyes shut. "Go ahead."

"There's some insect damage in two sections. If we don't take care of it soon, it'll spread to the rest of the crop and could kill the entire output for this year."

"Shit."

He nods. "I just need to know how you want me to handle it. Pesticides are probably the easiest—and cheapest—solution, but it can be done organically, too. Depends on whether you want to go the organic route."

"I have to ask Bianca." I lean my head back and look up at the night sky. A full moon is rising over the horizon, tinting the darkness with a soft glow. "She's the winemaker. She needs to have a say."

"If it helps, I have a lot of experience with the organic side of viticulture. The vineyard I worked on in Washington state was certified, and I learned a lot of good techniques there."

Maybe we should try to get certified.

What am I doing? We need to deal with the issues happening now, not dream about what we could do a year or three down the road.

"So why don't you call Bianca in the morning, see what she says. In the meantime, I can start removing the infested sections until we get her decision."

"Okay. Yes. Let's do that."

I really appreciate that he's not trying to force me to decide immediately or push me in one direction or another—letting me discuss it with Bianca first instead of telling me what I have to do right now. I know time is of the essence, but he's still giving me a moment to decide. I'm not used to that.

And isn't that a sad state of affairs?

"One last thing."

I groan. "There's more?"

"Just..." He tilts his head down and looks me straight in the eye. It's a little disconcerting. "Do I have your permission to hire a crew? Just two or three workers, for the rest of the season."

I can feel my face scrunching up as I go over the numbers in my head. We should be just about able to cover it. I nod, and his expression smooths out. Like he was holding his breath as much as I was.

I don't know how I feel about him being as invested in this venture as I am. Or maybe he's trying to prove something to himself.

But for now, I'm just going to appreciate having someone around to help shoulder the burden, at least for a little while.

"Thanks." He leans back again, squinting up at the darkening sky. "I'll head into town in the morning and see who I can find."

"It's been a few years since you were here for growing season," I remind him. "Don't know how many contacts you still have."

"A few." He smiles, low and easy, and I can feel it curling in the pit of my stomach.

"It may be tough to find anyone this late in the season."

"Don't worry. I can handle it."

His confidence doesn't surprise me. Maybe he won't run into the same brick wall I have this season. I consider saying something but decide to let it lie. It very well could be a gender-bias difference or the fact that I'm a newbie at this whole game. He could have a much easier time of it.

I'd resent that if it wasn't working in my favor.

I start gathering the dishes. He follows with the rest of the leftovers, and we work in companionable silence in the kitchen to put things away and wash the dishes. A couple of soap bubbles float in the air as I shut off the faucet, nothing left to be done.

The ease of cleanup shifts to something warmer, more dangerous. I clear my throat. "Well."

Jake smiles, like I've said something funny. There's nothing humorous about this, though. Nothing at all.

"I'll see you in the morning," he says abruptly, then disappears up the stairs, leaving me breathing out a gust of air like I've been holding it for hours.

Yeah, this is going to be one hell of a summer. And it's only getting started.

Chapter 6

Jake

I can't sleep.

And it's not because the room is too warm or the mattress too lumpy. I mean, those things don't *help*, but it's really more about being under the same roof as Rosa for the first time since—

Since our secret sleepovers in the Caparelli wine cave when we were teens.

And I can't let my thoughts wander in *that* direction, or I'll never fall asleep again.

I shift under the light covers, wondering how much it would cost to have air-conditioning installed in a house this old, then remind myself that one, Rosa doesn't have the money and two, I won't be around long enough to benefit from the hypothetical AC anyway.

The window is open, and the fresh scent of growing things wafts in on the cool breeze. I've missed this in my years away. Every wine-growing region smells a little different, and even after my many vineyard experiences, Oak Creek Canyon is my favorite scent in the world.

Sometimes I really regret letting the situation with Rosa chase me away from home.

The house settles, and I punch the pillow to get it into a better shape. Maybe I should get a glass of water.

I pad down the hall to the bathroom, barefoot, hoping Rosa is fast asleep. I don't want to wake her.

It's weird, being here at the Caparelli homestead, like watching shadow us circle and dart through the quiet hallways and giant backyard. I catch glimpses of us at eight and ten, playing tag and hide-and-seek. At eleven and thirteen, camping out in the backyard under the stars, confessing our deepest secrets to each other. At sixteen and eighteen, sneaking into the wine cave to make out, certain no one would ever know. At eighteen and twenty, with the whole world in front of us, bright and shiny and new.

And then...nothing. Nothing but regrets and anger and recrimination.

Until now. Seeing Rosa as an adult, after all these years, has been like adding yet another shadow us to the collection.

Something else to carry with me when I go away again.

Because of course I'll be going away.

Now that Mom and Dad have sold the place, there's nothing to keep me here ever again.

The ironic thing is there's nothing to keep me *away* from here, either.

But it's too late to focus on that. Even if I wanted to stay, too much time has passed, too much water under the bridge. I made the best decision I could back when I felt like I had no other choice, but I let go of so many other things in the process.

So I'll be moving on. And I've got lots of options. I'll still be working for someone else, of course, but it's not like I have a choice about that part these days.

Italy is nice. Francesco Manca should have an opening next year. Or I could hire on at a winery in the Bordeaux region. I've always liked playing around with the richer reds.

Maybe I'll head back up to Oregon. The Willamette Valley has a lot of opportunities. It's a growth market.

Or I could head back to Washington state, especially the region right over the border from British Columbia. I still have no idea why that region of Canada is such a big wine-growing area across the border while the Americans still run cattle on their side.

Wine is a much better proposition than beef these days.

Of course, beef makes me think of steak, which makes me think of dinner and sitting in the backyard with Rosa while twilight wrapped around us.

I know I should avoid her. I should do my job, hole up in my room, and stay out of her orbit. But that's easier said than done.

The water from the tap is cold and refreshing, so I fill my glass again and open the bathroom door, ready to take it back to my room.

And of course, because my luck is no luck at all, she's on the other side of the door.

She jumps back, startled, her hand dropping from the door handle as I swing it out of her reach.

"I, uh—sorry." I look up, over her shoulder, down the hall.

Anywhere but directly at Rosa.

And I'm lying, because there's no way I'm *not* looking at her. She's in shorts and a teeny tank with thin straps, both made of some pale, light material, and the moonlight streaming down the hallway turns them transparent in a way that makes little Jake stand up and take notice.

Her nipples are peaked, tight little buds under the almost-see-through fabric, and I can't stop staring at them.

The years have been good to Rosa.

"Jake," she whispers, and I realize she's looking at me looking at her, and wasn't there some promise I made to myself about staying professional and distant and *out of her orbit?*

And where the hell is the anger and disappointment and frustration that's followed every memory of Rosa since I left Oak Creek Canyon?

Jesus, one meal and a chance meeting in the hall and I'm collapsing like a cheap grape-collection basket.

I lift my glass, ripping my gaze away from her chest, and say, "Thirsty."

I'm such a goddamn moron.

And she's *not* a moron, because her next move is to cross her arms over her chest, blocking her gorgeous breasts from view.

But now her gaze is fixated on my bare chest, and I realize I'm not the only one who's appreciating the changes of the past ten years.

The bolt of lust that arrows through me almost drops me to my knees.

I want to keep looking at her.

I want her to keep looking at me.

And both of those things are probably a bad fucking idea.

"Good night," I murmur and slip past her where she's standing in the bathroom doorway. At the last second, she steps back so we don't actually touch.

At least one of us has their head on straight.

I'm just not quite sure which one of us it is.

"Good night," she whispers back, scurrying into the bathroom and closing the door with a little more force than absolutely necessary. I head to my room, clutching the glass of water like it's my last link to sanity.

Maybe it is.

Because all I want to do is turn around and step inside *Rosa's* room, slip into her bed, pull her into my arms, and fall asleep together.

Maybe some other activities before that point, too.

But it's not going to happen. I'm here to make Caparelli successful in a way I wasn't able to do for Take Flight. Preserve one more family winery before it's ripped away by outsiders trying to make a quick buck.

And if I can stick it to her uncle at the same time—well, that's icing on the cake.

But Rosa and me? I just don't see that happening.

I shake my head and take the last few steps to my bedroom, closing the door firmly.

I set the glass on the bedside table and crawl under the covers. Tomorrow I've got to be up at dawn, making sure the irrigation system is working as intended. Then I'll head into town and see about picking up a crew.

There's a lot of work to do, and I need to stop thinking about *what could have been* and *what might be* and focus on *what is.*

That's the only way I'm going to survive this season.

"Nope."

"Sorry, no."

"Lo siento, señor."

"All booked up, man."

I shove a hand through my hair and blow out a frustrated breath. I'm running into brick walls everywhere I turn, and I can't figure out why.

It's later in the season, but it still shouldn't be this hard to hire some temporary workers for the next couple of months. I've never had this much trouble anywhere in the world.

But the minute I mention Caparelli, any interest dries up faster than the irrigation ditches during a drought.

I have my suspicions—and no one to ask about them.

It's getting near lunchtime, so I head to the café down the street and grab a table outside. The server brings me a big glass of ice water with lemon, and I drink half immediately. It's hot out today.

"Welcome back," booms a voice from over my shoulder, and I turn to see one of my best friends from high school drop into the seat next to me with a grin. "Knew you couldn't stay away forever."

"Wade Jenkins," I say, grinning. "I'm only temporarily, brother." I give him a fist bump and gesture to the server. "Join me for lunch?"

"Sure," he says, accepting another glass of water. We both know hydration is key—for people and for wine grapes.

In high school, we competed for spots on the sports teams and scholarships. In college, before I transferred schools, we fought for class rank and the best internships. But now, with time and distance and our own meandering paths to success, we're just two guys who know a thing or two about the wine business.

"So, how's the family estate?" I keep my voice light, like I'm not jealous as hell that he's still got a family estate to run. The slight raise to his eyebrows tells me I'm not as successful at hiding it as I'd hoped, but he's kind enough to ignore it.

"Same old, same old." He wipes his brow and slaps his hat

back on his head, protection from the sun. "Dad keeps on pretending to retire. I keep pretending to believe him. I'll eventually get to make decisions on my own."

"Cheers to that," I say and clink my glass to his. The server swings by again, and we order.

He leans back in his chair and tilts his head. "So what brings you back to Oak Creek Canyon? Helping your folks pack up? Sorry about that, by the way."

I wave his sympathy away. "Nah, they're already moved into their new condo in San Luis Obispo."

He whistles. "Nice."

Yeah. At least the damn hockey player who bought the place didn't try to lowball them. Even with the medical bills they were able to afford a nice place to retire.

"I'm actually working with Rosa on Caparelli," I tell him, and the hairs on the back of my neck lift up at the expression that crosses his face.

"Oh," he says, shifting uncomfortably in his seat.

I stare at him. "What do you mean, oh?"

He winces, then says, "Nothing."

I can feel my brow furrowing. "What aren't you telling me?"

"I—" Wade looks around. "Never mind."

The thing is, what happened between me and Rosa is just that—between us. As far as anyone else ever knew, we were just your typical high school sweethearts who drifted apart.

Our marriage? Nobody knew about that except for Uncle Geno.

The couple at the table next to us gets up and settles their bill, chatting loudly as they leave the patio. As soon as the space around us is cleared, Wade leans forward.

"Look, Jake, I'm telling you this as a friend: You may want to cut your losses and find something else."

"What the hell is that supposed to mean?"

"Well, for one, working with your ex-girlfriend is just asking for trouble."

He's deflecting. I sit back and wait for him to continue.

After a long moment, he does. "I'm assuming you just got back?"

I nod, and he shakes his head. "Damn. So you've missed the drama."

Great. "What drama?"

He leans back and takes a long sip of his ice water. "You know Rosa's grandma died recently?"

"Of course." I have a sinking feeling I know where he's going with this.

"She left Caparelli to the girls. And you can guess how well that went over with Geno."

I nod, letting him think he's the first to tell me about this situation. Like Rosa wouldn't tell me up front what I was dealing with.

Amateur.

"He's been using those grapes for years and already had half the crop spoken for in Carleo presales. So when the girls chose to run the place on their own, he decided to make sure that's exactly what they have to do—run it on their own."

The server chooses that moment to bring our meals, and we set the conversation aside until prying ears wander away again. As soon as he's gone, I lean forward and murmur, "What exactly does that mean?"

His voice is pitched just as low. "His workers have been keeping that vineyard running for years. But now they're all working on Belmonte instead."

"Well, yeah. That's where I come in."

Wade takes a bite of his sandwich and shakes his head.

"Just don't expect any payment. Word is Rosa is broke. Nobody wants to take a chance on not getting a paycheck."

"Where did you hear that?"

He shrugs. "It's not like it's a secret. She tried to hire a couple of the guys that worked the fields for Geno, but he warned them she didn't have the money to pay them. Didn't want them to get ripped off."

I just stare at him, my mind going a thousand miles an hour.

So Rosa's uncle takes his workers off Caparelli, then warns people she'll stiff them if they go to work for her. Did he scare off the last guy, too? Yeah, money is tight, but not that bad. I've seen the spreadsheet. She could pay a handful of workers to keep the vineyard running—but not if those workers don't trust her to make good on her promises.

And Geno seems to be willing to ruin her reputation to get his hands on those grapes again.

That *bastard*.

Just waiting for the girls to come crawling back, begging him to take the grapes so they aren't ruined and worthless. After all, with Rosa on her own, she'd have no other choice.

"So it's just Geno's word, huh," I say, trying to keep my anger at bay. "Any actual evidence? Or is a rumor enough to scare everyone off?"

I level a *look* at Wade, who at least has the decency to glance down, a hint of red crawling up his neck. He may be a coward in this situation, but he's not a complete asshole.

"You know how it is. Geno's pretty respected in this town. Why would he make that up?"

"It'd be nice if Rosa was respected, too. But I guess that's too much to ask."

Part of me wonders bitterly why Geno couldn't have focused all that negative energy on the hockey player who's decided to play winemaker with my family vineyard, but in the end, it really doesn't matter. Right now, Rosa is being played by someone who should *want* her to succeed.

"Just be careful, man. You don't want to get ripped off."

"Thanks, but I know what I'm doing," I tell Wade.

"Good luck. Maybe you and Rosa have a shot at making it work. The winery, I mean."

"Appreciate it."

I dig into my pasta and turn the conversation back to Wade's winery, but in the back of my head I'm already plotting.

Geno's sabotaging Caparelli?

It's time to go to war.

Chapter 7

Rosa

I'm sitting in the office—again, still, always—when the front door opens. I'm still not used to someone else waltzing into Nonna's house like that. Even when Damien the Surfer Dude was working here, he rang the doorbell or knocked.

Not Jake. He just comes right in like he owns the place.

Or like he lives here, which he does, so I need to get over myself and accept that fact that there's no reason for him to knock like he's a visitor. It's not like he owns the place.

My face heats up as I remember my lack of freak-out when we ran into each other in the bathroom last night. Talk about owning the place—he filled the bathroom doorway with those broad shoulders and bare chest and low-slung pajama pants I suspect he only wore because I'm in the house.

I was startled to see him there, like I'd conjured him straight out of the super-sexy dream that had woken me moments before, but I wasn't bothered.

No, scratch that. I was bothered—*hot* and bothered, to be accurate.

I should have gone straight back to my room. Instead I stood there, drinking in the whole grown-up gorgeousness of the boy I let get away. The man I no longer know but who's sleeping under my roof anyway.

And I'm pretty sure he wasn't unaffected, either, if the heated look in his eyes was any indication. It was like his gaze stroked me from head to toe, a physical touch whispering over my skin. Which both thrills and terrifies me.

I shake my head and banish my inappropriate thoughts to the far reaches of my brain, even though I know they'll come out to torment me as soon as I let down my guard. Right now, I have to focus on the winery and our vanishingly small chances of making this whole operation work.

"How'd it go?" I call out before I can talk myself out of it.

Part of me hopes he ran into the same roadblocks I did, just so I know it's not all about me.

The practical part of me hopes he managed to hire a team. At least a couple of people. Maybe even one, if they're good enough.

Because I really want this harvest to be a success. I want this winery to be a success. And I can't do it all on my own.

His footsteps are slow as he approaches the office, and my heart sinks.

He comes in and throws himself into the chair across from my desk. "Hey."

That doesn't sound good.

"No luck?"

He sits there for a minute, his gaze somewhere far away. I wait. He'll tell me when he's ready.

Jake has always been like this—a combination of extroverted and pensive. His outgoing, friendly, over-the-top personality masks someone who likes to think things through. He's not the sort to blindly rush in without working out all the angles in advance.

Except when we got married, that is. That was the ultimate impulsive move—for both of us.

He clears his throat, and I realize that I'm woolgathering now, too. I glance at him and tilt my head, ready for his response.

"No. No luck."

I should feel some vindication, but I don't. Just frustration and a growing fear that we won't be able to keep the vineyard and winery afloat long enough to make a go of it.

I'll be squandering Nonna's birthright—the biggest, scariest gift I've ever received.

"You weren't able to hire anyone? At all? Not even one dude?"

He shakes his head, one corner of his mouth ticking up in a humorless smile. "Nope. Not even one dude."

Some of my panic must be showing on my face because he rushes to add, "I'm not giving up. We just need to—pivot."

Panic turns to humor as I masterfully hold back a snort of laughter while a scene from an old sitcom flashes through my mind.

Not so masterful, I realize, glimpsing the smirk on Jake's face.

Bastard.

"Okay, so we're—pivoting. That's good. What, uh, what exactly does that mean?"

He slaps his hands on his thighs and stands. My core clenches.

Oh, this does not bode well.

"I'm going to check with a friend tomorrow, see if I can call in some favors. We'll have a team by the end of the week."

I nod slowly, wondering just what kind of favors he's going to call in. How tangled is this partnership going to be?

But I don't have any choice if I want to avoid slinking back to Uncle Geno, my tail between my legs.

"In the meantime, I'll start trimming out the insect damage."

"By yourself?"

I don't mean to sound like I doubt his skills, but it's a lot for one person to handle.

"Of course."

"I can pitch in."

He shakes his head. "I've got it."

"I don't mind."

"It'll take me longer to teach you what to do than it would take me to go ahead and do it." He smiles and turns to go.

I take a deep breath. "Jake."

He stops and looks back at me.

"If I'm going to run this operation eventually, I need to know these things."

He pauses, head tilted as he looks at me. I force myself not to shift nervously under his gaze. It's like he can see inside me, see all the parts I never show anyone, except maybe Sasha. Not even my sisters.

I'm afraid he sees the part of me that thinks I'm not only not good enough but might never become good enough. It's not like I've ever achieved anything the way Bianca has. I've never put myself out there like Allegra. All I've done so far with my life is...nothing.

God, I hope he can't see that.

Finally, he nods once. "You're right. But not today. This one really is a one-person job, Rosa. But yes, I'll get you out in the field and show you what you need to know."

"Thank you."

Partly for taking my request seriously, and partly for not teasing me about that exhale that sounded excessive even to my own ears.

The glint in his eye tells me it's a big sacrifice.

"I'm gonna hold you to it," I tell him. "And if the job today ends up being bigger than you thought, come get me."

"I'll be fine," he says with a wink. "Don't worry about me."

But I do. I worry about him...and the vineyard and the winery and my sisters and...

I'm a worrier, all right? It's what I do.

And by the grin on his face, I know he's remembering that about me, too.

"Shut up," I grumble, and he barks out a laugh.

"It's fine," he says, tapping the door frame as he exits the room. "I've got everything under control."

Then he's gone, taking his energy and confidence and all-too-masculine presence with him, leaving me a little breathless and a whole lot keyed up.

I also may have just a teeny bit of a competence kink, and he's pushing all my buttons.

The sun is starting to go down when I shut off the computer for the night. I've spent most of the day working on my budget, and now that I don't have to pay Surfer Dude (and Jake is taking just room and board), I'll probably have enough to pay a couple of field-workers through the end of the season. But after that—after the grapes are harvested and pressed and set aside for maturing—I still have to figure out how to survive until they can be sold.

This is so fucking complicated.

I could sell the Cabernet grapes to Uncle Geno, let him keep producing Carleo for another year. But I just...don't want to.

I don't want to postpone this for another year or another two or probably a decade. Once he has the Cabernet grapes back, he'd never let them go.

And besides, he doesn't want to *buy* them. He wants me to give them to him free of charge. Because family.

Ugh. Enough mental strain for the day. I slap the laptop closed and stand, stretching all the muscles that cramped up while I sat at the desk for way too long. My stomach growls, and I check my watch.

Food. I need food, and now.

I wander down the hall to the kitchen, which has a light on. My first instinct is to worry about the power bill, if I'm leaving lights on all over the place and forgetting about them, but then I turn the corner and see Jake, bent over at the waist, head in the fridge.

God, his ass is a thing of beauty.

I take my time admiring it.

Hey, a girl can look, right?

And it's not like he didn't take advantage of the situation last night at the bathroom door. Turnabout is fair play, and all that.

I hear him clear his throat and realize he's looking at *me*, looking at his butt.

Busted.

"You want something?" He's got this way-too-attractive smirk on his face. He knows damn well what I was doing.

And he probably has a pretty good idea of what I want.

But I can't have it, not with all this history between us, so I gesture at the fridge. "Getting a little hungry."

His gaze sweeps me from head to toe. "Same."

No fair.

I shove my hands into my pockets and step closer to the fridge. "Anything look good?" I hold up a hand, cutting off a—no doubt—sexually charged double entendre. "Food, Jake. I'm talking about food."

He steps back, hands up in an *I surrender* gesture. "I was thinking about throwing together a salad with some grilled chicken. Join me?"

I nod and grab some stuff out of the crisper. "You grill the chicken; I'll make the salad."

"Deal."

A BOTTLE OF WINE, A LOAF OF CRUSTY BREAD FROM THE farmers market, and two massive salads tossed with homemade strawberry vinaigrette later, I push my plate away and prop my elbows on the picnic table. "So, how did the insect damage work out?"

"Got almost all of it." Jake mimics my elbows-on-the-table move and leans forward. "It's looking really good out there, if I do say so myself."

"Please." I wave a hand grandly at him. "Give yourself all the credit you deserve. God knows I wouldn't know what to congratulate you for if it was up to me."

"Hey." He tilts his head and looks at me again in that way that makes me squirm inside. "Don't sell yourself short."

"Come on, Jake. I don't know the first thing about keeping a vineyard alive. I didn't even know the irrigation system had been turned off."

"You've got good instincts, Rosa. You always have. Maybe you didn't know what was going on with the irrigation system, but you knew something was wrong. You were out there checking the soil because you tracked that the vines weren't in good shape."

I duck my head, feeling heat crawl up my neck.

"And you're doing a crap ton of research on that laptop of yours."

"How do you—" I snap my mouth shut as his smile grows.

"Lucky guess. But I was right, wasn't I?"

I take a long swallow of wine so I don't have to respond.

"I haven't forgotten your obsession with learning everything down to the last detail. Why write a two-page essay when seven pages of meticulously researched information is ready to go?"

"I hate you," I mumble, knowing it's a lie.

He throws his head back and laughs, which shows me he knows it's a lie, too.

"Anyway." Jake finishes his wine and sits back. "You know more than you think you do. But you *also* want to know more and do more, which is really on-brand for you, and I'm sorry I didn't recognize that earlier."

"I don't expect you to be a mind reader," I protest, but he's already shaking his head.

"Not a mind reader," he says quietly. "I just know you."

I clear my throat and look away. He hasn't known me since we were both barely adults.

And yet.

He's not wrong.

I need a change of subject before this gets too personal, so I lean back and look up at the darkening sky. "Nice night."

Jake hums an affirmative, letting the conversation turn without protest. "Nothing beats a summer night in Napa."

"Oh, come on." I stand and start gathering up the dishes. "You've been all over the world. You can't tell me this is better than—than Canada or Italy."

"Keeping tabs on me?" He slants me another one of his patented smirks.

"No." I snatch his plate off the table and add it to my stack of dishes with a clank. "Oak Creek Canyon's just a small town in a lot of ways. People talk. And your parents were always super proud of you."

His teasing smile fades away at that. "Yeah. I know."

Somehow I've killed the mood completely, and I don't even know how. "It's a good thing, you know." At his puzzled look, I add, "Having parents who are proud of you."

I don't think my mom has ever bothered to wonder what the three of us have been up to since she left with her new husband. Hard to be proud of people you don't even think of from time to time.

"There's a lot of pressure," he says quietly. "All that pride."

I just stand there, because what the hell do I do with that?

After a long moment, he sighs and changes the subject yet again. "Did you get a chance to talk to Bianca?"

I nod. "She's totally down for going organic. Actually, I think her exact words were *Oh my God, I was afraid if I told you I wanted to do that you'd have a coronary.* Apparently she's been learning a ton about different organic processes down in Argentina but thought it would be one more thing for me to stress about."

"One more thing? What is she talking about? You are a paragon of *calm and collected.*"

I wrinkle my nose and throw a napkin at him.

He catches it in one hand and drops it onto the little tower of dishes I've stacked on the table. "I'm glad to hear Bianca and

I are on the same page. I can start implementing some changes now, so she can continue it after…"

His voice trails off. Picking up the empty bottle and wine-glasses, he heads toward the back door. "Anyway. I'll get the foundation set for her. And you can join me in the vineyard tomorrow, if you want."

"Perfect," I murmur, following him inside.

The kitchen is warm as we clean up, suds drifting from the sink. I wash, he dries.

It's cozy. It's domestic. It's terrifying how right it feels.

Is this what I gave up?

I shove the traitorous thought away and wipe my hands on a dish towel. "Well, I should hit the sack."

It's barely eight thirty, but I don't dare spend more time with Jake tonight. I'm too weak, too tempted.

He raises one eyebrow but thankfully doesn't say anything. Even though he could totally call me on it. "I hope you sleep well."

I nod and hurry out of the kitchen and up the stairs. I really wish one of my sisters was here to run interference.

Not between me and Jake. Between me and my stupid, romantic self.

Chapter 8

Jake

When I walk into the kitchen early the next morning, Rosa is already there.

She's wearing old jeans, a concert T-shirt from who knows how long ago—the band broke up sometime in the past five years, so before that—well-worn Romeos, and a baseball cap. Her thick brown hair is in a ponytail somehow threaded through the opening in the back of the cap.

She's practically bouncing on her toes, ready to get to work.

"Morning," I grumble, reaching past her for the coffee pot. I need caffeine after last night.

I did not sleep well at all.

There weren't any middle-of-the-night collisions in the hallway outside the bathroom last night, but that didn't make it easier sleeping under the same roof with Rosa.

I thought I could do this. Do the job, stay cool and collected, keep my emotions out of it.

Show her what she's missed.

Instead I'm seeing what I could have had if Geno hadn't interfered.

If Rosa hadn't let him.

I grit my teeth and try to leave the past in the past. It's just not as easy as it was when I didn't have to see Rosa every damn day.

"Someone's grumpy," she teases, taking the pot from me and filling a large-size travel mug. She shoves it into my hands and adds, "Sorry I don't have a vat-sized mug for you. I know how important caffeine is to your daily existence."

I huff and take a sip of the coffee. "I'll have a decent comeback once I'm caffeinated."

Rosa wrinkles her nose at me. "Come on, whiner. Time's a-wasting."

I'm not sure when she became more of a morning person than me, but I dutifully follow her out the back door, grabbing my backpack along the way.

The sun peeks over the horizon as we trudge up to the vineyard. Well, I trudge. Rosa bounces along perkily.

"Why are you in such a good mood?" I scowl down at my coffee. "It's barely past six."

She shrugs. "I don't know...I'm just glad to get out of the house. Feel like I'm actually doing something for Caparelli."

"Hey." I stop in the middle of the road, blocking her from moving forward. "You're working your ass off. You don't have to be in the fields to be *doing something* for Caparelli. If you weren't here, holding everything together on your own, this whole place would be back under Geno's authority by now. So don't sell your contribution short."

She tilts her head and smiles at me. "Thanks. That's a really nice thing to say."

"It's the truth."

We continue up the road, the quiet of early morning wrapping around us like mist. This is the time of day I love vine-yards the most, when the air is cool and the land almost feels like it's sleeping.

We reach the lowest patch of vines, and Rosa turns to me again. "So, what are we doing today?"

I dig into my backpack and pull out the plat map I sketched up last night, another reason I didn't get much sleep. Then I hand Rosa a notepad and pen. "We're going to check the insect traps."

She nods and clicks the pen open. "Gotcha."

We spend the morning walking up and down the rows of vines, stopping every dozen yards or so to check the traps. I mark the locations on the plat map while Rosa writes down our findings on the notepad.

"What exactly are we looking for?" She peers over my shoulder at the trap I'm holding. "Is everything fine?"

I nod. "So far, so good. Only the typical insects you'd find this time of year. Nothing invasive, nothing super harmful."

"How often do we need to check the traps?"

"I like to check every week or so. Just to be on the safe side." I set the trap back in place and make a note on the map.

"So what's your favorite part?"

I blink at her. "Of checking the insect traps?"

"No." She rolls her eyes at me. "Of working on a vineyard. Being in the industry."

"Oh." I squint and tilt my head. "Is it cheating if I say all of it?"

"Yes. It's cheating." She marches off down the row to the next insect trap, turning around and grinning at me. "But seriously. What's your favorite job from the past ten years?"

I follow her, trying very hard not to linger over the swing of her hips, the swell of her breasts, the ponytail bouncing from side to side with her stride. "Sorry—the answer is still the same. All of it."

She waves a hand. "Fine. Why all of it?"

I open the trap and tell her what to write down. Then I answer, "I've had opportunities most people haven't, at least when you look at the breadth of them. I've done just about everything—design a vineyard from the ground up, manage a crew, take a crop from planting to harvest to actually making the wine. I've learned organic techniques; I've worked all over the world in so many different climates and wine-growing regions. That's why I can't narrow it down to just one."

She's quiet for a little while. "I guess staying in one place and doing one thing must sound pretty boring to you."

I answer immediately. "It sounds pretty awesome, actually."

At least if the place was here.

But I don't tell her that.

Rosa flashes a quick smile that doesn't reach her eyes and turns back to her notes. "So how are we doing so far, Mr. I've Done It All?"

I ignore the obvious discomfort she's feeling over our conversation and focus on the specifics of today's task. "Only two more rows to go, and we can break for lunch."

Rosa's head whips around, and she stares at me. "Lunch? Is it that late already?"

"Time flies when you're having fun." It's not just a saying— I actually am having fun out here with Rosa. She's a good worker and a great conversationalist, and the morning really has flown by.

If I'm not careful, I'll forget how she broke my heart without a second thought.

Rejection isn't easy under any circumstance, but when the woman you decided you wanted to spend the rest of your life with says she doesn't want you anymore, it kinda flies past "hurt" like a comet past the earth. After Geno brought me the annulment papers, I was almost comatose for three days. But Rosa...apparently nothing. So, yeah, I have to be way more careful here. Whatever I feel for her, she doesn't feel for me. Well, except maybe the lust part. But I want more than that from her. And I'm not going to get it.

My mood effectively killed, I clear my throat and take off down the row of vines, Rosa hurrying to keep up with me. I stop at the next trap and wait for her to catch up. This time, she reaches out and grabs the trap, opening it herself. "Ta-da!"

Despite my internal struggle, I find myself smiling. "And the student becomes the expert," I tease.

"Well." She squints at the contents. "I couldn't tell you what most of these bugs are. Except maybe the fly. I can identify a common housefly."

"It's a start." I point at the insects one by one and name them again, then clear out the trap for the next round. Once it's back in place, we head to the final trap of the day.

"So what do you want for lunch?" She smiles widely. "I can go whip something up."

"Nothing for me." I click the pen closed and tuck it into my backpack along with the map, then hold out my hand for Rosa's notepad. "Need to run some errands."

Her face falls slightly, but she masks it with another smile. This one isn't as bright. "Yeah, that's fine. I should get this data into the computer anyway."

"You and your computer," I try to tease, but my heart isn't in it.

We walk down the road to the house, the easy conversation from earlier replaced with an awkward silence.

By the end of this summer, I'm pretty sure both of us are going to have whiplash.

Can't be helped, though. I have a job to do, and I can't let anything interfere.

Back at the house, I drop my pack by the back door and grab the truck keys off the key holder. "I'll see you later," I tell Rosa and head for the truck.

See, this is why the place needs other workers. Having Rosa in the fields with me is a terrible, terrible idea.

The more space between us, the better.

"THANKS FOR EVERYTHING." I STAND AND REACH ACROSS Dr. Armstrong's desk to shake her hand. "I really appreciate it."

"I should be thanking you, Jake," she says, handing over a stack of papers. "It's not often we get intern requests this late in the season, and I always have students looking for field experience."

I remember those days. I always planned to intern at Take Flight, with my dad and his crew, but after everything with Rosa, I stayed further afield. Transferred as a junior to a different program upstate, which is where I met Dr. Armstrong, one of the top viticulture and enology experts in the field. She helped me get started solo, without depending on Take Flight and the guaranteed job there. Afterward I only came back for holidays and short visits to see my parents.

To look over the fields and wonder what Rosa was up to, then curse myself for still caring.

My parents always wanted me to come back to Take Flight after college, but I couldn't do that—not while Rosa was still in town.

Maybe if I had, things would have turned out differently.

Not just for me, or even Rosa and me, but for the family business as well.

Well. Probably not. Even if I were around, Mom's medical bills would have been too much to cover without selling the land.

I still feel so goddamn guilty, though.

Oh well. Nothing to be done about it now.

I was pretty happy to find out Dr. Armstrong moved here a few years back, though. She's been good for the viticulture program, and we've kept in touch over the years.

Sometimes it does come down to who you know.

And I know I can trust her to help us get the right people to keep Caparelli viable.

"It's a small world, isn't it?" Dr. Armstrong leans back in her chair. "Imagine finding out that one of my favorite students followed me down the coast." She glances at the documentation on her desk. "Oak Creek Canyon, right? Practically in my new backyard." Her grin shows clearly that she's teasing.

"Actually, I think *you* followed *me*," I tease back. "I was born and raised here. You're the newbie."

"Fair." She looks out her window, eyes narrowed against the bright sunlight, then turns back to look at me.

She's got her *I can see right through you* look on right now. I do my best not to shuffle my feet.

"So." She adjusts her glasses. "Finally settling down? Or is this yet another short-term position?"

"Short term," I answer immediately, ignoring the twist in my gut when I say it out loud. "Just helping out a friend."

She nods. "Well, let me know when you're ready to move on. I'd be happy to connect you with a colleague or two. Wherever you want to go. I wasn't kidding when I said you were one of my favorite students. You deserve to find a place where you can put down roots."

I nod. Once, I expected to put down roots here, tangled with the roots of so many generations of my family. Those days are gone, though.

"I'll fill the paperwork out tonight with Rosa," I say, tapping the forms on the desktop. "Gotta be sure these two get all the credits they'll earn."

"Perfect." She smiles and waits until I'm out the door before she turns back to her computer.

One of the best things about having a world-class viticulture program practically in our backyard is that the students aren't necessarily locals. Dr. Armstrong didn't blink an eye when I requested the interns for this job be from out of state and planning to work elsewhere after they graduate.

The less we're connected to the Oak Creek Canyon rumor mill, the better.

We'll have to work around their class schedules, but neither of them is carrying a full load during summer term, so it shouldn't be too challenging. And college credits plus a reasonable stipend is a small price to pay to have two more sets of hands helping me in the vineyard.

I swing into the driver's seat of the truck and pull out of the university parking lot. I've got to get back to the vineyard and finish up work on that insect damage before I lose the day.

Get back to resisting the urge to push Rosa against the closest wall and see if her kisses still taste the same.

ROSA IS STILL IN HER OFFICE WHEN I STOP BY THE HOUSE for some more water. It's hot out today, and hand-trimming vines under the afternoon sun is tiring work.

I'm filling the glass from the tap for the third time when she wanders in. Her eyes look tired, and I wonder if she had as hard a time sleeping last night as I did or if she's just tired from stomping through the vines with me so early.

Silently, I grab another glass and fill it. She smiles her thanks and downs half of it in one pull.

It's hot inside, too. In more ways than one.

"So." She leans against the counter. "How did it go?"

"Finished clearing out the damaged vines," I say. "Not as bad as I originally thought, either."

She closes her eyes briefly. "Oh, thank goodness. I don't think I can take any more bad news."

"What about some good news?"

I wasn't going to say anything until later tonight, but might as well give her something positive to hold on to.

"Yeah?" She's biting her lip, trying not to look too eager.

"We've got two workers ready to start. Just need to fill out some paperwork first."

"What? How? Where did you find them?"

I raise an eyebrow. "What makes you think I didn't hire them in town?"

"Maybe because nobody local will work at Caparelli?"

I hesitate. She's not wrong.

"Jake, I'm not an idiot. I wouldn't have hired the last guy if he hadn't been my only option. At the time, I thought it was a gender thing. Like, they don't want to work for a woman or some bullshit like that. But when you couldn't find anyone, either..."

Her voice trails off.

I don't like that look on her face. Sad. Defeated.

Rosa should never look that way.

"Why won't anyone local work here?" Her voice is low and pained.

I sigh. "I think you know why."

Her face tightens. "Yeah, I think I do, too. No one wants to be on the wrong side of Uncle Geno."

I nod. "I'm afraid so."

"Okay." She claps her hands together and looks me in the eye. "Where *did* you find workers for us?"

I shove down the happy little twinge at the word *us*. It doesn't mean anything. "I called in a favor from my viticulture prof," I tell her, pulling the conversation in a happier direction. "She took a local professorship a few years back. And she was able to recommend two upperclassmen looking for field experience. All we have to do is fill out the internship paperwork so they can earn credit, and then pay them a stipend."

"And by *we* you mean *me*," she teases, but her smile is genuine. "But are you serious? Just a stipend?"

I nod. "The credit is the biggest part of it for them," I add. "Well, that and the real-world experience."

"That's amazing," she says. "I can't believe I didn't think of it earlier."

I shrug. "Well, I wasn't kidding when I said I called in some favors. Usually you have to go through a vetting process to bring on interns. But Dr. Armstrong knows me and trusts me, so we were able to bypass some of the busy work."

"So when can they start?"

"As soon as the paperwork is completed and turned in." I hand her the packet I'd left on the table earlier and watch as she flips through the pages. Her eyes light up at one spot; I can tell by glancing at it that the stipend amount is making her really happy.

I get what it's like to work on a tight budget. It brings back uncomfortable memories of conversations with my parents right before they decided to sell.

If I can help it, Rosa and her sisters will be able to hold on to Caparelli as long as they want. Maybe I can do for them what I couldn't do for my parents: save their vineyard.

She grabs a pen out of the junk drawer and sits down, filling out the forms as she goes. "Are they locals? Not that it matters."

I shrug and fill my water bottle with ice to take back out into the fields. "Nope, both from out of state. Actually, Emi is from Canada."

"Cool." She flips the page, fills out another line. "A lot of vineyards seem to be opening up in northern areas."

"God bless global warming," I say, rolling my eyes.

She mock-glares at me. "Bite your tongue."

"Yes, ma'am." I screw the top onto my water bottle.

Rosa clicks the pen closed and stands, handing over the completed paperwork. "All done."

"I'll get them in as soon as I can." I turn around and stack them on the counter.

"Thank you, thank you, thank you. Seriously, I could kiss you right now."

Whoa. Sounds like I'm not the only one with kissing on the brain. I can't help myself—I take a step toward her.

She freezes. "I, uh... Just a figure of speech."

"Right." My voice sounds like gravel. "You just keep telling yourself that."

"I'm sorry. That was so unprofessional and...and wrong. I shouldn't have said that." She's almost babbling now, her eyes wide and her cheeks pink.

"Uh-huh." I take a step closer.

Rosa swallows, and I watch the movement of her throat. "I just meant *thank you*."

"Sure you did." Another step.

She sways toward me, almost unconsciously, like iron filings to a magnet.

Or maybe she's the magnet, and I'm caught, drawn forward with every blink of her eyelashes.

And somehow I'm barely a footstep away from her, close enough to feel the puffs of her breath on my face, to see her eyes flutter down.

"You can thank me however you want," I whisper into her ear, leaning forward so my cheek is almost touching hers.

Her face turns toward mine, and her lips are *right there*. But I wait, every muscle in my body tight with want. It has to be her choice. She has to make that move.

She closes her eyes, then presses her lips to mine. It's brief, barely a peck, but I feel it everywhere.

Ten long years.

I kiss her back, a little longer, a little harder, and she whimpers low in her throat. I fist my hands at my sides to keep from pulling her closer. Her mouth is soft and luscious, and I want to stroke my tongue at the seam of her lips, to see if she still tastes the way I remember. I want to pull her close, feel the warmth of her curves against my body.

I want.

I draw in a long breath and step back. "You're welcome," I say, and then I do the only logical thing. I grab my water bottle and get the hell out of there.

THE SUN IS DOWN BY THE TIME I FINISH WEEDING THE FAR section of vines. There's another spot I'll have to work on tomorrow, but most of it is cleared up for now.

What's not clear is my head. God damn, being this close to Rosa is messing with me in so many ways.

It was easy when there were thousands of miles between us, when I didn't have to see her or hear about her or think about her for years at a time.

Okay, that's a lie. I thought about her.

I thought about her a lot.

I resented her for finding it so damn easy to walk away from me, from *us*, without a backward glance.

I hated her for letting her uncle dictate the terms of our separation.

I hated myself for missing her.

And that's the hell of it all. I still missed her—after everything. At least after the annulment-that-wasn't I could convince myself I'd never really known her. That she was never the girl I knew, the woman I loved, the person I married. She was colder, more heartless. Someone who could walk away without looking back.

But now that we're working together, around each other day and night, I wonder.

And now we've thrown a kiss into the mix, which was a horrible idea and totally wrong and something I shouldn't be wanting to do again. And again.

I definitely want to do it again.

But I'm pretty sure Rosa won't. She's always been the practical one, up until I talked her into eloping. And I'm getting the impression that she spent the past ten years paying penance for that decision. Overall, this is not a situation that lends itself to more kissing.

I should take a page out of her book, focus on the here and now and leave the past in the past.

But I know myself. And I have a sinking feeling I'm not going to be able to do that.

I'm playing with fire, and I know I'm going to be the one who gets burned.

Chapter 9

Rosa

I'm still thinking about that kiss the next morning.

I hurry through my morning routine, keeping an eye out for Jake. His bedroom door is still shut, and the bathroom is empty.

Downstairs, though, there's a coffee cup on the side of the sink and a half-full carafe in the coffee maker. I ignore how thoughtful that is and pour myself a cup, doctoring it up with some creamer and sugar.

Jake always teased me about how my coffee barely deserved the name once I got through fixing it to my liking.

I shake my head and take a long sip, letting the warmth and caffeine soak into my bloodstream.

That stupid kiss is still on a loop inside my head, where it's been since last night. I tossed and turned for way too many hours with that memory playing over and over and over.

It was nothing, right? Barely even qualified as a kiss. Just a quick press of the lips as a thank-you.

But I know I'm lying to myself because that "nothing" of a kiss affected me more than any other kiss I've had in the past ten years.

Not that there are a lot to compare it to. I mean, I haven't been on the shelf. I've dated.

A little.

In my defense, I was always really busy. First college, then working for Belmonte. Didn't leave a lot of time to get out there and meet people. And in Oak Creek Canyon, everybody knows everybody.

When you watched a guy eat paste in first grade, it's hard to see him as a viable romantic partner as an adult.

A little voice inside me whispers that no one around here ever held a candle to Jake anyway, so why would I bother?

I groan and set the half-drunk mug of coffee in the sink. This is getting me nowhere.

Might as well head into town and take care of some errands.

And if that gets me out of the house so I won't run into Jake, all the better.

Downtown Oak Creek Canyon is bustling, locals and tourists mingling on the sidewalks as they wander in and out of the storefronts. A guy in front of the tourism-board office holds up a sign, trying to encourage visitors to sign up for a winery tour.

Maybe next year Caparelli can be part of something like that.

I pull out my phone and start tapping out a text to Bianca

and Allegra with the idea. I know we're barely clinging to the winery by our fingernails at this point, but nothing wrong with planning for the future, right?

A shadow falls over the phone screen, and I look up. Uncle Geno is standing there, looming over me.

I know—it sounds dramatic, but there's no other word to describe it.

For a brief, wild moment, I hope he's ready to wish me well. Tell me he's proud of us for making a go of it.

Then I notice the tightness around his mouth and the way he's trying to pretend he's relaxed. Casual.

Nope, no family pride forthcoming.

"Rosa." His voice is clipped, businesslike.

I nod. "Hi, Uncle Geno."

"Surprised to see you here." He glances around. "Are you sure you can afford—well, whatever you're window shopping for?"

Well, that's rude.

I bite back a snarky reply. "Just picking up some supplies. Window shopping isn't my speed."

"No, I suppose that would be more your mother's thing."

I smile tightly. I may have issues with my mother, but hell if I like hearing her own brother talk that way about her. "What are you up to?"

His smile is condescending as hell. "The chamber of commerce meeting just ended. It's important to give back to the community, you know."

If only he thought it was as important to provide some level of support for family.

"How are things at Caparelli?" He looks down at me, a fake look of concern on his face. "I was sorry to hear that you're struggling."

Yeah. *Sure you were, Uncle Geno.*

"Who says that?"

He waves a hand dismissively. "It's a small town."

"Yes, it is. But don't worry—we're doing fine."

"'We'?" His gaze is sharper now, somehow. "I heard your only employee quit last week. Who's 'we'?"

So he knows about Damien but apparently not Jake. Yet. And I don't want to be the one to tell him. "Allegra and Bianca," I say, because that's sort of true. "And I have a couple of interns starting soon."

He harrumphs. "Rosa, I admire your can-do spirit. But there's no way you're going to be able to make a go of this with your absentee sisters and a handful of students with no experience. It's time to bring Caparelli back into the fold."

I know he's not entirely wrong. I've definitely chosen the harder option. Handing the reins back to Uncle Geno and the cousins would be so much easier, so much less stress. But I don't *want* to assimilate, to see Nonna's legacy swallowed whole by the rest of the family business.

And with Jake helping me now, there's a glimmer of hope that it could actually work.

"At least give me the grapes for Carleo. Just this year. I have preorders. You must understand—it's our reputation. The family reputation."

I look at him for a long moment, my head tilted. *Give* him the grapes. Not sell them, not trade for something that Caparelli needs. He still sees Caparelli—sees *us*—as something that belongs to him, to Belmonte.

"We have plans for those grapes as well. You'll have to figure something else out this year."

And even though I'm shaking inside, I pull my shoulders back, turn on my heel, and walk away.

No Way, Rosé

WHEN I GET HOME, I'M STILL RIDING HIGH ON THE feeling of standing up to Uncle Geno. Other than deciding to take on the challenge of making Caparelli an independent winery once again, that's not something I've done before. I've spent my entire adult life doing what he's told me, hoping at some point he would see my worth. That he'd give me responsibilities, let me contribute to Belmonte like his sons do.

But it never happened. I stayed in the background, doing as I was told, never allowed to pull my own weight. My college degree—the one I chose *specifically* so I could contribute to Belmonte—was ignored.

I feel like I've been continually paying penance for my mistake ten years ago, and I'm done.

Now I have an opportunity to show my worth, prove I'm capable, and I'm not going to run back to Belmonte with my tail between my legs. I'm going to ensure that Caparelli is a success.

No matter what.

I pull into the driveway and turn off the car, sitting there for a little bit before getting out.

For the first time in my adult life, I actually feel like I'm in the driver's seat.

Then I get out and head to the front porch, where Jake is sitting in the late-afternoon shade.

"Hey, Rosa," he says, lifting the glass in his hand. "How's your day been?"

"Not bad," I reply. "Is that lemonade?"

He nods. "There's more in the fridge."

I walk past him, into the house, headed for the kitchen. Lemonade sounds really good right now.

Back on the porch, I settle into the remaining chair and take a long sip. "God, that's good."

"Right?" He finished his drink and sets the glass on the little table between us. "The perfect beverage on a hot summer day."

I nod. "Everything going well in the field?"

"Except for waiting on our interns to get started, it's great. Running smoothly." He pauses, and it seems like he's about to say more, but instead, we both sit in silence for a while. I squint out at the hazy view, the heat of the late-afternoon sun pressing down on the horizon.

"Ran into my uncle today," I say, glancing over at him. His mouth tightens, which isn't surprising. Geno was never his favorite person.

"Oh? And how did that go?"

"Pretty well, actually." I try to hide the grin threatening to break out. "I stood up for myself, for once."

"Really?" He smiles at me, and my heart clenches. "That's pretty awesome."

I nod. "He tried to bully me into giving Belmonte our Cab grapes, and I flat out told him no, we have plans for them ourselves."

Jake laughs, head tilted back, and I'm ridiculously proud of myself. This is all so small, so basic—but I can't help it. Everything about this feels good.

"I bet he had a coronary when he found out I was working here," Jake adds, and just like that, my good mood slides away.

"Uh." I twist my hands in my lap. "I didn't tell him."

There's a long pause. "Oh."

I glance sideways at him. "Bianca knows, of course. And Sasha. But otherwise, I haven't told anyone."

He nods.

"I thought we'd want to keep it quiet. You know."

"No, I don't." His face is impassive.

Flustered, I wave a hand in the air. "You know how gossip is in Oak Creek Canyon. People blow things all out of proportion and—" I snap my mouth shut. I'm babbling, and I don't like it. "I guess I just didn't want people to know you're here."

"But people already *do* know I'm here. At least working for you. I spent half a day going around town trying to hire people for your vineyard."

"Yes, but..."

"And I had lunch with Wade a couple days ago."

I do an actual double take. "Wait, you had lunch with Wade?"

"In town. At the café. Outside, at a table on the sidewalk. Sorry—I didn't know that I had to stay hidden from public view."

"That's not what I'm saying." I rub a hand over my forehead. "It's just...complicated."

"Nothing complicated about it." He shrugs. "Just your average married couple sharing the same address for a while."

"Jake."

"Totally innocent. Like that kiss last night."

I can't help myself—I whip my head around to make sure no one is listening. When I turn back, he's got this smirk on his face that makes me want to...

Dammit. It makes me want to kiss him again.

"I don't want to talk about that, either."

"Too bad. It was a good kiss. Definitely in my top ten."

I absolutely do *not* wonder how many of the other nine were after we broke up.

I also don't think about the fact that I can't even remember having nine other kisses in that same time frame.

"That's ridiculous," I say, because that was definitely too brief of a kiss to make his hall of fame.

He pins me with a *look*.

"There's no way that little kiss is in your top ten."

"You think that was a little kiss? A nothingburger? Okay, then. Maybe we should try again, see if we can get it right this time."

Oh, God. Every part of my body is saying *yes, please.* But that would be the worst idea ever.

I shake my head and change the subject. Again. "Look, Jake, when we agreed to this arrangement it was business only, and I want it to stay that way."

He raises an eyebrow but doesn't say anything.

"And even though people probably will figure out that we're working together, I'd rather not flaunt the fact that you're living here as well."

"Okay." He stands, picking up his glass, and heads toward the front door. "I'll keep that in mind."

The soft thud of the door closing behind him echoes in my head louder than a gunshot.

Chapter 10

Jake

The next day, I'm in the fields by sunrise and work until the sun is starting to set, until every muscle is screaming and I'm covered in dirt and sweat. I don't know if I'm mad at Rosa or myself—or maybe a combination of both. I do know that I hate being anyone's dirty little secret. Our elopement may have been a secret, but it wasn't dirty. Just something special for the two of us. We wanted to protect it, keep it safe.

We weren't wrong. As soon as her uncle found out, he destroyed it. Destroyed us.

But after our conversation last night, I feel like a dirty little secret, and I don't like it.

I head down the hill to the back of the house, stopping at the shed to clean and put away my equipment. The interns will start soon. I need to focus on getting this vineyard in shape so that once Bianca is back and harvest begins, they're in the perfect place to move forward.

And I can move on.

When I step inside the mudroom at the back of the house, I hear Rosa puttering around somewhere—probably the kitchen. I'm a mess, plus I don't really want to face her yet, so I head upstairs. A shower sounds nice right about now.

In the bathroom, I strip down, leaving my grimy work clothes in a pile on the floor. I turn on the shower, the bathroom filling with steam. Even though it was a warm day earlier, the evening chill is setting in, and the hot spray feels amazing on my sore muscles.

I soap up, washing away the dirt and stress of the day as I think back on my argument with Rosa. I shouldn't have thrown the kiss in her face like that, especially since I wouldn't mind a repeat performance.

I wasn't lying when I told her it was in my top ten.

Even though it was over almost before it started.

Kissing Rosa again, after so many years, was a revelation. I was so sure I was over her. Now I just don't know.

I turn into the spray, letting the water run over my head.

I can't lie to myself anymore. I want her more than ever.

A carousel of images flashes through my brain.

Rosa lifting up onto her toes, pressing against me, her mouth on mine.

I close my eyes, and my soapy hand drifts lower, pressing over my thickening cock.

Her lips wrapping around a forkful of dessert, her eyes closing in bliss.

I may have told her that living under the same roof was just a matter of location and convenience, but I lied.

Staying here, just down the hall, is pure torture.

The light from the hallway turning her pajamas transparent, her body lush and tempting.

Head bowed, I brace a hand against the shower wall and begin to stroke myself.

Rosa, naked and eager, arms wide, welcoming me to her bed.

My cock is hard and leaking precum already. This isn't going to take long.

Rosa underneath me, head tipped back in ecstasy.

Those last two may be a decade old, but they're enough. My balls draw up, and I come, breath shuddering out in great gasps as I try to stay as quiet as possible. The shower washes away the remnants of my orgasm as I scrub the guilt off my skin.

She deserves better than me. But I will never stop wanting her anyway.

THE LAST THING I WANT TO DO AFTER THAT IS SIT DOWN to dinner with Rosa and try to make fucking small talk, so I head for the front door, shout down the hall that she shouldn't bother to wait up for me, and leave.

The drive into town doesn't give me nearly enough time to figure out what I'm going to do that will keep me occupied and gone until she's asleep, so I just park and start walking around.

After today's argument, she'll probably be pissed off that I'm so visible in town yet again, but it's not like I have many other options. My parents live four hours away now, and most of my high school friends have either moved or are part of the gossipy wine community Rosa wants to keep out of the loop for as long as possible.

The shops are closed up, but the restaurants and bars are hopping, so I pick a hole-in-the-wall at random.

As luck would have it, Rosa's cousin Leo is the first person I see when I walk into the place.

I groan internally, because he's just about the last person I want to see, unless you count Rosa.

For completely different reasons, of course. I don't want to get into Leo's pants.

I debate turning around and leaving, but he's already seen me, and it would be too obvious I'm avoiding him if I leave now.

Instead, I let myself get waved over and sit down with his group. He was only a year ahead of me in school, so I recognize some—but not all—of the guys he's hanging out with as well. I order a beer and sit back, figuring I might as well see what the gossip mill has to say these days.

"Hey, Jake. Sorry to hear about your folks' place."

I nod at Leo, accepting the condolences, even though hearing that phrase over and over is like nails on a chalkboard. Everyone's sorry, but no one did anything to stop it from happening, now did they?

Not even me.

The rest of the group chimes in, and I do my best to be polite and gracious and shit. My beer arrives, and I take a long pull.

I'm pretty sure I'm going to need it.

The guy sitting next to me introduces himself. He's the new winery manager at Vintage Vines.

Well, not so new. He's been there seven years apparently.

"I'm actually a little surprised this is the first time I've met you," he says. "You don't get back to the Canyon much, do you?"

"Nope."

Bruce leans in. "Jake here couldn't wait to leave town."

I start to protest, but honestly, he's not wrong.

"Well, it's nice to put a face to the name," Steven says, then turns to answer somebody else's question.

I try to pay attention to the conversations around me, but half the time I don't even know who they're talking about. I guess there's been more change in Oak Creek than I realized.

"So what's Belmonte going to do without the Carleo?"

I glance side-eyed at the guy at the other end of the table, Mark or Matt or something. I try not to look like I'm interested in hearing about this, too.

Leo leans back in his chair, seemingly unconcerned. "We'll get the grapes."

"Not what I heard." Bruce props one elbow on the table. "Rosa's being a real hard-ass about it."

"She'll come around."

"Not like she can keep the place running solo," someone else adds, and Leo shakes his head.

"Not solo anymore," he says. "Or at least that's what she told my dad today. But whoever it is, they won't be there long."

Matt or Mark nods. "Nobody would be that stupid."

Leo shoots him a glare. Mark or Matt—or is it Mike?—snaps his mouth shut and looks down.

My spidey sense is tingling like whoa, but I can't say anything without drawing attention to the fact that *I'm* in town and qualified and Rosa's husband.

Or, as far as everyone at this table is concerned, her ex-boyfriend.

I'm really hoping none of them put two and two together.

"So what brings you back to Oak Creek, Jake?" Bruce shoves a handful of peanuts into his mouth and chews loudly. "I thought your parents moved out of town after the sale."

"They did," I say, thinking quickly. "But a lot of their stuff is in storage here. I need to go through it, make sure I've got everything that's mine."

It's a stupid excuse. I already told Wade I'm working with

Rosa, and if I'm still around a week from now they'll know I was just blowing smoke.

But for now, it'll do.

"Actually, I should get down there before they close for the night," I improvise, swallowing the last of my beer and standing. I toss a twenty onto the table to cover my share. "Nice to see y'all."

Then I get the hell out before they start asking any more questions.

I'm ON THE OUTSKIRTS OF TOWN WHEN I PASS BY THE storage facility. On impulse, I pull in and drive around to Mom and Dad's unit.

I wasn't lying, exactly. They *do* have a storage unit here, and I *was* planning to dig around in it, make sure I got all my stuff before leaving town again.

It just isn't in the top fifty reasons I'm here, is all.

I check my watch. The place closes in forty-five minutes. Might as well take a look around while I can. I dig the keys out of the glove box and turn off the truck.

When I lift open the garage door to the unit, my heart sinks. I was afraid of this.

It's the largest unit the place offers, and it is jam packed.

Boxes line every wall, up to the ceiling. Furniture, wrapped in plastic and resting on pallets to keep it off the ground, crowds the center of the concrete floor. There are plastic locking totes and several filing cabinets and, inexplicably, a *Lethal Weapon* pinball machine.

When did they get a pinball machine? And why are they storing it here?

Sighing, I reach for the closest box. There's a notation on it, in Mom's handwriting, that says *Holiday Dishes.* If I'm lucky, that's what will actually be in it.

If not, this crap could end up being enough to keep me here all summer, just like I told Leo and his friends.

I open the box and look inside.

FORTY MINUTES LATER, I'M STARTLED BY THE SWEEP OF A headlight beam as the manager of the storage facility drives up. He rolls down the driver's-side window. "Five minutes until close," he calls, and I nod.

Luckily for me, Mom was meticulous in her labeling, so I've been able to be organized in my digging. I pack up a few more pieces of childhood memorabilia and put them on the passenger seat. It's not everything—I'll have to come back again —but I did find the box I'd packed up the summer before I left Oak Creek Canyon, along with a few other things, and that's enough for now.

I grab the last item and turn off the light, closing and locking the storage-unit door. I follow the manager's car out of the facility, and he waves while he locks the gate behind me.

The local store is still open, so I swing into the parking lot.

I grin as I walk inside.

Rosa is going to be *pissed.*

Chapter 11

Rosa

J ake is gone when I wake up.

This is becoming a pattern.

I shouldn't be stressing about it. Fieldwork always starts with the sun, before it gets too hot later in the day. There's no expectation that someone who works on the business side of things would be up and working that early.

Doesn't make me feel any better, though.

I check the driveway as I head downstairs, something easing in my chest at the sight of his truck. I'm not sure why I keep thinking he's going to be gone for good each morning.

Probably a little leftover trauma from ten years ago.

To be fair, he didn't actually leave until after Uncle Geno handed him the annulment papers, but he was still the one to walk away. Eventually.

I head to the kitchen, eager for some caffeine. I pour a mug, thankful again that Jake made enough to share, and pull a yogurt out of the fridge. It's still a little surprising every time I open the fridge and find a selection of food, even though I'm the one who put it there.

I could get used to this.

But that would be a bad idea. I should know better than to pin my hopes on a mirage.

I grab a spoon out of the silverware drawer and dig in. Then my eye catches on something on the kitchen table, and my blood runs cold.

The blue-and-yellow gift bag glints in the morning sun, sitting atop a white envelope.

What fresh hell is this?

I approach it like it's a bomb or something, my jaw clenched. I slide the card out from under the bag and open the envelope.

Happy Tenth Anniversary, it reads.

I blink and look over at the calendar. That *bastard.*

I'm out the door and down the road before I remember I didn't even bother to see what was in the bag.

THE EARLY-MORNING SUN IS BRIGHT ON THE HORIZON AS I stalk through the vineyard, ducking between rows of greenery and scanning up and down the dirt paths for Jake.

Jake, who's saving the winery, who leaves a gift on the breakfast table, who's making me *hope.*

Who's leaving at the end of summer anyway.

How dare he.

"How dare you!" I shout as the top of his head comes into view across the vines. I force down the hope and hold tight to the indignation as he straightens up, pulling off his gloves. "That was a shitty thing to do."

"Huh." He shrugs. "Not the usual reaction I get when I give someone a gift, but okay."

"An *anniversary* gift."

Jake nods. "Ten years ago today."

"Would you stop?" I ignore the flutter in my heart at his words. "We're *not married*! How many times do I have to tell you that?"

"Saying it doesn't make it true," he parries back, wiping the sweat off his brow.

I do my best to ignore his forearms and barrel on. "And pretending we didn't get an annulment doesn't make that true, either!"

A rustling in the row next to us distracts me, and I turn my head to see what animal is wandering through the vines.

A pair of bright blue eyes meets mine, and I stumble backward, choking on an inhaled breath.

Jake looks over as well. "Oh. Right. Rosa, this is Emi. Emi, meet Rosa."

Wow, I've definitely made a *great* impression on the new intern.

A young woman wearing leather gloves and a baseball cap comes around the end of the row and nods at me, her expression a little pained. "Nice to meet you," she offers. "Thanks so much for giving us this opportunity. We won't let you down."

We?

"And this is Javier," Jake adds, waving at the young man following behind.

Make that *both* interns.

"Welcome to Caparelli," I say faintly, wishing the ground would open up and swallow me whole. "Jake, a word? In private?"

"Sure." He turns to the interns and gives them a couple of instructions on what to do next, then heads in the opposite direction, not even turning back to see if I'll follow.

Dammit. I follow him, if only to ensure no one else can hear our conversation.

"What the fuck, Wright?" I'm whisper-shouting because I don't want those two hearing any more than they already have. I can feel the blush burning my cheeks.

"Good morning to you, too," he says, taking a long drink from his water bottle.

"You couldn't have warned me?"

He looks over toward the interns, toiling away out of earshot.

"About Emi and Javier? I told you they'd be starting as soon as possible."

"I didn't think you meant this soon! And you didn't even try to stop me from barreling on about stuff no one else should ever know about."

"When, exactly, would I have had time to say something?" He waves a hand. "You were pretty hell-bent on saying what you wanted to say. It's not like I could get a word in edgewise."

"I didn't exactly plan to say it with an audience," I splutter. "And how the hell did you get them here and working so quickly? I thought there was paperwork to file or something."

"I got final approval from Dr. Armstrong yesterday and invited them out right after." He shades his eyes and looks up the hillside. "No time to waste, really."

He's right. I'm still embarrassed, though. And afraid. And hopeful. And a little turned on, to be honest

"I'm going back to the house," I tell him.

Jake doesn't say anything as I head down the row to the road. But as I turn back toward the house, I hear him call after me, "You never mentioned if you liked the gift."

I sigh and continue walking without turning around.

It's mid-afternoon before I can bring myself to open Jake's present.

Initially I was going to just take it, pretty gift bag and all, and toss it into his room. I don't want it, don't want anything to do with an anniversary that doesn't exist, for a marriage that stopped being real nine years and three-hundred-sixty-two days ago, from a man I still don't know if I can trust.

But the truth is?

I'm tempted.

I go from stalking past it on the way to the fridge to glancing over while I toast a bagel for lunch to poking at it with my butter knife after I finish my meal.

Is it something ridiculous, dragging out the humor that only Jake seems to find in this situation? Or is it generic, from someone who really doesn't know me at all anymore?

Or—scariest of all—is it something personal and intimate and sweet?

I can't take it anymore. I pull the bag toward me and reach inside, holding my breath. I don't know why it feels like something bigger than it is, something the rest of this summer hinges on.

I dig through the tissue paper until my fingers brush against something solid. I pull it free, and I have to choke back a gasp. I can't believe it.

Oh, God. I am so in over my head.

Chapter 12

Jake

I drag out my end-of-day routine as long as humanly possible, but eventually I have to go back to the house. Emi and Javier are long gone, headed back into town with big grins on their faces alongside the streaks of dirt and sweat, and bursting with excitement about the days to come.

I remember those days, when I was finally able to put everything I was learning into practice, the sheer joy of being out in the fields working the vines. I may have had a leg up from being part of a winery family from birth, but there was still something magical about that first internship.

I know it's Rosa's vineyard—well, hers and her sisters'—but I'm still pretty pleased to be part of this journey for Emi and Javi, to give the next generation of viticulturists an opportunity.

Next generation? What the hell? I'm not nearly that old. Yet.

Can't deny that I *feel* old sometimes—like now, when every

muscle in my body aches. It's hard work getting this vineyard back into shape, and even with helpers I'm working my butt off. Times like this, I wish Caparelli had a hot tub in the backyard. Pull on some swim trunks, sink into the heated water, soak away all the aches and pains.

Or no swim trunks. Suddenly, in my nonexistent-hot-tub scenario, Rosa is there with me, her curves slick and bare, her leg brushing mine as she lowers herself into the water. Steam rises around us, enveloping us in a warm, wet paradise just for two.

I shake my head and keep trudging forward. It's clear that it has been way too long since I got laid.

The house comes into view as I turn the curve in the road, and I can't help but wonder—not for the first time—what Rosa thought of my gift. I know it wasn't fair, throwing our shared history in her face like that, but I'm tired of being the only one of the two of us carrying that weight around.

She doesn't want to face it, but we're married. And if she wants that to not be the truth anymore, she's going to have to be the one to do something about it.

I walk in the front door, fighting the urge to call out *Lucy, I'm home!* in a truly awful accent. It would just be another reminder of our past together, when we used to watch old sitcoms here on the black-and-white TV in the family room, arguing about which of us was better suited for a comedy career.

Me. It was me.

The light is on in the kitchen, so I follow its glow down the hall and step inside. Rosa is there, her ever-present laptop on the kitchen table in front of her while something amazing-smelling bubbles away on the stovetop.

"Soup's ready," she says, not looking up from what is no

doubt yet another spreadsheet. "Bread's warming in the oven. I'm sure you're hungry, so feel free to get started."

"Thank you," I say, my stomach growling as I wash my hands. I dry them on the towel hanging on the dishwasher, then reach for a bowl. I get one down for Rosa, too, and a couple of plates for the bread.

"Hmm." She clicks her mouse and types a couple of numbers. "Don't get used to it."

The reminder of my limited time at Caparelli pulls me up short for a moment, but I shake it off. I grab the butter dish and place it on the table. I ladle up soup and cut slices of almost-too-hot bread, pour a couple glasses of white from the bottle in the fridge. Then I sit down in the seat across from Rosa and wait for her to look up.

She finally does, her gaze catching mine across the table. "I'm not ready to talk about it," she says, then sets aside the computer and digs into her dinner.

Okay, then. I tip my head in acknowledgment and start eating, both of us silent as we enjoy the meal. Before I even realize it, I've emptied my bowl. The soup is fantastic, and I don't think it's just because I'm that hungry.

I get up and fill my bowl again. I hold up the ladle, an unspoken question, but she shakes her head.

"I'm good," she says, finishing off the last of her bread. She carries her dishes to the sink and starts washing up.

I sit again, digging into my second bowl, and watch as she pulls out a container for the leftovers.

"This isn't an anniversary dinner," she says, wrapping the remaining bread in foil. "Because we are *not married*. No matter what you say."

I say nothing, because I know by now I'm not going to convince her. She's going to have to figure it out on her own.

"But. Thank you for the not-anniversary gift." She glances

at the wall behind me, and I turn, realizing belatedly that she's already put up the 1950s-era tin Caparelli advertisement.

It's almost embarrassing how happy this makes me.

"You're welcome," I say. "It's yours anyway. Well, your family's."

She nods again, not looking at me. "Where did you find it?"

I swallow another bite and say, "In the storage unit my folks rented after selling Take Flight. That's where I was last night—looking for some of my stuff that I left behind when I...well." I cough briefly. "Anyway, my folks cleared out their stuff a while back, after it sold, and they gave me a key to the storage unit when I told them I was going to be in town for a while. Apparently my mom fancies herself something of an Oak Creek Canyon historian. Collected a whole bunch of memorabilia over the years."

Rosa finishes putting away the leftovers and stands at the sink, looking out the window into the darkened yard. "I remember seeing one like it, years ago. Hanging on the wall in the entry to the wine cave, back when it was still open. Then Uncle Geno closed down the wine cave, consolidated everything into Belmonte, and—I never saw it again."

"I'm glad my mom was able to save this one for you, then."

Even with my side view, I can see her swallow. "Nice of her to let you give it to me."

"It wasn't even a question. She was happy it would be back in Caparelli hands when I called her last night and asked."

"Well." She flashes me a quick smile, but her face settles back into something—pensive. Almost sad. "Your mom was always really nice. Thank her for me."

I joke, "Story of my life. I give you the gift, my mom gets the credit."

Rosa rolls her eyes, gathering up her computer. "At least

your mom wasn't trying to troll me with a fake-anniversary gift."

I open my mouth to argue, but she steamrolls right over me. "It's a lovely piece of Caparelli history, and I'm glad to have it. But you have to stop this nonsense about us being married. It just makes working together all the more complicated."

I hold my hands up in surrender. "Fine. I won't mention it again."

She turns to go.

"But hey, you don't have to take my word for it. Go look it up yourself."

"What?"

I shrug. "You have to file an annulment for it to be valid, right? Go verify the filing information. Prove it to me."

"I don't have time to go on a wild-goose chase, Jake." She swings the arm that's not holding the computer wide, encompassing the house, the vines, the massive job we've both taken on. "There's too much to do. As you well know."

"Okay." I hang up the dish towel and turn the stove light on in preparation for closing down the kitchen for the night. The soft glow will light the way if one of us wants a midnight snack or something. "But I know you, Rosa. And I know you're going to fixate on this until you know the truth. You don't believe me? Get the legal proof, one way or another. That's all I'm saying."

I can't help myself—I touch her shoulder as I pass her on my way out of the kitchen. It's stupid and self-sabotaging, but I guess that's just how this summer is going to go for me.

"Good night," I murmur, then turn off the overhead light on my way out of the kitchen. I look over my shoulder and see Rosa still standing in that same spot, the glow of the stove light behind her. "Just—think about it."

Then I head upstairs, taking the steps two at a time, putting as much distance between us as I can manage in the same damn house.

Chapter 13

Rosa

I shake my head and shove my hair out of my face, no doubt getting dirt on my forehead from the gardening gloves.

But I can't stop thinking about everything, so much so that I finally gave up on trying to work in my office and decided to clean up the front yard instead.

Most of the time, a little physical labor gets me out of my head and turns off the thoughts whirling around inside.

Today? Not so much.

Jake wants me to prove we're not married. I'm pretty scared whatever I find will prove the exact opposite.

Either way, I'm ignoring the whole mess for today. Hell, I've been ignoring it for the past week. I just can't bring myself to do anything about it. Not yet.

When my cell phone rings, I'm tempted to ignore that, too. But curiosity gets the best of me, and I check the screen.

"Hey, Legs," I say, clicking the Accept button. "What's up?"

"Rosey Posey!" Allegra chirps, her voice light and cheerful. "Just missing my big sister. How are things at Caparelli?"

I tuck the phone between my ear and shoulder and tug at a stubborn dandelion. "It's fine," I say. "How's...what country are you in right now?"

She laughs. I can hear the bustle of city sidewalks in the background. "Croatia at the moment. The Dalmatian coast is mind-blowing. You should come hang with me! You'd love it."

I'm sure I would. I bite the inside of my cheek to keep from lecturing her—I'm her sister, not her mom. "Little busy at the moment," I say wryly.

"Later, then," she says blithely. "I'd love to see you."

"Ditto," I say, shading my eyes from the sun that's burning overhead. It's probably time to go inside before I get the world's worst sunburn. "Do you know when you'll be coming home?"

I can almost hear her shrug over the phone. "At some point. Don't worry, though. I'll be there eventually."

I could use the help now, but I don't say that.

She'll keep working temporary jobs and crashing on couches across Europe until she's ready to pitch in at Caparelli.

I just have to wait until that happens.

"So, what are you working on at the moment?"

She sounds like she's actually interested, not just making small talk, so I set aside my resentment and put on my partnership cap. "Currently I'm pulling weeds in the front yard," I say, wandering over to the porch and sitting in the shade. "Not my favorite chore, but needs to be done."

"Oh, yeah! You're staying in Nonna's old place, aren't you?" A car honks in the background of her call, and I hear a conversation in a language I don't understand as I assume people walk by. "Hang on—I'm going to change this to a video call. I want to see how it looks!"

I start to protest that it's not that impressive yet, but the request to shift to video pops up on the screen, so I sigh and accept. "Keep in mind I'm mostly focused on the business side of things," I warn her.

She waves a hand dismissively. "I'm sure you're rocking it. So good to see you, Rosey Posey! You look far less stressed than I expected."

It's a backhanded compliment, to be sure, but I'll take it.

"Seriously, you've got a nice glow about you."

I hope the blush isn't obvious on the tiny phone screen. "You know the California sun," I deflect.

"It looks good on you," she says. "And things are really going okay? Caparelli's a big job, Rosey. I've been worried about you."

"Thanks," I tell her. "It's a lot, but I'm okay for now." And oddly enough, it's not a lie. Up until Jake arrived, it was hard handling this without my sisters here. But sharing the burden with someone else—someone who cares about Caparelli almost as much as I do—has been a game changer.

I can feel the heat rising in my cheeks at the thought of Jake, so I shove that train of thought aside and focus on Allegra. "You look gorgeous as ever," I tell her.

She smiles and pushes a hand through her riot of curls. They're lighter than the last time I saw her, and she's lightly tanned as well. "I think it was the two weeks on a yacht in the Adriatic that did it," she says with a laugh. "Sun, surf, and the food! You'd love it."

"Sounds amazing," I say honestly, because if I can't be out there adventuring, at least my sisters are, and that counts for something. I can keep the home fires burning and Nonna's legacy alive for all three of us.

"So show me everything," she says now, dodging out of the way of a scooter that's weaving its way through traffic on the road beside her, motoring onto the sidewalk briefly. "I want to see what you've done with the place."

I turn the phone so she can see the front yard. I'm about halfway done with the weeding, so it looks slightly better than it would have if she'd called yesterday. "Still a bit to do here," I say, then walk up the steps to the porch. "Eventually I'll need to have this porch evaluated, maybe replace the wood in some places. But so far it's holding up."

She hums in agreement. "I used to love playing out there in the evening," she says. "Such a beautiful view, and so peaceful."

"Now it's a great place to have a glass of wine and watch the sunset," I agree. "I'll probably get a new seating setup at some point."

"Sounds good." Allegra leans out of camera range and rattles off something that definitely isn't English to someone I can't see. She pops back into view. "Sorry—just finishing up plans for later tonight."

"No worries," I reply. "If you need to go, I understand."

"Not yet! You haven't shown me the inside."

I plaster on a smile once again and head for the door. "Again, manage your expectations. I don't have a lot of time to remodel." *Or funding,* I think but keep that part to myself.

The interior is dark after the brightness outside, and I blink a few times to adjust. "Okay, the main room I've fixed up is the office."

Allegra oohs and aahs as I turn in a slow circle in the middle of the room, showing off the workspace setup. "Oh, I remember that chair! Is it still as comfortable as I remember?"

I nod. "Yeah, but I had to leave it on the porch for a few days to air it out."

She wrinkles her nose. "Ooh, I bet. Probably smelled like an old museum in there when you started out."

"Exactly." I look around. "So what else do you want to see?"

"Kitchen," she says immediately. "My favorite room in the whole place."

It probably was for all of us, back when Nonna would bring us down to bake cookies or enjoy some fresh-pressed grape juice during harvest time. "It's not quite up to speed yet, but it's getting there."

She exclaims as I walk the phone into the kitchen. "Rosey! It looks amazing. So homey!"

I turn in a slow circle, letting her see the tidy little room and the few touches I've been able to add—cheerful towels with a grape-cluster design on them, sheer yellow curtains over the kitchen sink to brighten up the plain white blinds.

"Wait, what's that?"

I stop turning and look at the wall in front of me. "Oh. That's—that's just an old advertisement for Caparelli," I say haltingly.

"Where did you find it?" She leans close to her phone, her face getting bigger as she peers through the screen. "Take me closer. I want to see it."

I take a deep breath and move closer to the tin hanging. It really is gorgeous—and makes me feel warm and happy every time I look at it.

But I really, really don't want to tell her Jake gave it to me.

"Wow." For a moment all I can hear is the background noise of the city behind her. "I've never seen it before. Where on earth did you dig it up?"

"It was in storage," I say, crossing my fingers behind my back. I'm not lying. I'm just not including the fact that it wasn't in *our* storage.

"I can totally see that as the foundation for our new roll-out," she muses.

I'm a little startled. "I was thinking the same thing!"

"Great minds think alike," she teases. Then she looks over her shoulder again. "Okay, I've got two more minutes. Show me upstairs, and I'll let you go."

"Checking to make sure I made my bed this morning?" I tease as I climb the stairs.

"As if you'd ever leave your bed unmade," she jokes back. "Not our Rosey Posey."

God, I hate that nickname. But my family will stick with it until the end of time.

Also, she's not wrong about the bed.

I turn left at the top of the stairs and head into my bedroom. She makes positive comments on how it looks, which is gratifying.

Looking at the house with fresh eyes, I realize I've actually gotten more done than I thought. In some ways, I miss my studio apartment back in town, but in other ways, this feels more like "home" than anything has since Nonna passed away.

Maybe since Mama left all those years ago.

"Wait," Allegra says as I pass the bathroom door. "Let me see how you upgraded the bathroom, too. Knowing you, it's amazing."

I don't know that I'd call it amazing, but I am pretty proud of how it turned out. "The shower curtain was ridiculously on sale," I brag, showing off the thick white curtain with grapevines trailing down either side. "I love it."

At some point I want to paint those grapevines on the walls as well, but for now I'm content with the green-and-purple matching towels and the grapevine-design toothbrush holder and cup.

"Hold up," Allegra says abruptly, and I stop mid-turn.

"What is it?" I look around.

She's quiet for a minute. "Rosa, why are there two tooth-brushes by the sink?"

Oh. *Shit.*

"And two towels. And an extra hairbrush." She bursts out into delighted laughter. "Rosey Posey, do you have a *man* staying with you?"

I open and close my mouth a couple of times before words actually come out. "I, uh, it's not what you think," I stammer.

"It better be what I think, or I'm going to be seriously disap-pointed in you."

I'm silent for a minute.

"Rosa, turn this phone around so I can see you."

I'd pull the older sister card, but she'd just tell Bianca and they'd gang up on me, so I sigh and rotate the phone.

"Do you or do you not have a man staying in the house?"

"I do. But it's complicated."

"I have time." She walks over to a sidewalk café and sits down at an empty table.

I back out of the bathroom and go into my bedroom, taking a seat in the comfy chair in the corner. "You said you had two minutes before you had to go."

She waves a hand. "Eh, they'll wait for me. This is more important."

Dammit.

"I don't know if Bianca told you about the first guy I hired...?" At her nod, I continue. "Well, after he took off, I needed someone to manage the fieldwork, and I was getting desperate. So when Jake Wright offered to help out for room and board, I agreed. He's staying here for a little while as we get our feet under us."

"Wait, Jake Wright? As in Take Flight?"

I nod. "He was in the area after his parents sold their place. He's got the experience to handle it."

"I don't doubt that. So just room and board, huh? That's very...*generous* of him." She leans into the last part, filling it with innuendo, but I ignore it.

"Yeah, I know. We're very lucky."

We really are, even more than she knows.

"But that's all it is? Housemates while he works for Caparelli?"

"Yep," I lie. No way I'm telling her about the whole he-thinks-we're-still-married thing.

She purses her lips. "That's too bad."

"What?"

"Oh, come on, Rosey. He's hella fine. Or at least he was back when he was in high school. Wait, is he a troll now? Did he have an unfortunate disfiguring accident and now has to hide himself on a vineyard, away from society?"

I laugh despite myself. "No, he's still good looking."

Understatement of the year.

"And he's single?"

No, but not in the way she's thinking. "Allegra."

"Is he?"

I nod, reluctantly. Too complicated to explain.

"You should go for it, then."

"Stop it. He's my employee."

She rolls her eyes. "Whatever. You guys were, like, hashtag RelationshipGoals in high school. Maybe now is your opportunity."

Downstairs, the door slams, and I jump. "I gotta go," I say in a rush.

"Wait, is that him?" She sits up, her eyes sparkling. "Let me talk to him."

I shake my head so hard I can feel the start of a headache coming on. "Nope. I've kept you long enough."

"Please, please, please? I just want to say hi." She makes puppy-dog eyes at me, but I ignore her.

"We'll talk again later," I say, glancing toward the hall. "Take care, Allegra."

I go to push the End button as Jake reaches the top of the stairs.

"Hey, Rosa," he says, his voice low and seductive.

"Hi, Jake," Allegra yells over the phone, her voice tinny through the speaker. "Don't let Rosey hang up on me."

He walks down the hall, the hair at his temples dark with sweat. He tucks his work gloves into his back pocket. Peering over my shoulder, he smiles at Allegra through the video call. "Hey, A," he says. "Wow, it's been a while."

"Years," she says, leaning back in her café chair and grinning. "I was just a bratty kid last time I saw you."

"Still bratty," I mutter, but she just laughs.

"So I hear you're saving us from disaster and ruin," she continues, turning all her attention to Jake and ignoring me completely. "Thanks for that, by the way."

"Happy to do it." He scratches the back of his neck. This close, I can smell his earthy, just-got-in-from-the-fields scent, and it's driving me insane. "The three of you deserve a fighting chance."

"Hope you're still around when I get back," she says, and I straighten my spine.

Jake slants a look at me, then turns back to the phone. "It's possible," he says. "Depends on when you're planning on being here."

"Well." She waves a hand dismissively. "Who knows about that. Eventually, though." She turns and looks off-camera again, and her shoulders slump. "Sorry, guys. Duty calls. I've gotta go. Chat with you later, Rosey?"

I nod and blow her a kiss. "Take care, Legs," I say. "Don't be a stranger."

She waves at both of us and says, "Ciao," then clicks out of the call.

The silence once she's gone is loud.

"She still calls you Rosey?" Jake shakes his head. "I thought you hated that nickname."

"Oh, I do," I say with a groan. "But it's stuck, despite my best efforts. I think my family is going to call me that until the day I die."

"And you still call her Legs?"

I pull up short at that. "Yeah, I should probably make sure she's still good with that nickname," I say.

"Makes sense." He's too close to me, both physically and emotionally. I take a few steps toward the staircase. Jake steps back, giving me a little room.

I'm both happy and disappointed about that.

"Everything good with Allegra?" He tilts his head toward my phone. "Sorry to interrupt, by the way. I didn't realize you were on the phone until it was too late."

"No worries." I start down the stairs and sense more than see him follow. "Yeah, she's fine. Better than fine. Definitely living her best life."

"You're not doing so bad yourself," he says.

I can't help but scoff a little at that.

"No, I'm serious. Yeah, things are stressful right now, but you're putting in the work that will pay off down the line. You're managing a full-on business with very little support—besides Emi, Javier, and me. Seriously, I'm impressed. And someday soon, everyone else will be as well."

I swallow past the lump in my throat. "Thanks."

"So I guess the cat's out of the bag with Allegra about me staying here, huh?"

"Well, she saw your toothbrush and got ideas."

He laughs, his footsteps echoing down the stairs behind me. "Caught out by oral hygiene. Who would have thought."

I can't help but laugh a little as well. "I told her you were helping us out for room and board."

"Hmm."

I reach the bottom stair and turn around. He's got this look on his face that I can't interpret.

"I'd better get back to weeding," I say, stuffing my phone into my back pocket.

"A little outdoor time. Good call," he says, heading toward the kitchen. "I'm just grabbing some snacks for the crew."

He washes his hands at the kitchen sink and fills a tall glass with water from the fridge.

I feel a little guilty. Shouldn't I be the one bringing snacks out to the team that's saving our vineyard?

He narrows his eyes and waves a finger at me. "None of that."

"None of what?"

"None of your overstimulated guilt complex. The three of us in the field are fully grown adults who can see to our own needs. You are not responsible for the world, Rosa."

No, but it does feel like it sometimes.

He finishes his water and sets the glass down with a thunk. Then he opens the fridge and starts rooting around in it.

I open the cabinet and pull down a box of crackers and some cookies. Then I grab the big wooden tray Nonna used when she would bring out a midday snack to the workers back in the day.

Jake smiles when he sees it. "Man, that takes me back." He adds mandarin oranges, apple slices, and some bottles of water to the mix.

"Remember when we'd sneak fresh-baked cookies off this

tray when we thought Nonna wasn't looking?" I put some napkins on the side. "I'm pretty sure she put extra just for us."

"Of course she did." He hefts the tray and starts to leave. "And Rosa?"

"Yes?"

He looks me in the eye until I start to squirm. "It's okay to set the burden down for a little while and let someone else carry it."

He's gone before I have a chance to respond.

OF COURSE, BIANCA CALLS WITHIN THE HOUR.

"Are you kidding me?" she screeches. "Jake is *living* with you?"

"Hello to you, too," I say drily, giving up on yard work for the foreseeable future. "How's Argentina?"

"Forget about Argentina. Jake is living at Caparelli with you?"

"Yes, and you knew he was working for us. We talked about it last week, remember?"

"*Working for us* and *living together* are two very different things," she says.

"I'm aware of that, yes." I grab a yogurt and a spoon from the kitchen and head to the backyard. Somehow I missed lunch completely. "He needed a place to stay. His parents sold their place, you know."

"Yeah." She's quiet for a minute. "That sucks."

"It does." I sit at the picnic table, grateful for the arch of tree branches overhead, shielding me from the worst of the sun. "Anyway, he agreed to stick around and help us out but didn't have anywhere to stay without spending a fortune. And it's not like we could pay him enough to make that worth his while."

Bianca says, "Our budget's still a disaster, isn't it?"

"It's not the greatest, no." I take a bite and swallow. "Especially after I paid the permits to take Caparelli out of inactive status. But Jake was willing to work for room and board, and I couldn't say no."

"Just be careful," she says. "I don't want him breaking your heart. Again."

"He didn't—" I start, but she interrupts.

"You graduated high school, and he fucked off to parts unknown almost immediately. After years of dating. I'm surprised you're even talking to him, to be honest."

"It's complicated." I shove another spoonful of yogurt into my mouth. I'm almost tempted to tell her about the whole *We might actually be married—surprise!* thing, but it's too convoluted for a phone call.

Plus, I'm starting to wonder if the broken heart was mutual and not just me.

Maybe I need to face the situation head on, finally, instead of shoving my head in the sand and pretending it'll go away.

"I bet." She sighs. "Well, if he screws you over again he'll have to deal with me."

"Change of subject, please." I finish off the yogurt.

"Okay, fine. Actually, I was hoping I could talk to Jake. Is he around?"

I sit up straight, my eyes narrowed. "Why?"

"Jeez, suspicious much, sis?"

"Maybe the fact that you just *threatened him* has something to do with it," I argue.

"Whatever. I just want to talk with him about harvest and what he thinks we should do with the grapes this year."

"You're the winemaker," I remind her. "You don't need anyone's approval."

"But I would like his input. Let's face it, he has years of experience we don't, thanks to Uncle Geno, and I'd love to brainstorm some ideas with him. So could you pass my number on to him tonight, please?"

Well, when she puts it that way... "I'm sure he'd be happy to bounce some ideas around."

He would, I know. He's just that kind of guy.

"Okay, thanks. Love you!"

I hang up and take my empty yogurt container into the kitchen, turning the conversations with my sisters over and over in my head. Yeah, I can't keep ignoring the elephant in the room. It's time for me to do what Jake challenged me to do and look into our annulment myself. At least then it won't be a question mark anymore.

Chapter 14

Jake

Emi and Javier kill off the snacks in record time, and we're nearing the end of the workday, so I send them home a little early. Not enough time to start a new task before quitting time anyway.

Rosa texted me an hour or so ago, letting me know her other sister, Bianca, wants to chat with me about plans for after the harvest.

Allegra hopes I'll still be around when she gets back.

And Rosa?

I can't read her, at least on this. Does she want me to stay? Does she want me to go?

That's my fault, of course. I haven't even hinted at the idea of sticking around. And my track record after our ill-fated wedding wouldn't inspire her to believe I'd be willing or able to put down longer-term roots.

I think I could. Maybe. I've just never let myself want it before.

And I shouldn't now, either.

Whatever frustration I'm feeling, I have only myself to blame.

That's not the only frustration, either. Even cold showers and thinking of our seventh-grade history teacher, Mrs. Collins, in hair rollers and a cold-cream face mask isn't enough to distract me from the aching desire I feel every time we're in the same location.

Hell, she doesn't even need to be nearby. The scent of her bodywash lingering in the shower, fresh-picked flowers on the table in the morning, snacks and water waiting in the fridge when Javi, Emi, and I come barreling in from the fields at the end of the day.

I wander down to the edge of the vineyard, feeling that combination of bone tired and energized that I only ever feel at the end of a day in the fields. I'm ready to take a shower, eat a good meal, and go to bed.

I'd just rather I wasn't going to bed alone.

I take in a deep breath, pulling that Napa Valley scent right to the bottom of my lungs. There's a light breeze that does nothing to reduce the heat haze over the road, but I don't mind.

It's the perfect recipe for grape growing.

I check a couple of vines, birdsong hovering in the background. I really should head back to the house, but things with Rosa are, well, weird. We aren't ready to strangle each other anymore—but I hate not knowing where I stand. Where *we* stand.

If there even is a "we."

Gravel crunches on the road, and I realize that while I've been standing here pondering, someone's managed to almost sneak up on me.

On a wide, open gravel road.

I really need to start paying more attention.

I turn to see who's headed this direction, but the guy walking toward me doesn't look familiar. Or, rather, he does, but not in a *which Oak Creek Canyon family does he belong to?* way. He's clearly not from around here.

Or maybe it's me who's not from around here anymore.

"Hey," he says as he gets closer, pushing his hat back on his head. "How's it going?"

"Fine," I answer, still wondering who this person is, walking the private road between Caparelli and Take Fli—the other vineyard. "You?"

He shrugs and holds out a hand. "Thought I'd come over and introduce myself to the neighbors," he says. "Jansen Beck."

The neighbors? I glance over his shoulder at what used to be my family's vineyard. "Ah," I say, begrudgingly shaking his hand. "The athlete."

I notice a slight double take, but he holds it together far better than I can at the moment. Shit, I'm being an asshole.

"Once upon a time," he says tightly, shoving his hands into his pockets. "And you are?"

"Jake Wright." I glance over again at what's now his property, and when I look back, I see the moment he clocks the last name.

Jansen nods. "So, *not* the neighbor." His expression is sharper now, more alert. Like I'm lurking around here trying to find a way to—what? Sabotage him? Steal the property back?

Internally, I roll my eyes. "Nope. Just helping out at Caparelli for a while."

"Well." He tugs his hat back down, covering his forehead, and tilts his head slightly.

I feel like I'm underneath a microscope or something. It's not a pleasant feeling. But my mom instilled better manners in me than I'm showing at the moment, so I lift my chin and say, "Welcome to Oak Creek Canyon."

One corner of his mouth quirks up in an approximation of a smile, and he huffs out a breath. "Thanks. See you around."

He turns to go, and so do I, fighting the urge to look over my shoulder to watch him walk back onto the property I spent all my life assuming would one day be mine.

By the time I hit the back door at Caparelli, I'm feeling even shittier than I did when I was talking to whatever his name was. I was rude and obnoxious, and for what? It's not like he stole the property out from under me. My parents needed the money, they put the place up for sale, he bought it. No harm, no foul. I probably owe him an apology.

In the mudroom, I toe off my shoes and toss my socks into the washer. I can hear Rosa typing away in the office, so I call out a hello on my way up the stairs to take a shower.

I'm still in a fucking piss-poor mood even after I've washed away the dirt and sweat of the day, so I decide not to inflict my attitude on Rosa and head into town for the evening instead. She waves me off when I pop my head into the office to let her know, mumbling something about the end of the fiscal quarter or whatever.

"Oh, wait a sec," she calls out when I'm halfway out the front door. "Bianca wanted to talk to you about plans for the harvest."

I'll probably be gone by then. I don't know why that makes my chest ache—it's not like there hasn't been an end date on this situation from day one. "That's more up to the two of you. Well, three, if Allegra's pitching in."

"That's what I told her, too," she says, coming out from behind the desk and leaning on the doorway of the office. "But I think she'd like your input anyway."

I'm conflicted. Every day, I feel myself getting more and more entangled in Caparelli, thinking about the future and what's going to happen down the road. The more I'm invested, the harder it will be to leave.

But treating this like just one more temporary placement doesn't feel right, either.

"Fine," I say, forcing a smile. "Give me her number, and I'll call her."

She grabs her phone off the desk and taps on the screen a couple of times. "Here you go."

On cue, my cell beeps with the incoming text.

"Thanks," I tell her, my hand on the doorknob. "I'm not sure when I'll be back, so, you know. Don't wait up."

"Okay." She reaches up and tightens the band on her ponytail. I do my best not to pay attention to the way that lifts her breasts so they strain against the fabric of her T-shirt. "Oh, and I'll be out tomorrow morning. So I guess I'll see you after lunch-ish?"

I nod. "What's going on tomorrow morning?"

She pauses. "Nothing big, just hanging out with Sasha."

There's something more there, but I let it go. "Sounds good. Have fun."

I head out the door and climb into my truck, plugging in Bianca's number before heading down the drive toward town.

"Hey, B," I say when she picks up. "Rosa said you wanted to talk about post-harvest plans?"

We chat the whole drive into town.

I GRAB A CHICKEN SANDWICH AT THE FAST-FOOD PLACE IN
the center of town and decide to walk around for a bit, maybe
get rid of that itch beneath my skin that's been there since I ran
into Jansen what's-his-face who bought Take Flight. It feels like
a combination of frustration, embarrassment, and—jealousy?
Yeah, probably. Goddamnit, I hate admitting it, but I'm jealous
as fuck.

He's got a winery—*my* winery—to run the way he wants.
He can make plans and implement changes and develop long-
range strategies to keep it going well into the next decades.

Or he can run it into the ground and walk away. Doesn't
matter—it's his winery. His choice.

And what have I got? A temporary job with a temporary
living space, spending twenty-four seven with the woman I
once wanted forever with. And in a matter of weeks, all of that
will be going away.

Hell yeah, I'm jealous.

Bianca has some great ideas for Caparelli. I can tell from
our conversation how passionate she is about winemaking, and
whoever gets to work with her is a lucky person.

I found myself getting excited about the possibilities as we
talked, and I had to keep reminding myself that I wouldn't be
around to help make those plans come to fruition. It's probably
time to start making some plans of my own.

I just don't want to. Not yet.

The sidewalks are crowded as I wander down the street,
eating my sandwich and glancing into store windows. I see
some people who look familiar and we nod at each other as we
walk by, but the majority seem to be out-of-towners. Or maybe
residents who've moved in since I left.

Oak Creek Canyon has definitely grown in the past ten
years, and in a good way. The shops are bustling—tourists are
buying souvenirs and bottles of wine. As I watch, a group of

about half a dozen women sign up for a winery tour at the tourism-board office.

It would be great to get Caparelli on that rotation once we start selling wine again.

They. They, *not we,* I have to keep reminding myself, and it sucks.

"Jake Wright? Is that you?"

I shake off my maudlin mood and look around to see who's talking to me. A woman with dark brown skin and tight curls is standing at the corner, a big smile crinkling the corners of her eyes.

"My God. Carol?" I stride over and wrap my arms around her, laughing a little. "How long has it been?"

She pulls back and smacks me on the arm. "Too damn long, young man."

I roll my eyes. "Okay, yeah. You're not wrong. What are you up to these days?"

"Still working at..." Her voice trails off. "Actually, I don't know what he's going to call it."

I wince inwardly. Carol has been Take Flight's accountant since I can remember.

"He's lucky to have you," I say, holding back that wave of jealousy I've been fighting all evening. "Nobody better to help run the place."

Her smile softens, grows fonder. "Thank you, Jake. I loved working for your family, I hope you know. Best winery in Oak Creek Canyon."

I nod. Once upon a time, it was. And I can't fault her for sticking with a job she knows like the back of her hand and does well.

"So what are you up to these days? Just visiting?" She looks around. "Are your folks here, too?"

I shake my head. "No, they're enjoying retirement in SLO."

"Oh, right, I heard something about that. Tell them I said hi next time you see them."

"Will do."

"And you?"

I smile and shove my hands into my pockets. "Actually, I'm helping out at Caparelli for the summer. Getting it ready for harvest now that Rosa and her sisters have taken over."

"Are you, now!" She tilts her head. "Those girls are lucky to have you."

"It's just Rosa at the moment, but thanks. It's nice to be home for a little while."

"Just a little while?"

I nod, even though it feels like a lie. Or maybe I just wish it was. "Yeah, only until harvest. Then it's time to move on to my next gig."

"Oh, that's too bad. I know your folks always hoped you would come back, settle down here. It's never too late to come home, you know."

I smile tightly. It certainly feels too late for me. Take Flight is sold, my parents have moved, and Rosa...

Well.

It's all water under the bridge.

Carol's expression brightens. "Maybe while you're here you can stop by and meet the new boss. I think Jansen could use some friendly neighbors. Maybe someone to bounce ideas off of."

I swallow. "Maybe."

It would be the neighborly thing to do. I just—can't do it. Not yet. Not while the loss is so fresh.

"Anyway, you know me." I smile again. "Always moving on."

She sighs and places a hand on my elbow. "Maybe it's time

to put down some roots, Jake. Oak Creek Canyon will always be your place, no matter how far you travel."

I make some sort-of-agreeable noises and give her another hug, then head down the sidewalk, rolling that last sentence over and over in my head.

Maybe Oak Creek Canyon is my place. But I don't know where I fit in it anymore.

Chapter 15

Rosa

"Thank you so much for coming with me," I say to Sasha as she slides into the passenger seat. "There's no way I could do this on my own."

"Of course!" Sasha hands me a white bakery bag and eases two hot drinks from Rise 'n' Wine into the cup holders. I love their business plan—coffee shop by day, wine bar by night. And their pastries are to die for.

I peek into the bag and see several doughnuts inside. "Bless you," I tell her as I set the bag on the center console and ease away from the curb.

"Couldn't resist." She rifles through the bag before choosing an old-fashioned with chocolate frosting. "They just smelled too good."

"Always do." Traffic isn't too bad this morning, and I get onto the highway headed out of town without too much hassle.

My coffee order is perfect, as always, and I shoot Sasha a grateful smile. I'm so lucky to have her by my side.

"So are you going to tell me where we're going, or is it going to be a complete surprise until we get there?" Her face lights up with pretend glee. "It's a surprise party, isn't it? On a Wednesday morning, eight months before my actual birthday?"

"You caught me," I deadpan. "I knew you'd never suspect it this way."

"Perfect." She takes a big bite of her doughnut and sighs happily. "Actually, you don't have to tell me. Giving me an opportunity to play hooky last minute is payment enough."

Sasha works in a salon, which helps out with the constant hair changes. Today she's got a stick-straight bob, black hair with a streak of bright red underneath. I called her last night, at the end of my rope, and asked if she was free this morning.

Sasha being Sasha, she immediately rescheduled one appointment and canceled another—*She's a pain in the ass anyway and never tips. Let someone else deal with her blowout and roots.*—and was waiting on the sidewalk outside the salon right at 10:00 a.m. when I pulled up.

And no, I didn't tell her last night where we were going. I was still feeling so raw and mixed up, and confessing it over the phone felt too—impersonal.

Although now that we're in my truck going sixty miles an hour down the highway to the county seat, I'm realizing this isn't the most typical situation, either.

"Do you know what eight days ago was?" My hands tighten on the steering wheel. "I mean, other than a Tuesday."

"Damn. Stole my answer." She shoves the rest of her doughnut into her mouth and chews thoughtfully. "I'm guessing it's something significant."

I turn on the blinker and ease into the next lane over. "Yeah, you could say so. According to Jake, it was our ten-year anniversary."

"Ohhh." She leans over and pats my knee. "Should've

151

warned me. I would've asked Inez to add a couple of shots to our coffee orders."

To my horror, I feel the start of tears prickling at my eyes. Dammit, I am *not* going to cry over this shit. "Give me a doughnut," I say instead, holding out my empty hand.

She drops a Bismarck into my palm, then digs a napkin out of the bag and places it on my lap.

I take a bite, savoring the sweet filling and fluffy pastry. After swallowing, I say, "We're going to the courthouse to prove I'm not married to Jake anymore. That I haven't been for almost ten years."

"Okay."

I glance over. Sasha's brow is furrowed, like she's trying to work something out in her head. I focus on traffic while I wait for her to spit it out.

"Why do we need to go to the courthouse, exactly?"

I set the half-eaten doughnut on the napkin and take a long sip of my caramel latte. "Because I need a copy of the annulment filing. I figure that's the best place to get one."

She nods. "Got it."

I finish my coffee and doughnut as we pull up to the old courthouse, a gorgeous three-story brick building with a wide staircase sweeping up to the entrance. I park in the lot across the street, and we make our way to the front of the building. For some unknown reason, my stomach swoops a little as we climb the stairs.

Maybe I should have passed on the coffee and doughnut.

Once we get inside, old craftsmanship turns to modern technology, so we drop our keys and purses into little boxes for x-raying and pass through the metal detectors. I collect my stuff and cross to the directory on the opposite wall. I squint at the tiny letters and numbers.

Sasha comes up and bumps me with her hip. "Public Records," she reads off the board. "Second floor."

I toss her a grateful smile, and we head up the stairs to the right, then follow the signs to the office I need.

There's a line for the counter, so we join the queue and talk quietly as we wait. Or, at least, I try to talk quietly. Sasha keeps showing me ridiculous memes on her phone, and I have to fight the impulse to snort-laugh at half of them.

See, this is why I asked her to come with me. She's doing her best to distract me, and I appreciate it.

"Next," says the bored-looking woman at the counter, and I realize with a start that she's talking to us. Sasha gives my elbow a squeeze as we step forward.

"Hi," I say with a nervous laugh. "I, uh, need an annulment record."

"Names of spouses," the clerk says in a monotone voice. Her septum is pierced, and her name badge reads *Millicent*.

"Um. Rosa Maria Isabella Martinelli and Jacob Linus Wright." I elbow Sasha in the side as she snickers at Jake's middle name. I whisper, "It's his great-grandfather's name."

Millicent ignores us as Sasha mimes zipping her lips. "Date and location of birth for both spouses," she intones.

Five minutes later, her long list of questions is over and we sit on the bench across the room while Millicent slouches off to the back to work her magic.

Or at least I hope she's working her magic. For all I know, she could be scrolling on her phone while we wait.

She returns from the back, and I pop off the bench like a windup toy. I may have had a little too much caffeine today already. "Thank you so much for—"

I stop abruptly as she shakes her head. "No records. Sorry."

My head swims. "I'm sorry—what?"

"No annulment was filed for that marriage. We have no records."

Jake was telling the truth.

"I do have a record for the marriage if you want," she adds helpfully. "Filed in Las Vegas, Nevada, just over ten years ago."

"No, thank you," I say faintly. "Sorry to bother you."

She shrugs and looks away. "Next."

"Come on." Sasha wraps her arm around my shoulders and steers me out of the room. "Let's get out of here."

Next thing I know, I'm in the passenger seat of the truck and Sasha is pulling out of the parking lot.

"Why are you driving my truck?"

Sasha turns on the blinker and rolls her eyes at me. "Because I'd like to not die on the way back to Oak Creek Canyon," she says drily. "Lord knows you're in no condition to be behind the wheel."

She's not wrong.

I lean back in my seat and close my eyes. "Oh my God," I moan. "We're still married."

"So it seems."

I squint at her. "You don't sound surprised."

"Don't forget, I know Jake, too. He's the stubbornest man alive. If he didn't want an annulment, he wouldn't get the annulment. Geno's big mistake was leaving the paperwork with Jake rather than filing it himself."

True. If Uncle Geno had handled it, our marriage would have been over when I thought it was over.

"But I'm pretty sure you can't file for an annulment by proxy," she continues. "Unless you're a lawyer handling the case. And Geno is a lot of things but definitely not a lawyer. It had to be one of the two of you."

"How do you know this?"

She lifts one shoulder as she merges onto the highway. "I listen to a lot of true-crime podcasts."

Which—I don't even want to go down that rabbit hole, not right now.

"It's just so stupid, Sasha," I complain, everything that's been crowding my brain for days finally spilling out. "We had an agreement. I signed the paperwork. Why wouldn't Jake file it? It doesn't make any sense."

She doesn't say anything. But I know Sasha, and she's not saying anything really damn loudly.

I groan. "Fine, out with it."

When she finally does speak, it's gentler than I expect. "Did you actually have an agreement? Like, did you talk to Jake about it before having your uncle deliver the signed paperwork to him?"

I swallow. "No."

"Well." She's watching the road, but I get the feeling she's watching me, too, out of the corner of her eye. "Maybe that's your answer. Maybe he never agreed at all."

We're both quiet for a while as Sasha drives us back to Oak Creek Canyon. She turns the radio on to a pop station, and the music plays quietly in the background as I ponder.

Then I do what I always do when I'm overwhelmed.

I make a list in my head.

One: I'm apparently still married to a man who, until recently, I hadn't seen since a couple of days after our wedding.

Two: I've hired my—well, my husband to work on the winery/vineyard I just inherited with my sisters. This means we'll be seeing each other every day until he moves on.

Three: He's actually living *in my house*, which means we will continue to be in each other's orbit around the clock instead of being able to keep our time strictly professional.

Four: He's made it clear that he's still attracted to me, and I...

Five: I'm still attracted to him. Even though the rational side of me is screaming it's a bad, bad idea.

Six: The rational side of me is losing out to the barely-able-to-keep-from-jumping-his-bones side.

But.

Seven: If we act on our attraction, I don't know if I'll be able to survive the heartbreak when he leaves me behind. Again.

I groan and rub my temples. "Can you distract me? I'm getting a nasty headache."

"Of course." Sasha launches into a story about one of her more amusing clients, and by the time we roll up to Vineyard Vixen Salon, I'm laughing so hard tears are rolling down my face.

Sasha puts the truck in Park, unbuckles her seat belt, and leans over the console to give me a hug. "I'm here for you, babe," she whispers into my ear, and the tears turn to something more emotional.

I nod, not trusting my voice, and get out of the truck to switch to the driver's seat. As we cross on the sidewalk, she leans in again and puts her hand on my shoulder. "It's gonna be okay. I promise."

I don't believe her, but I smile and nod anyway.

She gives me a thumbs-up and turns to go. Then she whips around again.

"What?" I ask.

She shakes her head. "Rosa, babe, you're in big, big trouble."

"That's not news," I shoot back.

"It will be when the IRS figures out you've been filing

incorrectly for the last decade." With a cackle, she disappears into the salon.

The IRS...?

Realization hits me.

FUCK.

Chapter 16

Jake

By the time lunch rolls around, I'm starving.

I pull off my gloves, wipe the sweat off my forehead, and wave Emi and Javier over. "Let's head down to the house and grab a bite to eat," I tell them.

By their enthusiastic response, I can tell I'm not the only one ready for a break.

It's been a crazy morning, filled with lots of hard physical labor and on-the-job instruction. They're both quick learners, though, and I'm so glad Dr. Armstrong recommended these two. It's still going to be a slog, managing everything with a skeleton crew instead of the full team we'd be using under normal circumstances. But for the first time since I impulsively volunteered for this, I feel like I can actually make it work.

We can make it work.

Back at the house, we clean up in the mudroom and I show the interns to the kitchen. Javier and I put together sandwiches while Emi grabs the bowl of fruit in the fridge and a bag of chips out of the cabinet. Remembering Rosa's reaction to finding me on the front porch the other day, I lead them to the backyard and set up the picnic table for lunch.

It's better for a meal anyway.

Emi and Javier sit down and dig in, chattering away, while I return to the kitchen for pitchers of ice water and lemonade and some glasses. I'm trying to figure out how to open the back door with my hands full when I hear the front door.

Rosa's home apparently.

"Hey," I call out, not wanting to startle her. I hear her drop something by the front door—probably her purse—and she follows the sound of my voice to the back.

"Hi," she says with a fake smile. There are worry lines around her eyes and her face looks paler than usual, and I wonder what happened this morning to make her look that way. Then her gaze drops to my overfull hands. "Here, let me take some of that."

I give up the pitcher of water with a smile, and she opens the back door.

"Oh!" She spots Emi and Javier, who both look up from their lunch as we walk out. "Sorry—I didn't realize..."

I put down my pitcher and glasses and take the water from her. "No, my fault. I should have let you know we were having a lunch break."

"I hope you don't mind us barging in," Emi says, twisting her napkin between her hands. "We probably should have asked first."

"Of course not," Rosa says, her smile genuine this time. "This house is as much a part of the operation as the vineyard is. You're always welcome to stop in for a meal, something to drink, or a bathroom break. Seriously."

Javier lifts the platter of sandwiches. "Want to join us? We've got plenty."

Rosa shoots me a look I can't interpret, then squares her shoulders and says, "I'd love to. I'll just go grab another plate and cup."

I wave her off. "No, sit down. I'll take care of it." I hurry inside before she can turn it into a battle of wills, and come back out to find her deep in conversation with Javi and Emi.

If a part of me is a little annoyed that she's not talking to me, well, it's better if I ignore it. I'm just happy she's not looking like someone stole her favorite toy anymore.

I spend most of lunch watching as Rosa ignores me while chattering away with Emi and Javier. They pepper her with questions about growing up on a winery, being part of a wine-making family tradition, what it's like being a woman in a traditionally masculine field. Emi is hanging on her every word.

I'm doing my best not to be jealous, but it's a close thing.

She subtly shifts the conversation to how the internship is going for Javier and Emi, and in no time the two of them are stumbling over each other to tell her how much they're loving their experience on Caparelli so far.

It's only been a week, but I'm feeling pretty damn good about it, too.

But I'm not feeling good about this lunch. Something is wrong.

As they tell her about everything they've done today, I watch Rosa's face. She's listening to them and smiling, but there's something bothering her.

Even after ten years apart, I can still tell.

I'm not sure what she and Sasha were up to this morning, but it looks like something happened to upset her. Did she run into her uncle somewhere?

"Anything exciting happen this morning, Rosa?" I wince inwardly as I watch three heads turn in my direction. I've completely derailed the conversation, and not in a delicate, considerate way like Rosa just did.

Subtle, I am not.

"What?" She's frowning now, a wrinkle between her eyebrows.

I shrug. "Just wondering how your day has been so far. You and Sasha get up to anything interesting?"

She shakes her head. "Just grabbed coffee."

"That's nice." I flash a smile at her, but her frown grows deeper.

"What do you mean by that?"

"Just that it's nice you spent some time together. Aren't you...best friends?" I'm completely out of my depth, and I have no idea why.

"Yep." She stands and starts gathering the dishes.

"Here, I'll help." Emi grabs a pitcher and follows Rosa into the kitchen.

Maybe it's just me, but that seems like a weird reaction to a perfectly normal question. I wonder if there's some bad blood between her and Sasha these days; they've been friends forever, but who knows what's happened over the past ten years.

Clearly, not me.

Javier looks at me, baffled. I shrug and stack some plates, clearing the rest of the table. We walk back into the kitchen where Rosa stands at the sink, washing up dishes and studiously avoiding me.

Fine.

"All right, crew, let's get back to the vines." I clap my hands together. Emi folds the dish towel and leaves it on the counter, and Javier puts what's left of the lemonade in the fridge.

"Thanks again," Javier says, and Rosa shakes off the comment with a smile.

"Anytime," she says, looking pointedly at Emi and Javier.

I roll my eyes and turn to go. Whatever's put her in this mood, at least I know it wasn't me.

BACK IN THE FIELDS, I SHOW EMI AND JAVIER HOW TO trim the excess leaves and shoots of summer growth to allow the clusters of grapes to grow correctly, and we each take a different row to focus on. A lot of people consider it tedious, repetitive work, but it's not something you can skimp on if you want a decent crop. I fall into the rhythm of it easily, letting my mind wander a little as I run my fingers up each shoot, pinching off the side growth and thinning out the leaves. It's as much art as it is science, finding the right balance of shade and sun to let the grapes reach their highest potential.

Every few minutes I check on Emi and Javier in their rows, pointing out the best cuts to make and the optimal shade coverage to leave behind. They're both picking it up really quickly, and I can't help it—I'm fucking proud of the work they're doing.

I clap Javier on the back and head over to my row, mentally composing an email to Dr. Armstrong thanking her again for sending us these superstars, when a noise at the bottom of the hill catches my attention.

Dust is rising from the gravel road, and I realize the noise is made by a vehicle driving our direction.

There isn't a lot of traffic on this road, for good reason—it's more of a private spur between Caparelli and *the winery formerly known as Take Flight*, a quick cut-through between the two properties. I shade my eyes with my forearm as a sheriff's truck pulls to a stop at the base of the vineyard.

I'm already headed down the hill as a guy in full sheriff's uniform gets out of the truck and shuts the door. He's wearing a white cowboy hat and mirrored shades and looks a bit uptight. He also looks vaguely familiar, but I can't place him beyond that.

His work boots crunch on the gravel as he rounds the back of the truck. I stop at the end of the row and nod at him. "Hello, Officer. Can I help you?"

"It's *Deputy*." He takes off his sunglasses and inclines his head. "Are you in charge here?"

That's a loaded question, but I just answer, "Yes. What's going on?"

"I'm afraid I'm going to have to shut you down."

By this time, Emi and Javier have walked up beside me, and I can see their worried glances out of the corner of my eye.

"I'm sorry, Deputy..." I pause and wait for him to tell me his name.

"Romero."

"Deputy Romero, what do you mean, *shut us down?*" None of this makes any sense.

He flips open a tablet and scrolls down the screen. "Lack of proper permits, lack of payment for said permits, unapproved size of operation..."

I hold up a hand. "Okay, hang on."

Turning to Emi, I lean down and say, "Go get Rosa."

She nods and sprints down the road to the house.

Facing the deputy again, I say, "Those are some serious accusations. Do you have evidence?"

He sighs. "I'm not a lawyer. I've been asked to follow up on some complaints, so here I am. And until I have proof otherwise, you and your crew will have to cease operations."

I fucking hate bureaucracy, but I hate the idea of losing

precious workdays even more. "What kind of proof do you need?"

He opens his mouth, probably to launch into more bureaucratic nonsense, but we're interrupted by the sound of Rosa and Emi running up the road to join us.

Rosa stops in front of the deputy and smiles politely, even though she's breathing hard from racing up the hill. "How can I help you?"

"Who are you?"

"I'm one of the owners of Caparelli."

He looks between us. "Okay, who's actually in charge here?"

She waves a hand casually at me. "Jake is my vineyard manager. I'm Rosa Martinelli. As I said, I'm an owner."

"Yes, I'm familiar with your family," the cop says cryptically.

Rosa furrows her brow at him but lets the comment pass. "What seems to be the problem, sir?"

He repeats the complaints while I watch Rosa's face. She listens intently, and when he's done, she just nods. "I'll be right back."

Javier, Emi, Deputy Romero, and I stand in the road and watch her hustle back to the house. I'm not quite sure what's going on in her head, but she seems to have things under control, so I turn back to the interns and tell them to take a water break.

Romero looks at me suspiciously, but I just shrug and say, "Gotta stay hydrated."

I don't know what to make of him. He looks like he's probably older than Javier but younger than me, and he's now holding that stupid white cowboy hat in both hands, which—whatever makes you happy, buddy.

Though come to think of it, he doesn't look very happy.

He slaps the hat on again as Rosa comes back up the road, clutching a file folder in her arms.

"Okay." She stops next to me, her chin tilted up in challenge. "Here are the permits." She takes a couple of pages out of the folder and hands them over. "Canceled check for payment." Another sheet of paper smacks his palm. "Survey of vineyard property, dated right after we inherited, that shows we are officially a *small* winery, not a *microwinery*." She holds out the folder. "Don't worry—the originals are back at the house. You can keep the copies."

He opens his mouth to speak, then snaps it shut.

I don't blame him. That was pretty hot.

"Thanks," he says, his mouth a thin line. "Looks like you've got all the bases covered."

"Yes, I do."

Pretty hot? Beyond that. *Way* beyond.

"Sorry to bother you. I'm required to follow up on complaints, you understand."

She crosses her arms. "Any chance you could share where the complaints are coming from?"

He shakes his head.

"That's what I figured." She tilts her head. "Are we free to continue working?"

"Yes, ma'am."

She nods. "Let me know if you need anything else." Then she turns to me and says, "You and the crew can get back to work."

Then the four of us watch as Romero tips his hat, swings back into his truck, and drives off down the road.

"That was pretty impressive," I say, smiling at Rosa. "But then, you were always a whiz at paperwork."

She just looks back, her face impassive. "Some things are too important to leave up to someone else."

I don't think she's talking about the winery right now.

"I'd rather take care of it myself and make sure everything is done right. Otherwise I could find myself in a huge mess with no way out."

Definitely *not* the winery paperwork.

She smiles at Emi and Javier. "Enjoy the rest of the afternoon. If you need more water, come on down to the house. Don't want you two to get heat stroke."

That *two* makes her feelings about me pretty damn clear. I'm just not sure what I've done this time to deserve it.

Without looking at me, she turns on her heel and heads back to the house.

Chapter 17

Rosa

I can't believe I said that.

I don't even want to deal with it myself, let alone get dragged into yet another conversation with Jake about our marriage and non-annulment.

So why would I all but tell him *you fucked up everything—* in front of witnesses?

Ugh.

And then there's the visit from Officer Not-So-Friendly. What the hell was that about? Someone made a *complaint* about Caparelli?

As much as I hate to admit it, I wonder if Belmonte had something to do with it.

It's almost too horrible to consider.

And it could have turned out so badly, too.

Thank God I'm as anal about paperwork as Jake made me out to be.

If there's one thing I can take full pride in, it's my ability to research. The rules and regulations surrounding winemaking in Oak Creek Canyon are complicated at best, arcane and indecipherable at worst. As soon as Allegra, Bianca, and I decided to take on our inheritance for real, I dove into the morass of requirements to make sure we had all our ducks in a row.

I filled out every document, paid every fee, kept copies of everything.

That was a very good call.

I'm still a little shaken, and I don't know what to do about it.

Part of me wants to figure out what to do about Caparelli suddenly being targeted and how to prevent it from happening again.

Part of me wants to figure out what I'm going to do about my—*hell*—my husband.

Part of me wants to crawl into a barrel of wine and forget everything that's happened since Nonna died.

But I don't have the time—or the mental energy—to do any of those things, so instead I refile the paperwork I got out for the deputy, put a load of laundry in the washer, scrub the downstairs bathroom, and try not to think about anything for a while.

I'M REMAKING MY BED WITH FRESH SHEETS WHEN I HEAR the door open downstairs. "Jake?" I call down. "Just you, or are Emi and Javier with you?"

"Just me," he says, exhaustion coloring his voice. The sun is going down, and he's been in the vines for a very long time today. Other than lunch and the interruption by Deputy Romero, I haven't seen him all day.

"What are you in the mood for for dinner?" I shake the comforter and let it drift down onto the mattress. "Or should we just order a pizza?"

His heavy footsteps sound in the upstairs hall, and he pokes his head around my doorframe. "Pizza sounds amazing."

"Sausage and green pepper?"

He nods. "And sun-dried tomatoes," he adds.

That's new. But it sounds good.

"I'm gonna take a quick shower."

His hair is damp against his forehead, and a smudge of dirt runs across one cheek where he probably brushed something away with his work glove. His T-shirt is plastered against his chest, and I can see the edges of his six-pack through the light fabric.

I swallow and turn away, gritting my teeth in an approximation of a smile. "Okay. I'll go ahead and order."

He nods and heads into the bathroom, and I hear the door shut with a click. Moments later, the water turns on.

I shove the pillows back on the bed and hurry downstairs so I won't end up standing in my room like a creeper, listening to him shower.

Earlier, I put together a list of items for us to talk about, business-wise, trying desperately to keep my focus on the winery and not all the other ways my life is imploding right now. Maybe if we keep our conversations professional and organized, the rest of our time together will be, too.

Item one: Timeline on harvest.

Item two: How long do we have the interns?

Item three: Any items needed in the next three weeks that I can order?

Item four: Why the hell Jake kept our non-annulment a secret all this time. What if I had wanted to get married to someone else?

Nope. Strike that. I'm not ready for that conversation yet.

By the time he comes downstairs, wearing gray sweatpants and a UC Napa T-shirt, the pizza is ordered and I've uncorked a Merlot from a nearby winery. I'm sipping my first glass, sitting at the kitchen table, and staring at the sheet of paper in front of me.

At least it keeps me from looking at him in those damn gray sweatpants. Almost impossible to resist.

Jake drops down into the seat across from me. Behind him, I can see the Caparelli sign he gave me a couple of days ago, and my stomach knots again at the knowledge that it really was an anniversary present.

Just think, if we hadn't parted ways thanks to Uncle Geno's interference, we could have celebrated that date every year. Together.

And now he's here, temporarily, and our togetherness is just a—a mirage. A fantasy.

Isn't it?

I take another big sip.

He pours some for himself and takes a taste, swirling the ruby liquid around in the stemless glass. Picking up the bottle, he looks at the label. His face brightens. "This is from Wade's family winery! Not bad. I'll have to let him know we enjoyed a bottle."

"How is Wade doing these days?" I haven't seen him in ages.

Jake leans back in his chair. "Pretty good. Still waiting for his dad to hand over the reins."

If I wasn't watching his face as closely as I am, I would have missed the way his mouth tightened over that sentence.

"It must be hard."

I didn't mean to say anything. I have a damn meeting

agenda right in front of me to help me keep our conversation from getting too personal. But it slipped out anyway.

Why can't I keep my distance from him?

Should I even try?

Jake sighs. "I've had time to get used to it."

I tilt my head and look at him.

He laughs. "Okay, fine. I've had time to convince everyone around me that I'm okay with it."

"When did you know?"

He looks down. "That they were going to have to sell? After the second round of chemo." He lifts his glass in a mock salute. "All hail the American healthcare system."

"Medical bills." It's not a question. They're not the first family around here to lose their winery due to medical debt.

"At least they had insurance. That paid for most of it. But even so, it wasn't enough, especially after the fires a few years back. They didn't have enough savings to make it through."

"I know I've said it before, but I'm sorry."

"Yeah." He props an elbow on the table. "At least mom is cancer-free now."

"Thank God."

"I just wish..." He sighs, his eyes going unfocused. "I wish it hadn't come to that."

"Me, too," I whisper.

He shrugs. "It's part of why I'm glad I'm here. If I can help prevent this from happening to you and your sisters, it'll be worth it. I don't want to see another family-owned winery sold off to some celebrity playing at winemaking."

"Maybe he's not so bad," I offer, and he laughs, shaking his head.

"Wishful thinking."

"I still haven't met him. Have you?"

He nods. "A couple days ago, in fact. We...well, let's just say we didn't exactly hit it off."

Of course they didn't. I'm sure Jake has a lot of feelings about the guy who bought his parents' winery, whether he deserves it or not.

"Still, probably best to give him a chance."

"That's so Rosa. Always seeing the best in people, regardless of the circumstances." His lips quirk wryly. "Except maybe me."

"Wait, what?"

"Lately it seems like all you can see is the worst in me."

I open my mouth and close it again. What do I say to that?

Before I can formulate an answer, the doorbell rings, and I reach for my purse on the counter behind me.

But Jake pops up and holds up a hand. "Nope. I've got this one." He strides out of the room and down the hall to the front door before I can protest. I can hear him charming the delivery person while I grab some plates from the cupboard, shaking my head.

"I was going to pay for that, you know," I grumble as he brings the box into the kitchen and places it in the center of the table.

"And I beat you to it," he says with a grin. "Come on, sit down. Can't let it get cold."

I open the box, letting the smell of our favorite pizza—plus sun-dried tomatoes—fill the room. Jake grabs a beer out of the fridge ("It goes better with pizza—don't tell Wade.") and puts two large slices on his plate. I take a big bite of my slice and groan as the taste fills my mouth. God, I love Divino Pizza.

When I look over, Jake is taking a long pull from his bottle and a muscle is jumping in his jaw.

"Everything okay?"

"Yup." He shoves half a slice into his mouth and chews.

No Way, Rosé

They must have worked their asses off this afternoon for him to be this hungry.

"So, we have a few things to talk about," I say as I start on my second slice of pizza.

I take a pen and pull the list toward me.

"What are you doing?"

I shrug. "Just keeping track." I tap the sheet of paper.

Jake starts choking on his pizza.

"Are you okay?" I jump out of my seat and round the table, ready to try out the Heimlich maneuver if necessary.

He coughs, waving me off as he clears his throat. "I'm fine," he rasps. He takes another swig of beer and sets the bottle down on the table with a thump. "Are you actually telling me you created an *agenda* for dinner?"

I can feel heat crawling up my neck. "Um...sort of?" I drop back into my seat.

"That's so you." Jake shakes his head, laughing. "Everything itemized and organized and turned into a list."

"Hey!" I wave the paper at him. "My organization and list-making saved us when that cop showed up today."

He sobers. "Yeah, it did. Nice job."

Slightly mollified, I slap the paper down and finish the last of my wine.

Without asking, he picks up the bottle and fills my glass again.

I don't protest.

"Honestly, I just didn't want to forget anything," I tell him, nodding at the list in front of me. "There are a lot of moving parts."

He nods. "Okay, hit me. What's your first *item*?"

He's teasing me, but I ignore it and clear my throat. "What's the timeline on prepping for harvest?"

I PUT THE PIZZA BOX IN THE FRIDGE, AND JAKE TAKES THE rest of the wine out to the front porch. I've given up on hiding the fact that Jake is living here, so I follow him out and sit in the Adirondack chair where I can see the sun dipping below the horizon. We're most of the way through my list-slash-agenda, and things are going well.

Of course, I have to blow things up. "So who do *you* think turned us in?"

Jake glances at me. "You know who." His voice sounds— careful, like he's afraid to say it out loud.

I can feel the tension between my shoulders. I don't want to say it, either. I don't want to make it real. "Maybe it's just something that happens when you're starting up," I say, sounding more like a question than a statement. "Not that Caparelli hasn't been around forever, but separating it from Belmonte kind of made it a new place."

"Really?" His voice is dry. He's looking forward, eyes shaded in the deepening twilight.

"It makes as much sense as anything else," I try. Which it doesn't, but I'm desperate to find a reason that isn't the most obvious one. Because if it really is who I think it is...

I don't know how I'll bear it.

He's quiet for a long moment. "Do you really think the athlete across the way got the same treatment?"

My stomach tightens. "Is it horrible if I say that I hope so?"

Jake shakes his head. "I get it. At least you wouldn't be the only target if that was the case."

"Exactly." I lean forward and prop my elbows on my knees. My stomach is in knots.

Jake clears his throat and tips his head toward the piece of paper in my hand. "Okay. What's next on the agenda?"

I roll my eyes. "It's just a damn list, Jake."

"They're never just *damn lists*, Rosa. You live your life by lists. Even when we eloped, you had to prepare a list first." His voice is fond.

And he's not wrong. I worked on that list for weeks—what our cover story should be, what we needed to bring, which chapels on the strip were more likely to marry two young people, one of whom had barely turned eighteen.

Who would be taking care of our responsibilities while we were gone.

I had it all planned out to the last detail. Except I hadn't counted on Nonna having the heart attack that put her in the hospital while I was off in Vegas marrying Jake.

Jake reaches out a hand and covers mine, resting on the arm of my Adirondack chair. God, even that little touch feels so good. "There was nothing you could have done," he murmurs, and I'd be startled at how well he can read my mind, except—

It's always been like that between us.

The hell of it is I was so *happy*—until we got home. We drove back from the airport together, holding hands on the bench seat of Jake's pickup truck, and I remember looking at them tangled together, joy swelling in my chest. I had a simple gold band on my finger that we'd bought in a pawn shop off the strip right before the ceremony, and I watched the sun glint off it as we headed back to Oak Creek Canyon. I couldn't wait to tell everyone.

And then we pulled up to Caparelli, and Uncle Geno was waiting in the entryway as I dragged my suitcase inside. He'd been going through Nonna's papers, looking for her insurance information to bring to the hospital when he'd heard the truck pull up, and the fury in his eyes when he saw us made me take several steps back. I bumped into Jake, who put his hands on my shoulders and asked Uncle Geno what was going on.

It all tumbled out then, in a torrent of words I could barely track. How Nonna was sick, and Allegra and Bianca had tried to call me but I wasn't answering, and they'd panicked. How Geno had tried to track me down on the grad trip only to discover that I'd bailed on it for parts unknown. How disappointed he was in me—for lying, for being so irresponsible, for not being there when they needed me.

And then he saw the ring, and everything went even more to hell.

"It was a nightmare," I say softly.

"You know, if Geno knew I was here, he'd probably have a coronary," Jake muses, scrubbing a hand through his hair. "Remember how he ordered me off the property that day?"

I huff out a laugh. "I wonder if there's a statute of limitations on something like that."

"Doesn't matter." He leans back in his chair, looking out at the night sky. "It's your property now. He doesn't have a say on it anymore."

Sometimes that's hard to remember. I've spent so many years deferring to Geno and what he said, the idea of being solely responsible for what happens at Caparelli is a little frightening. So much responsibility on my shoulders.

And even scarier is how nice it is to have someone shoulder it with me. Especially when his time here is limited.

He's done so much for me, for us, for Caparelli. Even when he had no reason to.

The least I can do is tell him I was wrong.

I take a deep breath and let it out. "Sasha and I didn't go for coffee today. I mean, yes, we got coffee. But that's not why we spent the morning together."

He waits for a moment. "Okay," he says carefully.

"We went to the courthouse."

I glance over. He's nodding but not looking at me.

"You were right." I suck in another breath. "We're still married."

"Yep." He doesn't sound arrogant or gleeful or like he's ready to do a victory dance.

He sounds sure. Solid. Calm.

Why wouldn't he be? He's had ten years to get used to the idea. I've had a couple of weeks.

And only a handful of hours since I confirmed his story.

I open my mouth, ready to ask him why he never filed the papers, but then I snap it shut. I'm afraid of what he'll say.

Did he still want to be married to me?

Does he still want that now?

What do I want?

I want Jake. In my arms, in my bed.

I can admit that to myself. But something still holds me back from admitting it to him.

At this point, though, I'm not sure what. We're married. We're living in the same house. What would it hurt?

I'm so, so tempted.

"So what do we do now?" I ask him.

He laughs softly and shakes his head. Holding up the bottle, he says, "Finish the wine, for one."

"Yeah, okay." I hold out my glass for another pour, and he fills his own with the remainder.

He toasts me with an ironic quirk to his left eyebrow. "To the happy couple," he murmurs and takes a long drink, keeping eye contact with me the whole time.

"Asshole," I reply, drinking up as well.

He chokes on the wine, sputtering as he laughs. I grin into the glass in my hand.

That felt good.

"Holy shit, Rosa," he says finally when he catches his breath. "I was not expecting that."

"Gotta keep you on your toes," I quip and set my glass down. When we both stop laughing, I sigh. "This is a mess."

"Maybe." He finishes the last of his wine and puts the glass on the little table between us. "But it doesn't have to be."

I look at him, confused, and he lifts one shoulder. "It's been a mess for ten years, Rosa. We don't have to fix it tonight. Maybe we shouldn't even try."

I tilt my head. "What do you mean?"

He stands and holds out his hand. I place my palm in his, shivering a little at the heat that travels up my arm at that innocent touch. Tugging lightly, he pulls me to my feet. "I mean, why don't we forget this mess, forget all the ins and outs of our tangled past, and focus on the here and now?"

"Here and now," I repeat, swaying toward him just a little.

He nods. "And right here, right now, I'd like to kiss you. What do you think about that?"

Chapter 18

Jake

For a long, silent moment, I hold my breath. Rosa's backlit by the last remnants of the setting sun and the dim porch light above. Her hair glows rich brown, framing her shadowed face. Even in the growing twilight, I can see the gleam in her eyes.

She lets go of my hand, and I swallow. If she doesn't want this, I can respect that. I'd never force myself on anyone, let alone the woman I—

Rosa steps forward, wraps her arms around my neck, and pulls me down into a fierce kiss.

Hunger surges through me as she strokes her tongue into my mouth. This isn't a soft, tentative kiss like the one in the kitchen the other day. No, this is heat and fire and passion, her teeth nipping at my lower lip, her hands gripping my hair. Her fingers tug at the strands, and I groan into her mouth.

She pulls back, eyes searching mine, and nods once. "Let's

go upstairs," she whispers, and it takes everything in me not to drop to my knees.

Instead, I grab her hand and pull her to the door, ignoring her laughing protest at leaving the glasses and wine bottles outside. "I promise you—I will come down and clean up. After."

"After?" Her voice is breathy, a hitch to it that tells me she's as aroused as I am.

"*After* whatever you're up for, darlin'." I tug her inside, closing the door behind us before I turn her around, press her up against it, and kiss her.

Just because I can. Just because I've wanted to since the day she agreed to take me on.

Just because.

I trail kisses down her jaw, her throat, dipping my tongue into the hollow at the base of her neck. She moans and tilts her head back, giving me better access. "Soft," she whispers.

"What?" I murmur, arms full of a warm, sexy Rosa.

"Your beard is soft," she says, tipping her head to the side so I can hear her better. "I've never kissed someone with a beard before. I thought it would be more—wiry, or something. Scratchy."

"If you think my beard feels good when I'm kissing you, just wait until it's between your thighs," I growl, and suddenly the teasing is replaced with something darker, more heated. She tightens her arms around my neck and whimpers.

I can't wait.

I kiss her again, deeper this time, one hand stroking down her spine until I'm cupping her perfect ass. I squeeze lightly, and she practically melts against me.

"I thought...we were going...upstairs," she gasps, her body plastered against mine from shoulder to knee. I can feel her chest rise with every breath.

"Yes, ma'am," I say, pressing an open-mouthed kiss to the swell of her left breast. My other hand joins the first, and I lift her up, urging her wordlessly to wrap her legs around my waist. She giggles, clinging to my shoulders as both of my hands grip her butt. I carry her up the stairs, then stop at the landing.

She pulls back, looking at me quizzically. I tip my head to the left, then the right. "Your place or mine?"

She rolls her eyes.

I don't want to admit it, but I like that we're able to have fun with this, too. It's hot and sexy and tantalizing, but it's also goofy and playful.

Just like Rosa herself.

At least the Rosa I knew. The Rosa I married.

"I've got the bigger bed," she answers, and I turn toward her room. Once inside, I kick the door shut and stride forward, the light of the moon rising over the hills behind the house dappling the comforter through the gauzy drapes. I press one more hard kiss to her luscious mouth—and drop her right onto the middle of the bed.

Rosa throws her head back as she laughs, bouncing on the mattress. Her hair drapes along the pillows piled up at the headboard, and her eyelashes look a million miles long, fluttering against the tops of her cheeks.

She leans back on her elbows, looking at me through those gorgeous lashes, lips curving up in a seductive smile. "Well? Aren't you going to join me?"

With a growl, I climb onto the bed and crawl forward until I'm hovering over her, my knees on either side of her hips. Leaning down, I stop a breath away from her mouth and whisper, "Tell me what you want."

"You," she says simply, then puts a hand in my hair and pulls me down.

Chapter 19

Rosa

Jake's mouth is hot and eager against mine, and I open to him immediately. The brush of his beard against my cheek sends a shiver down my spine. Like I told him downstairs, it's soft and tickles just a little, and I bite back a groan as I imagine that touch in other, more intimate places.

Just like he promised.

In the back of my mind, I'm sure "Do the Right Thing" Rosa is freaking out, but there's something freeing about letting go of all the *must*s and *should*s and responsibilities and just doing what I want, for once.

Reaching out and taking what Jake is so freely giving.

It's not love or romance, but I don't need those in my life. He'll be leaving at the end of the harvest season anyway.

We're both going into this with our eyes open. Scratching an itch that's been hovering under the surface of our skin since the moment we saw each other under that tree on Take Flight's property.

I want Jake, and he's made it clear he wants me, too.

Why not take what we can get while we can?

After all, we *are* husband and wife.

I smother a giggle.

"What?" Jake leans back, hands gripping the base of his T-shirt. With one smooth motion, he strips it off over his head and tosses it into a corner without even looking.

Jesus, how does he make that look sexy?

"You're so...God."

"Nope. Still Jake." He smirks as I roll my eyes. Then I reach out and place my palm on that solid, muscled bare chest, and the smile falls away, replaced by a heat in his eyes that I can almost feel.

He looks so different, so *masculine*. The last time I saw Jake naked, he was barely twenty, all lean gangly limbs and adolescent frame. Now he's filled out, broad shoulders and taut stomach, with more chest hair than I remember.

His flat nipple tightens under my hand as I stroke him from the shoulder down. His knees, on either side of my waist, hold me in place, and I wriggle impatiently. I want to put my mouth on that nipple, suck and lick and tug at it with my teeth.

I want to press a kiss to his stomach, watch the muscles ripple as I explore. I want to follow that thin trail of hair from his navel, disappearing down under the waistband of the gray sweatpants he put on after his shower when he finally came in from the fields, washing off the dirt and sweat of the day.

I want to get dirty and sweaty with him.

I *want*.

As if he can read my mind—and maybe he can; at this point I'm not ruling it out—he shuffles back and swings his leg to one side of the bed, so he's no longer holding me down. Not that I'd object, under the right circumstances, but right now I want to be able to touch him back. He stretches out by my side, his body heat radiating where he's pressed up against me. I lean forward, kissing his collarbone, breathing in the faint scent of bodywash and clean, fresh male.

He trails a finger along the neckline of my tank top, leaving goose bumps all along the skin. He slides his hand over my breast, cupping it in his palm, and my nipple beads under his touch. I can't help it—I arch up, pressing into his hand, wordlessly begging for more.

Jake swears under his breath and pulls the tank top off, throwing it in the opposite direction of his shirt. By the end of this my bedroom floor is going to be covered with clothing items in random locations.

And I love it.

I sit up, reaching behind me to unhook my bra, sending up a silent thanks to past me for choosing something a little sexier than usual this morning. I told myself it was for a boost of confidence on the way to the courthouse—nothing like cute lingerie to add a little spring to your step—but I wouldn't be surprised if some part of me expected, or maybe hoped for, this outcome.

Jake swears again as I drop the bra off the side of the bed, leaving my breasts bare. I start to cover them, but he stops my hands with a gentle squeeze. "Don't hide," he says. "You're beautiful."

And yeah, it's not like he hasn't seen me naked before. He'd been my first, back when we were teenagers. We'd found places all over both our wineries to have sex where no one would find us. But I'm not going to lie—I've changed over the years, and I'm not that tight-body teen anymore.

I glance at his face, looking for any hint of disappointment. But all I can see is *want*.

I can feel heat race over my neck and chest. He smiles, almost predatory in his gaze, and traces the blush across the tops of my breasts with his fingertips.

Then he replaces his fingers with his mouth, and my head drops back with a groan.

His lips explore the swell of my breasts, tongue dipping out to stroke and taste. He traces circles around my nipple, getting closer with each pass until he takes it into his mouth and sucks gently.

My hands fly up to his head, fingers threading through his hair. He pulls off with a soft *pop*. "You can pull my hair," he says, his voice like gravel. "I like it."

Huh. That's new.

I give a gentle tug, and he moans around my nipple, sucking even more enthusiastically. He switches sides, and his hand strokes the first one, thumb brushing over the damp, beaded nub, while his mouth works the other. His free hand slides down my stomach, under the waistband of my shorts, and teases me there.

I'm surrounded by sensation, pleasure rushing through me from multiple angles, and I whimper. His beard brushes against the underside of my breast, and it sends shivers throughout my body.

Dimly, in the back of my mind, I wonder where the hell he learned how to do all this, but I lock it away. If I can benefit from his skill, it really doesn't matter.

Jake pulls back, his fingers toying with the button on my shorts. "Do you want me to take these off?"

I blink at him. I'm so turned on I can barely understand the spoken word.

"Rosa." He smiles softly at me. "I'd like to see you naked. Is that something you're interested in?"

Oh. Got it. I nod eagerly. "Yes. Yep. Uh-huh."

He laughs, shaking his head. "Good to hear it." With a teasing smile, he unbuttons my shorts and slides the zipper down, the sound loud in the quiet of my bedroom. I do my best not to squirm when his knuckles brush my hips as he pulls the shorts down my legs.

He drops them off the end of the bed—yet another location for our wayward clothing—and then leans down and presses a kiss right on top of my lace undies.

God.

He smiles up at me, his eyes hooded, and he hooks his thumbs under the edges of the underwear and drags them slowly down my legs. Following the fabric down, he kisses the inside of my thigh. The side of my knee. The outside curve of my calf. My ankle.

"Jake," I whisper, my throat tight.

He looks up from the bottom of the bed, and his eyes soften. He crawls up the mattress, hovering over me again, and kisses my forehead. "I've got you," he murmurs against my skin.

I blink against the sting of tears at the corner of my eyes, then squeeze them shut.

This is supposed to be a fun, mind-clearing romp, not something sweet and thoughtful and soft. I need to nudge it back into romp territory before my heart gets involved.

"I believe you promised me a new beard-related experience," I tease when I can get my voice under control. I squint one eye open and see his face above mine, the soft smile turning into something more heated, more hungry.

"That I did," he agrees, smoothing his hand down my side, tracing my curves. "And I keep my promises."

He settles between my legs, his shoulders pressing my thighs wide. Then he leans forward and licks.

That does it. Every worry, every stress flies out of my head with each pass of his tongue. It's heat and slick, perfect pressure. It's the gentle brush of his beard against my thighs, the tease on my mound.

He takes his time, his tongue and lips and hands exploring me with a single-minded focus that overwhelms me.

I grip his head with my hands, and yeah, I tug a little. The groan that rips from his mouth makes me clench in the most delightful way.

Too soon, I feel my orgasm building, spiraling from my center out. I tug his hair again, a silent warning, but he just dives in even more enthusiastically. And that's it—I break, wave after wave of pleasure washing through me. When it ends, I'm wrung out. Sated. Empty in the best way.

Jake kisses his way up my body, finally stretching out on the pillow next to me. He grins. "Hi."

I grab his head and kiss him, pouring everything I can't say out loud into the kiss. I taste myself on his tongue, and a spark rolls through me. My hand slides down his chest, past his stomach, down to his gray sweatpants. I break the kiss and pull back, my mouth in a pout. "You're not naked yet."

"Definitely an oversight." He shoves his hands into the sides of his sweats and pushes them down, along with his underwear. He lifts his hips to pull them all the way off, and I bite back a groan.

Then he drops back onto the comforter, his cock hard against his belly. I wrap my fingers around it and give it an experimental stroke.

Jake's head drops back onto the pillow, and he groans. "Give me your hand, sweetheart."

I look at him quizzically but let go and place my hand in his.

He raises it to his mouth and licks it, thoroughly. Twinges of pleasure ripple through my body.

When my hand is well lubricated, he lets go, and I take him in my grip again. This time the slide is easier, slicker, and my movements speed up as I watch his expression. I can see his pleasure build, and I shiver.

"I'm close," he warns, but I redouble my efforts. I want this —I want his pleasure as much as I wanted my own. His body tenses, and he comes, painting his stomach and chest and spilling over my hand.

He lies there for long moments, breathing hard, while I curl into his side and wonder what's going to happen next.

Apparently what happens next in Jake's world is he gathers himself, swings his legs off the bed, and disappears out of my room. I'm just starting to spiral when he returns, carrying a warm washcloth. He cleans my hand and between my thighs and winks at me as he takes it back into the bathroom. When he comes back, he pulls down the comforter and maneuvers me under the sheets.

He leans down and kisses me on the forehead. "Sleep well, Rosa. I know I will."

"You're going?" My voice cracks, and I wince. "I mean, yeah. Of course."

He nods and grabs his sweats off the floor. "I need to clean up the front porch first, as promised. Don't worry—I'll close up downstairs."

"Thanks," I say, injecting some false cheer into my voice. "Appreciate it."

"Anytime." He finishes pulling up his sweats and winks at me again. "And believe me, I mean it."

I listen to his footsteps fade as he goes downstairs, then the front door opens and closes.

I'm not sure how I feel. I mean, physically, I *definitely* know how I feel. It's been a long, long time since I've had an orgasm with someone else. I feel more relaxed, more sated than I have in a long while. Little sparks still zing under my skin.

But emotionally—hell, who knows? I should be happy Jake

is keeping it on a physical-only level. Sex is one thing. Sleeping together—something else completely.

It's a good reminder that whatever we get up to for the rest of this summer, it has an end date. And I'd better keep that in mind instead of harboring happily-ever-after fantasies.

WHEN I WAKE UP THE NEXT MORNING, JAKE IS GONE.

Not only from my bed—as promised, he went back to his own room as soon as he finished tidying up the porch—but from the house as well.

I can't explain it, but when the house is empty, I can tell. The silence is different, the energy lowered.

I pull on a bathrobe and head downstairs, nodding to myself when I confirm Jake's absence. The coffee pot is half-full, my favorite mug sitting next to it. There's a cereal bowl in the sink, and the milk carton has been rinsed and is ready for recycling.

I *hmph* a little and open the fridge. Thank God I've got half-and-half, because if Jake had finished off the last of the dairy products before I got my coffee, there would be hell to pay.

On the other hand, I need to get groceries, so I pull out the notepad and a pen and sit down at the table with it—and my perfectly doctored coffee.

List completed, I take a shower and get dressed to go into town. Then I shoot Jake a text, letting him know that if he or our interns want anything from the store, message me back with the requests.

The parking lot at the grocery store is mostly empty when I

arrive, a benefit of shopping early. With any luck, I'll be able to avoid running into anyone I know this time.

My luck runs out in the produce department.

"Hi, Rosey," Aunt Janet says, swooping over to kiss me on the cheek. "How are you, dear?"

At least one person at Belmonte still treats me the same way they did before we inherited.

She probably still sees me as that little kid who had to be "mothered" to within an inch of her life once Mama moved to Europe.

She lifts her thumb and scrubs at the bright pink mark I just know she left on my cheek.

Still at it, then.

"You look..." Her voice trails off as she really looks at me. "Actually, you look like you're doing well."

I plaster on a closed-lip smile. "I *am* doing well, thanks. How are you?"

"Oh, you know." She waves a hand, encompassing everything I'm apparently supposed to know. "Busy, busy. You'd think with fewer vineyards to manage, Geno would have more time on his hands, but..."

So that's awkward.

I turn around and grab a piece of produce at random, just for something to do. I'll have to figure out what exactly cactus leaves can be used for. Later. "It's good to hear things are going well," I say, even though she's said nothing of the sort.

"Well." She fidgets with the strap of her purse, which confuses me. I've never seen Aunt Janet fidget with anything. "I just wish you would stop pretending to run Caparelli and join up with your uncle and cousins again."

Pretending to run Caparelli? I breathe in, count to three, breathe out. "Aunt Janet, I *am* running Caparelli. And it's going really well, too."

Okay, maybe I'm exaggerating a little, but it *is* going well. Thanks to Jake and our interns.

She tilts her head, a sad look on her face. "Is it really? Trying to handle everything on your own?"

"I'm not on my own," I blurt out. "Jake is doing an amazing job."

Oh. Oh, shit. I wasn't going to say that.

"And the interns," I rush to add. "Emi and Javier are a great addition to the team."

"You should be on your *uncle's* team," she argues. "Like you've been for the past ten years. This is a family business. The family needs you."

I sigh. "Aunt Janet, I love you, but we both know the family never needed me. Not for the winery business anyway."

"Of course we did! How can you say that?"

"Has Uncle Geno hired someone to replace me yet?"

There's a long pause. "I—I'm not really sure..."

"Mm-hmm." I toss a bag of onions into my shopping cart. Why I think I need a dozen onions, I can't be sure, but it gives me something to do with my hands.

Aunt Janet's mouth opens and closes a couple of times, like she's trying to come up with something more to say, when her eyes narrow and she asks, "Wait a minute. Jake? Who's Jake?"

I was hoping she'd be distracted away from that topic. I clear my throat, try to inject a casual tone into my voice. "Jake Wright."

"Your ex?"

Wait, how much does she know? Did Uncle Geno say something to her all those years ago?

Then I remember he was my boyfriend before he was my husband, so it's not an unreasonable question. "Yes, my ex-boyfriend. Since Take Flight was sold, he offered to help out on Caparelli."

"That's—nice of him."

"Yes, it is." I flash a wide smile. "It's been great seeing you, but I have to get back to Caparelli. Say hi to everyone for me!" And with that, I make a run for the freezer section.

On the way, I check my messages, but there's nothing shopping-related from Jake, so I finish getting everything on my list and check out. I have to get out and get home without any more awkward family encounters.

It's closing in on noon by the time I get back to Caparelli, so I put together a fruit salad and an easy chicken-wrap recipe. I'm pouring a bag of chips into a bowl when the back door opens. "Wash up," I call out, putting the chips on the table next to the fruit. "Lunch is in the kitchen when you're ready."

Emi breezes in, her hair falling out of a ponytail and a sunburn across her nose. "I'm famished," she says, pulling the lemonade out of the fridge. "But you don't have to feed us every day. Really."

Javier and Jake follow her into the kitchen. "Now, don't be hasty," Jake teases, putting a hand on my waist as he slides past me to the table. "Rosa's food is really good."

Just like that, I'm on fire again.

Then he turns to me. "She's right, though. It's not your obligation."

There's heat in his eyes, so obvious I'm surprised Emi and Javier haven't picked up on it yet. My thighs clench.

I turn away and fuss with the food on the table, hardly able to breathe. "Either you help me eat it or I have leftovers for days. Up to you."

They fall on the food like they haven't eaten for weeks, even though I had dinner with Jake last night and saw the evidence of his breakfast this morning.

There was other eating going on last night, too, my brain helpfully supplies. I choke on my chicken wrap, and Jake has to pound my back so I can breathe again.

"Wrong pipe," I croak, clearing my throat. I take a long swallow of lemonade and do my best not to look anyone in the eye until the end of the meal.

Emi and Javier chatter about the new pruning technique Jake's been showing them. I turn to him and tilt my head. "Sounds like something I should know how to do," I say.

He lifts one eyebrow. "You're welcome to join us this afternoon."

This man is going to be the death of me. "Can't wait."

Two hours later, sweat is dripping down my back, I have blisters on my thumbs, and my mouth feels like it has never experienced liquid.

And I'm having the time of my life.

It didn't take long for me to get the hang of pruning the vines, and Jake gave me my own section to work on, just like Emi and Javier. The four of us work in silence mostly, shouting out a comment or observation from time to time across the rows of vines. With every row I complete, I feel more and more like a part of the team, like I'm making a difference.

Every few minutes, Jake makes the rounds, checking on us

newbies (and yes, I'm counting myself as a newbie, too). He leans over my shoulder, watching as I trim a side shoot or pinch away some extra leaves. I can smell his shampoo this close and the leather of his work gloves. If I turn my head, I could press a kiss to his bearded cheek.

I face the vines, though, and try to focus on his directions, the minor adjustments that make the work that much more effective down the line. Jake leans in, murmurs praise into my ear, and walks down the row to see how Javier is doing.

I do my best not to melt into a puddle right there in the vineyard.

At least Javier doesn't want to jump his bones every time he comes near. I mean, probably. The man is so damn sexy, I wouldn't blame him.

Focus, I tell myself. There's something different about the vines, something I can't put my finger on, but I shake my head and let it go. It's the growing season; I'm sure things change every single day.

It's heading toward sundown when Jake finally calls an end to our work, and we troop down the hill to the house. There's only a small section left, and the three of them are confident they'll be finished early tomorrow.

Emi and Javier clean up and head home, while Jake and I take turns showering. I manage to avoid asking him to help me conserve water and shower with me—something I regret when I'm under the spray, alone.

I'm on edge, practically vibrating with the need to get my hands on Jake again.

But by the time I get downstairs, Jake is eating leftover pizza out of the box. "Sorry," he mumbles around a bite. "I would have waited, but I'm meeting up with Wade tonight."

"Of course," I say. I'm not disappointed. I'm not. "Tell him I said hi."

He shoves the rest of his pizza into his mouth, glances at his watch, and swears. "Don't wait up," he says as he heads to the front door. "And thanks for helping today. I really appreciate it."

I wave goodbye and close the door behind him. Okay, yes, I was hoping for a repeat of last night.

Maybe he isn't as interested in another round as he said he would be last night.

Oh well. If our bedroom games are just one and done, I can live with that.

Or at least I'm working really hard to convince myself that it's true.

I clean up the kitchen and look around, trying to find something to keep me busy for the night. Finally, I decide it's time for a bubble bath, a new book on my e-reader, and a mug of tea.

If I toss and turn until I hear him unlock the front door late that night, well, I'll never tell.

Chapter 20

Jake

"Hey, boss man." Javier claps me on the shoulder as he passes by, heading to the corner of the vineyard where he left off last Friday. "How was your weekend?"

I shrug. "Not bad," I answer. "You?"

"Nice to have a couple of days off," he replies as he heads up the hill.

I nod and keep weeding. Emi and Javi had Saturday and Sunday off, but I worked over the weekend, partly because there was work that needed to be done, calendar be damned, and partly to keep myself busy and out of temptation's way.

So I worked from dawn until sundown, ate standing up in the kitchen, then found reasons to be out of the house—and out of Rosa's orbit.

My get-together with Wade was fine but nonproductive. At least when it came to getting proof that Geno was behind the complaint about Caparelli. He either didn't pick up on my hints or isn't as tied into the rumor mill as he seemed last time we talked.

He did, however, notice how frequently I mentioned Rosa. And gave me all sorts of shit about that.

Wade, like pretty much everyone else in this town, thinks she's just my high school sweetheart and ex-girlfriend. If he knew we're actually married?

Now, *that* would be material to power the rumor mill for the next ten years, if not longer.

I didn't fill him in, of course. The knowledge that Rosa finally accepts our current state of matrimony is too tenuous, too new for me to start blabbing it all over town. Instead, we talked about crops and harvest plans and who in our graduating class is pregnant or moving out of state or finally got married. Wade said Ben and Danny's wedding was the social event of the year.

It was a good catch-up and I'm glad to be reconnecting with Wade, but I'd be lying if I said I wasn't itching to get back to Caparelli.

Back to Rosa's bed.

Which is why I stayed out the next two nights as well, finally heading home well past midnight. Much as I want to spend every waking moment rediscovering her body, figuring out what makes grown-up Rosa gasp and moan and squirm under me, it would be dangerous to give in to that urge. I have to parcel out those moments, pace myself. I don't want to get addicted to her breathless sighs, and the other night I realized pretty quickly that it would be really, really easy to get to that point.

I'm leaving, and she's staying, and we still have this goddamned mess of a marriage to untangle.

And yes, I'm aware that the mess is of my own making. But I didn't realize how hard it was going to be dealing with it now that Rosa knows and what I want *us* to look like when the marriage part of it is untangled.

I move over a row and pull some more weeds, glad for the physical labor to help clear my head. That's the plan, at least. Emi calls out a cheerful hello as she clomps her way up the hill to finish the last section with Javier.

Mid-morning, they're done, so I call them over for a water break and pull a clipboard out of my backpack. "Next job is tracking pests," I tell them and go over the different insects that are common to the area as well as the invasive and dangerous ones to keep an eye out for. "Start in the bottom left corner, work your way up and down the rows. The traps are numbered, so write down the number of the trap, the insects caught in it, and put the date at the top. Bring the clipboard over when you're done."

They nod in unison and head down to the lower left-hand corner of the fields, chattering as they go. Emi's pulled out her cell phone and is showing Javier pictures of some of the more invasive insects, if their conversation is anything to go by.

Or it could be the latest viral video. Who knows.

My own phone buzzes in my back pocket, and I pull it out and frown at the screen. I don't recognize the number, but I decide to answer it anyway.

"Hello?" I push my hair off my forehead and squint up at the clouds scudding overhead.

"Jake? It's Tomás."

I straighten. I haven't heard from him since I was foreman for his vineyard in southern Oregon a couple years back. "Tomás! It's been a while."

"It has," he says. "What are you up to these days?"

I fill him in on what's going on with Caparelli, and he tells me all about his new property in Washington state, just over the border from Canada.

"So, do you have any plans for after harvest?" he asks. "Because I have a proposition for you."

By the time we hang up, my mind is spinning.

I file it away to think about later and settle back into my weeding routine—bend, tug, toss. Bend, tug, toss. The rhythm helps me focus, pulling my thoughts away from the phone call and my relationship issues and onto the state of the vineyard.

Even with our skeleton crew, things are looking up for Caparelli. The vines are thriving, the grapes well past the tight green baby-marble stage. They've doubled in size in the short time I've been here. Soon, they'll swell even more and start taking on color. Rosa and I will have to decide whether to water again soon or wait until later in the season. Too much water and the grapes could burst before harvest; too little and the vines will wither.

There's a reason so few wine growers go to Vegas; growing grapes is one of the biggest gambles around.

Of course, Vegas makes me think of Rosa again, more, *still*. Our elopement was a gamble, too, but one I'd been so sure of before we ran off together.

I didn't realize I'd rolled snake eyes until we got back home.

Although...

No, I can't let the ceasefire that's temporarily happening between us fool me. There's an end date to my time here, just like there was an end date to our happily-ever-after.

I just didn't know it back then. I'll be more vigilant this time around.

As if my thoughts have conjured her, I catch sight of Rosa climbing the hill to the vineyard, a pitcher of ice water in one hand and some cups in the other.

I kick myself—again—for passing up the opportunity to spend time with her last night.

And by "spend time," I mean "fool around."

I wipe the sweat from my forehead and tug off my work gloves. I wave, and the way her face lights up when she sees me...

I know I shouldn't read anything into it.

I don't *want* to read anything into it.

I can't help myself.

"You've gotten so much done today already!" Her eyes are shining as she looks around the fields. She sweeps an arm, indicating the vines and the tidy rows and the grapes that are just starting to turn color. "This is actually working!"

"Thanks for the vote of confidence," I say drily, but I know what she means.

I also know the look on her face was for Caparelli, not me.

It's for the best.

She pours a generous amount of ice water for me, then calls over Emi and Javier. They tromp on over, smiling at Rosa and draining the cups of water twice over before finally joining the conversation.

"That was a lot," Emi says, still breathing a little hard. "But we finished up right before you got here, Rosa."

"Finished what?" Rosa glances down at the clipboard Javier is holding. "Oh, were you doing the insect report?"

"Yup." Javier hands me the clipboard. "Got 'em all."

I frown, checking my watch. There's no way they got through all the traps this quickly. I flip through the pages. "Looks like you missed some," I say.

Emi shakes her head. "We walked every row. That's all of them."

"No—see?" I point to the rows of data. "The numbers aren't sequential. There are a bunch of them that were, well, skipped."

Javier looks at Emi. "We checked every trap that was out

here. I noticed the numbers weren't all in order but figured those were just the ones you used."

"That's what was bugging me the other day!" Rosa says suddenly, then grimaces. "Pun not intended."

I frown at her. "What?"

"When I was out here helping with the pruning, I couldn't figure out what looked different. But that must be it. Some of the traps are missing."

I look closer at the trap numbers on the clipboard, then stomp over a couple of rows to check.

She's right. About every fourth trap is just—gone.

"Holy shit," I mutter under my breath. Someone's actually *stolen* our insect traps. "Do you have extras in the shed?"

Rosa shrugs. "Maybe? There's a lot of crap in there. Sorry—I didn't take inventory when I moved in."

Right. Fine. I nod and turn to Emi and Javier. "Okay. One of you take my truck and go into town. Buy about—" I check the clipboard. "About thirty more traps at the farm store. We have an account there you can charge it to."

Javier takes the keys out of my hand and jogs down the road to my truck, parked outside the Caparelli house.

"Emi, go check the shed to see if there are some we can start putting back up, fill the gaps. And Rosa, do you still have that trap map you made last week?"

"Of course. I'll go grab it and give Emi the key to the shed." She slings an arm around the younger woman's shoulders. "Come on, let's go."

I watch them walk down the road together, chattering away, while my mind races.

Someone, probably on Geno's orders, pulled our traps—not all of them, and not all in one spot. Just enough to make it look like we still had traps if you didn't look too closely. Enough to make sure we're out of compliance with insect control if someone were to—

The growl of a truck engine at the bottom of the hill grabs my attention, and I groan.

Not again.

I wait at the edge of the vineyard for Deputy Romero to pull to a stop and get out of his truck. "Hello," I say tersely.

He nods. His eyes are hidden behind his sunglasses, so I can't read his expression very well. But something tells me he's not happy to be here.

"What can I help you with, sir?"

He coughs. "We've received a report of invasive vine mealybugs on your vineyard."

"Oh, *really*."

The deputy raises one brow, arching over the upper rim of his sunglasses. "Yes, really. I need to inspect your traps."

How convenient.

"Lucky for you, we just completed this week's insect survey." I hold up the clipboard. "But we noticed—"

He steps forward and takes the clipboard out of my hand. What a jerk.

"As I was saying," I start again, but he's frowning at the paper and striding off to the next row of grapevines. I roll my eyes and follow behind, watching as he looks from the first trap in that row to the documentation in his hand, then back again.

He walks forward several paces and looks around. "You're missing some traps. These are too far apart."

I grit my teeth and hold on to my temper. "Yes, I know. We discovered that this morning. It's being handled."

He crosses his arms over his chest, clipboard trapped between his elbow and his side. "So you're out of compliance."

"Technically, yes, but—"

He pushes past me and heads back to his truck. He's

opening the passenger-side door when Rosa walks up to join us, paperwork in hand.

"You're back." Her voice is halfway between ingratiating and wary. "Anything we can help you with?"

He turns and holds out a hastily scrawled ticket to her. "You can shut down until the invasive pest control board has a chance to verify your place is back in compliance."

Her mouth drops open. "What?"

I jump in before he can continue. "Amazingly enough, Rosa, there's been another complaint about Caparelli. This time, that we're hiding invasive insect activity. Mighty convenient that it happened the same day we discovered a quarter of our traps are missing."

"Are you kidding me?" She glares at Deputy Romero. "Another complaint?"

"Yes, ma'am." He stands there, impassive. "Another complaint."

"Wait." She whirls toward me. "It's about the traps?"

I nod. "Apparently so."

"Oh, for heaven's sake." She whips out the documentation from last week and shakes it at Romero. "Here's the trap map and results from last week's study. You can see exactly where the traps are supposed to be—and *were*, up until recently."

He looks at the papers in her hand skeptically. "You're saying there are supposed to be more traps."

"I'm saying we *had* more traps. We documented their locations and everything. And somehow they end up missing right before you're sent out to check them?" She pauses and glances at me. "You know who did this, don't you?"

I shrug one shoulder. "Seems like it."

She turns back to Deputy Romero and glares at him. "What are you going to do about it?"

"Do about what?" He looks like he'd rather be anywhere than right here, right now.

"About the missing traps! Someone obviously stole them. And then called in a complaint."

"You have no proof of any kind of sabotage."

"And you don't have a warrant."

He crosses his arms over his chest. "Do you really want to go there?"

"If necessary, yes." Rosa shakes the papers at him again. "I would also like to make an official complaint about the missing traps. Our proof is right here! We had the traps, we have the locations marked, there are obviously traps missing, and now you show up? It's clear as day."

He sighs. "It's circumstantial at best."

"I don't care. I want a record that we reported it."

He throws his hands up. "Fine. Get the new traps in place by nightfall, and I won't shut you down. But I'm only doing this because you have documentation of coverage as recently as a week ago."

"And you'll make a note of our concerns?"

"Yes," he grinds out through gritted teeth.

"Thank you for your generosity," I say, with only a hint of sarcasm.

He whips his head around and looks over the top of his sunglasses at me. I guess that wasn't as much of a *hint* as I'd intended.

"Can you tell us who reported us?" Rosa manages to hold on to her temper better than I did.

"No." He crosses his arms. "And I'll need copies of the insect reports. The control board will still need to verify that you aren't hiding a mealybug infestation."

"We aren't," I say. "But you're welcome to send someone from the control board to go over our results."

"Let's just start with the insect reports, shall we? Have them ready by five p.m. I'll stop by then to verify you're back in compliance."

He turns on his heel and saunters over to his truck, swinging into the driver's seat without knocking his cowboy hat off his head. I'm almost impressed.

Rosa watches him drive off, her eyes narrowed. "He knows more than he's saying."

"Of course he does. He's not going to share his sources with us. We're the bad guys apparently."

Emi passes the truck on her way back up the hill, arms filled with insect traps. Rosa and I head down to meet her, each of us taking some of the traps.

"I think that's all that was in the shed," she says, digging into her pocket for the key. She hands it to Rosa. "Pretty sure it's not enough to make up for the missing ones."

"It'll be fine. Javier should be back with some more soon, too. We just need to get these traps up today."

She nods, then gestures with her head toward the end of the drive. "Was that the deputy from the other day?"

"Yep. But don't worry about it—we've got everything handled."

My eyes meet Rosa's, and I can see the worry she's trying to hide.

We have everything handled?

God, I hope I'm telling Emi the truth.

Chapter 21

Rosa

I'm filing papers in the office when Jake comes through the back door, yelling something about taking a shower.

Earlier, Deputy Romero's truck rumbled by the house, headed toward the vineyard. Half an hour later, it made the opposite journey.

I was tempted to walk up there to see what transpired, but I restrained myself. I didn't want to give Emi and Javier the impression the situation is more serious than it really is.

The problem is I'm not quite sure just how serious this situation actually is.

Jake and I both know who's behind this. It's time to stop hiding from the truth and figure out how to fight.

I close the filing cabinet with a sigh and maybe a little more force than necessary. I'm angry. Livid. But not at my husband.

This inheritance—this quixotic, overwhelming, brilliant project—should have been a chance for me to show my competence. To prove to everyone that I'm capable of putting in the work and making Caparelli viable again.

But if I can't protect Caparelli from sabotage, especially from my own damn family, how capable am I really?

I shut down my laptop and close the lid, knowing I won't get any more work done tonight. At least not until we have a plan.

I head into the kitchen and grab a bottle of Chardonnay out of the fridge. I hold it in one hand, two glasses and a bottle opener in the other, as I wander into the front room we rarely use.

When we were kids, Jake and I would sometimes hang out in here, escaping from the summer heat on the wide wooden floors. We'd play board games and cards, maybe watch a cartoon or two on the old beat-up black-and-white TV that used to sit in the corner.

It's gone now, and the floors are even more scarred and dusty than they were back then, but Nonna's old couch is still comfy and it's still one of the cooler rooms in the house.

I can hear the shower turn on in the distance, water rushing through the pipes to the upstairs bathroom. I try to ignore the image of Jake standing under the spray, water pouring in rivulets over the sculpted muscles of his chest. And after the other night, I know exactly what that body looks like. The fantasy is based on reality.

I swallow, hard, and pour a little wine.

I take a sip of Chardonnay and swirl the golden liquid in my glass. It's one of my favorites, from Take Flight before Jake's family had to sell. I only have a few bottles left, and I've been trying to stretch it out, keep a little for a future treat. But today feels like a day to crack one open.

Before too long, it'll be gone. Just like Take Flight itself.

The water shuts off, and I sit on the couch, scrolling

through my phone until Jake appears a few minutes later. He drops down onto the opposite end of the couch, giving me a distracted smile. He's wearing joggers and a well-worn T-shirt with the neck stretched out, and I have to dig my fingers into my thigh to keep from reaching for him.

I keep replaying the other night in my mind, the way it felt like he was worshiping my body with every move.

And then he left and stayed out the next night, and the one after that, like he was avoiding temptation.

Or maybe he was just avoiding the inevitable awkward conversation. *It was fun, you're a great girl, but...*

But. He's leaving soon. In the long run, it's better if it was just a one-night thing.

Maybe if I keep telling myself that, I'll eventually believe it.

I hand him the bottle, and he pours himself a glass, leaning back with a satisfied sigh. I put my phone down and turn to him. "What did Officer Friendly have to say on his return visit?"

Jake snorts, taking a long swallow of Chardonnay. "Very little," he says eventually and pulls a business card out of his pocket. "He wants me to contact him if we think of anything we can share with him."

"Gee, how thoughtful." I roll my eyes.

"But in the end he decided there wasn't enough evidence to shut us down or report us to the invasive species board."

"Thank God for small favors," I mutter, and he nods.

Jake picks up the bottle off the floor and turns it in his hand, a fond smile playing at the edges of his mouth. "I loved this year," he murmurs, and my heart squeezes.

"Sorry. I didn't mean to—" I say, but he shakes his head.

"No, it's fine. Better than fine. A good memory." He tilts the bottle and studies the wine, gleaming gold in the early evening sunlight streaming in through the plate-glass window. "Take Flight had a good run. A long one."

I nod; there's not much I can add.

We sit quietly for a moment. Finally, I take a deep breath and turn to Jake. "So, I'm ready to fight back. Are you?"

He heaves a sigh. "Finally."

"We're obviously being sabotaged." I wave my hand. "The complaints, the impossibility of finding workers, someone messing with our equipment, everything."

"The hard part is finding proof." He twirls his glass by the stem, then puts it down on the coffee table and props his elbows on his knees. He stares out into the distance. "Without that, who's going to believe us?"

I nod. "Okay, then. Let's go over what we do know."

"Sure. Tell me what you've noticed."

I hold up a finger. "First. As soon as I take over Caparelli and Uncle Geno pulls his crew, I can't manage to hire anybody. It's like there's a 'do not work for' warning out in the laborer community. I have to go with the only candidate available, who ends up bailing in under two weeks."

"Yeah."

I add a second finger. "Then, you come along and discover he hadn't been watering the vines while he was here and shut off the irrigation system completely before he left. If you weren't around, that could have been a disaster."

"Also true."

"And then..." My voice trails off. "Then you come on board. What happened under your watch?"

"I can't hire anyone, either." He's quiet, still looking away. "And then I was warned not to work with you."

My heart stops. "What?" My voice sounds weak, pained, even to my own ears.

He slants a look at me. "Apparently word in town is that you don't have any money to pay people."

"Shit." I dig my hands into my hair and lean forward. "You're kidding me."

"Unfortunately, no." He lifts a hand, then drops it to his lap. "I've done what I can to convince people of the opposite, but it's a pretty solid rumor."

"It's not true," I say when I can gather my wits around me. "We don't have a lot of cash lying around, but I pay my bills."

"I know," he says. The conviction in his voice helps me calm down.

I shake it off and move on to the next issue. "Then, Mr. Law and Order shows up with a complaint about Caparelli's paperwork, of all things. Like I don't do everything by the book."

Jake laughs softly. "Your lists have lists," he adds.

I narrow my eyes at him, but he's not *wrong*.

"And then the traps." My breath hitches. "Someone actually came onto our property and stole equipment."

I almost can't bear to think about it.

And then I realize what I just said. *Our* property. I'd backtrack and say something about it being mine and my sisters', but enough time has passed since I said it that I'd just make it all the more awkward.

Not only that, but the last few weeks working together, it really has started to feel like our property. Mine and Jake's, together.

It's a mirage, not a marriage, but it's one I can't help but wish was real. I wish both were real.

I hurry to move the conversation along. "And again, Deputy Romero shows up with a complaint."

He looks out the window, pondering, then throws back the rest of his wine, leaving the glass empty.

I watch as his Adam's apple bobs and fight back the wave of want that surges through me.

"That seems more than a little convenient," he says, and I take a moment to figure out what the hell he's talking about. I was distracted, okay?

"Actually, it seems designed to be the most *in*convenient thing possible," I grumble.

Jake tips his head to the side, acknowledging my point. "So we've got rumors in town, anonymous complaints to authorities, and theft."

"Of the missing insect traps," I add. "And who knows what's coming next?"

Because once you lay it out there like that, it seems pretty apparent that this isn't over.

I know who's behind it. But I don't want to voice it. I barely want to *think* it because it's too awful to consider.

But based on the look on Jake's face, he knows, too.

So much for family, I think bitterly. Because there's no one else in the realm of possibility who stands to gain so much from the sabotage of Caparelli.

If I can't make a go of it, Uncle Geno's absolutely waiting in the wings to take over. He's made it abundantly clear that his goal is to take Caparelli back. And what better way to ensure Caparelli is back under Belmonte control than to have poor, naive Rosa fail at running it on her own?

Things happen, you know. Sometimes the odds are against you.

And right now, Geno is stacking the deck.

"There's no hard proof," Jake turns sideways on the couch, gently taking my hands. "But we'll get through this. I promise you."

I let the words wash over me, like *we* is a thing that's going to continue after harvest. If only.

His hands are warm and solid, gripping mine. I take a deep breath and let it out. "So where do we go from here? It's not like we have time to become amateur detectives."

"I think the best thing we can do is to stay alert. Watch for anything out of the ordinary. Stay on top of it so that we're not caught off guard by the next thing." He grins then. "And you can keep being your list-making, rule-following best self."

"Fuck you," I mutter, shoving him to the side, and he laughs, tipping his head back. I kind of want to lick the long, tanned length of his neck.

"Come on." He plants a hand on my knee and levers himself off the low-slung couch, then holds his hand out to me, palm up. "Let's go find something to eat and forget about this bullshit for the rest of the night."

"Sounds perfect."

As I follow him into the kitchen, trading insults and laughing, I realize that it really is.

It's perfect.

And when he takes my hand at the end of our meal and leads me upstairs to my bedroom, that's perfect, too.

Chapter 22

Jake

We're both quiet as we walk up the stairs together, the fifth one from the top squeaking a little as I step on it. She flashes me a quick smile at the sound, and I make a mental note to take a look at it later.

Much, much later.

Her room is bathed in the golden light of a late summer sunset in the valley, and when she grabs the hem of her shirt and tugs it off over her head in one smooth move, her skin turns golden, too.

I have to touch her. My palm skims from her wrist up to her shoulder, then down over the curves of her breast, her breath hitching as my thumb grazes her nipple through the lacy bralette. My hand settles in the dip of her waist, tugging her closer as my mouth descends upon hers.

It's softer than the other night, gentler, as if the frenzy that gripped us then has mellowed to something almost reverent.

She snakes her hands under my shirt and slides them up, up, bringing the softly worn fabric with them. I raise my arms obediently as she pulls it off and tosses it across the room. Then she leans forward and places a kiss right in the center of my sternum.

My breath hitches. I wrap my arms around her and grab the edge of her bralette, tugging it off. Her breasts pillow against my chest, and I hold her close, drinking in the sensation of skin on skin.

I'm almost giddy, which is not an emotion I expected to feel this summer.

I hadn't expected any of this.

But hot damn, I'm glad it's happening.

Her hands slide down my back and cup my ass, and she growls "Fucking gray sweatpants" into my ear, which is both a little confusing and makes me laugh way too hard. I lose the sweats, and she strips the rest of the way, too, and we're finally naked, tumbling onto the bed, both of us still laughing.

She makes me hot, and she makes me laugh. Something squeezes in my chest, and I close my eyes for a moment to get myself together.

"Where?" I ask hoarsely.

Rosa looks at me quizzically. "Where what?"

"Condoms. Where are they?"

"Oh!" She leans over to the bedside table and pulls out the drawer. With a triumphant grin, she holds the still-sealed box aloft.

She doesn't owe me anything, especially not her fidelity. It's not like you can break marriage vows when you don't know they're still technically in effect. But damn, if something warm and triumphant doesn't surge in my chest at the thought that the box hasn't been opened. That she chose, of free will, to go out and buy it. Because of me. Because of the possibility.

And if there's a similar box, also unopened, in my bedside table down the hall?

Just shows we're on the same wavelength here—that's all.

"I, uh, went shopping," she starts, then starts to laugh again. "God, I'm so bad at this."

"I don't think you're capable of being bad at anything," I tell her, then stretch over and gently tug the box from her grip. "Rosa. Are you sure?"

She nods rapidly, her hair swaying around her shoulders. "Yes. I am. But only if you are, too."

I set the box of condoms aside and pull her into my arms again, settling her naked body over mine. My cock strains between us. "Absolutely yes," I whisper and sink my fingers into her thick brown hair as I kiss her with all the *yes* and *please* and *now* surging through me.

I reach out my hand for a packet, but she shakes her head and opens it herself. "Let me," she says, her voice low and heated.

Flopping back onto the pillows, I throw an arm over my eyes as she grasps my cock by the base, her fingers warm and tight. Then I lever my shoulders up and look, because in what universe would I *not* want to watch as she covers me?

Rosa rolls it down my length, her gaze avid and fixed on my cock. A full-body shiver runs through me, and she glances up and bites her lip. "Can I..."

"Anything." I lean on one elbow. "Anything you want, sweetheart."

That shiver echoes through her now, and she tilts her head. "Can I ride you?"

In response, I spread my arms wide, lean back on the pillows again, and say, "Please."

I didn't mean it to sound like a plea, but she doesn't seem to mind. She rises onto her knees, swings one leg over my hips to straddle me. Then, holding my gaze, she takes me in hand again and slowly, deliberately sinks down.

We both blow out a breath when I'm fully seated inside her. Every inch of me feels like fireworks, like light and heat are traveling through my body at breakneck speed. I'm desperate to move, to thrust up into her tight warmth, but I hold myself back.

"Rosa." I slide my hand up her neck, cupping her cheek. She looks at me, her eyes slightly unfocused. "Baby."

She shudders.

I draw her down for a kiss, then whisper into her ear, "Ride me."

With a moan, she lifts up, then presses back down, her hands braced on my chest. She does it again, her breasts bouncing a little, and then again. She sets up a rhythm that's steady and strong and just this side of too much. I feel her everywhere—the smooth skin of her legs gripping me, her hands sliding through my chest hair, tiny puffs of air as she breathes above me. She rises and drops back down, over and over, her wetness sliding over my cock, her pussy surrounding me.

"Jake—I—" She gasps, her movements growing more frantic as she chases her orgasm. I grip her hips, thrusting up into her warmth, my balls drawing up.

"I'm close," I pant, and she nods, her head dropping onto my shoulder as I fuck up into her.

"Yeah," she says. "Me, too."

I can feel her tighten around me, and I speed up my movements. She turns her face into my neck, keening as she falls apart. I thrust up twice more and tumble after her.

Rosa slumps over me, her head tucked into my shoulder, her breasts pillowed on my chest. She rises and falls with the rhythm of my labored breaths. Damn, that was intense.

I trace patterns on her back, my fingers trailing over her heated skin. She smells good. She feels good. This feels right.

This feels bigger, more meaningful, than it should.

Let me, she said.

And I know, despite all my efforts to protect myself, I'll let her do whatever she wants. Whatever she needs.

Because I need it, too.

I WAKE UP PREDAWN, MY ARMS WRAPPED AROUND A NAKED, warm Rosa. I press a kiss to the back of her head and slip out from under the duvet. She grumbles in her sleep, forehead wrinkled as she burrows under the covers.

I fight back a fond smile as I sneak back to my own room and dress for the day.

God, I am in so much trouble.

I trudge up the road to the vineyard, steam rising from my travel coffee mug. I take a long sip and watch the sun start to peek over the hills.

It's going to be a hot one.

I visit each section of vines in turn, checking the status of the Merlots, the Grossos, the Chards, the Cabs and Sauv Blancs. They're all shifting over into veraison, the early stages of ripeness that's a precursor to harvest. The whites are shifting from green to a translucent yellow and the reds to a gorgeous purple ruby. I measure the Brix levels with my refractometer, then pull a couple grapes from each grouping and taste.

It's getting closer.

I'm filled with a combination of excitement and dread. Excitement because I love this part of the winemaking cycle—

the day-by-day watching and waiting for that perfect moment when harvest time is here. Dread because each day takes me closer to leaving Oak Creek Canyon.

And some small, traitorous part of me wonders if I really do have to go.

Waking up with Rosa in my arms every day wouldn't be the worst thing to ever happen to me.

In fact, I could get used to it pretty damn easily.

But I'm not the only one who has to be on board with that.

Easier to just stick with the plan.

SEVERAL HOURS LATER, I'M WEEDING IN THE MIDDLE OF the Cab vines when Emi calls from the edge of the vineyard closest to the road. "Hey, boss-man," she shouts over the rustle of leaves and birdsong. "I have a question for you."

I slide my gloves off and stick them into my back pocket, jogging over to her. "What's up?"

She points over at the vineyard formerly known as Take Flight, shading her eyes with her other hand. "What are they doing over there? And should we be doing the same thing?"

I take a look at the far rows of vines, as familiar as my childhood bedroom, and see workers busily putting up nets. I frown and dig my phone out of my pocket. Has the weather report changed since this morning?

Shit.

I shove my phone away and call Javi over as well. "Looks like there's a hailstorm predicted for later this afternoon," I tell the two of them. "The team across the way is putting up hail nets—good catch, by the way, Emi—and we need to do the same. I don't care what you were working on just now—this takes priority. Javi, let's get the nets out of the shed and inspect them quickly. Emi, go grab Rosa. This is an all-hands-on-deck situation."

We fall into step on the gravel drive, the two of them chattering away with enthusiasm. I'm trying to shove down the sense of dread that has been welling up since I saw the hail warning a minute ago.

We've got acres to cover and not enough time—or people—to get it done, if the weather report is correct. I glance over at the horizon and see dark clouds starting to gather.

Shit, shit, shit.

We enter the house through the back door, Emi calling out a greeting to Rosa while I grab the shed key off the board in the mudroom. Javi and I head out to the shed and unlock it, dust spilling out as the door swings open.

It's a mess in here, a jumble of old equipment and detritus from the years the vineyard was in service to Belmonte. Theoretically, the hail nets could be on the bigger property, but when time is of the essence that wouldn't make any sense. When you need hail nets, you need them now. We start digging through the piles, the dim light of the bare bulb swinging overhead giving us little to work with.

"I think I found them," Javi says from the back corner of the building, waving me over. I step over a rake and several bags of fertilizer to join him and bend down to look at the stack of nets he's uncovered.

My heart sinks, and I swear again.

"Is everything okay?"

I turn and look at the doorway of the shed, Rosa's worried face barely visible in the backlighting of the midday sun.

Even in a dire situation like this, my breath catches at the sight of her.

"That depends. Any chance you've got more hail nets hidden around here somewhere?" I pick up the top one and shake it out, inspecting it as closely as I can in the dim light. "Shit. Let me rephrase that. Do you have any *usable* hail nets hidden around here somewhere?"

Javi leans over and sticks his hand through the gaping hole in the center of the netting. He whistles low. "Insect damage?"

I shake my head. "Nope. The edges are too clean. This netting's been cut."

"What?" Rosa is picking her way across the littered flooring, Emi right behind her. "Someone sabotaged the nets, too?"

"Looks that way." I pick up the next one, pointing out additional cuts and tears in the fabric. "And that's only counting the ones that are actually here. We're about three-quarters short of what we'd need to cover all the vines."

Her eyes meet mine, and I can see her worry matches mine. "How much time do we have?"

Emi is already opening the weather app on her phone. "Looks like about...two hours?"

A brief silence descends on the shed as we all try to map out the next two hours.

Rosa's voice is tight and low when she speaks again. "Do we have time to buy more nets?"

I shake my head. "Possibly, but that assumes they aren't sold out already. Dammit, we should have bought them weeks ago."

Rosa winces, and I immediately regret saying anything. "Hey, it's not your fault. I should have thought of it earlier, checked the supplies when we weren't up against an emergency situation."

"My budget didn't help, though," she says quietly.

"Neither did the Belmonte crew taking the hail nets when they abandoned the property."

Her gaze narrows. "Uncle Geno."

I wave a hand at the shed. "There's not a chance in hell that your uncle didn't store hail nets here back when he was running both vineyards."

Rosa looks out the shed door. I can tell her mind is churning as she ponders the situation. "Right." She claps her hands together. "I guess it's time to call Uncle Geno."

"Hey, wait." I put a hand on her shoulder. "You don't have to do that."

Emi and Javi are looking back and forth between us, like we're some conversational tennis match, but I can't bring myself to care.

"Those hail nets, if he's got them, belong to Caparelli. We need them, they don't. I'm calling."

I let my hand drop. "Okay. In the meantime, Javi, take my truck into town and see if there are any nets left at the farm store. Buy any they have, put it on our account." I shove my keys into his hand, and he nods, already heading out of the shed before I'm finished.

Rosa holds up her phone. "I'll let you know what I find out."

I nod, and she walks away, already squaring her shoulders for the fight ahead. My heart aches for her, and at the same time, I want to punch someone. This whole thing sucks.

Emi steps forward. "I'll see if there are any nets worth saving. Maybe I can stitch up some of the holes."

"Thanks. That's helpful." I dig my own phone out of my pocket and start looking up numbers. "In the meantime, I'm going to call in some favors."

"Not that I'm not happy to hear from you, man, but I'm a little busy right now," Wade says as he picks up my call, not even bothering with hello. I can hear muffled voices in the background, footsteps on dirt, wind whistling through leaves.

"I figured you would be," I say. "So I'll keep this short. Any chance you have some extra hail nets lying around?"

"Uh-oh." His voice is clearer, like he stopped what he was doing and held the phone a little closer to his mouth. "Trouble at Caparelli?"

"Yup. Most of the nets are missing, and those we do have are full of holes. Not the type of holes that are supposed to be there, but bigger ones. Deliberate ones."

"Someone sabotaged your nets? Damn, Jake."

"Yeah. So if you have any you can spare, we'd appreciate it."

"Hang on a minute." The sound from his end of the phone call suddenly cuts off, and I'm hoping it's because he muted it and not because he's hung up. I feel itchy, restless, like there's anxious energy inside me burning to get out. I sit on the picnic table, my boots on the long bench below, and try to figure out who to call next. Time is running out. "Okay," he says abruptly, sound rushing back. "Give me half an hour and I'll see what I can do."

"Thank you," I say, relief making my voice rough. "I appreciate it."

"Later."

He clicks off the phone, and I scroll through my phone for another number to call.

"Hey, boss," Emi says. She's holding up two hail nets, the holes awkwardly stitched together. "These were the only ones with enough material left to fix."

It's not perfect, but it'll do for a start. We've got less than an hour and a half.

I heave myself off the table and tilt my head toward the vines. "Let's get a move on, then."

Chapter 23

Rosa

I drop down at the desk and scroll through the numbers saved in my phone. It's a long shot, but I start with the main office number for Belmonte.

"It's a great day at Belmonte," my aunt chirps as she picks up the phone.

"Hi, Aunt Janet," I say, trying desperately to keep my voice level. "Is Uncle Geno available?"

"He's a little busy, dear," she says, the words friendly but her tone definitely not. "I'll tell him you called."

"No, wait!" I take a deep breath. "It's really important that I talk to him right now."

I can almost picture the pursed-lip expression on her face. "He's out in the vineyard right now, helping to put up hail nets with the crew. He doesn't have time for a call."

They're probably using Caparelli's nets, too, I think bitterly, but instead of saying that I ask her for his cell phone number.

She refuses to give it to me. "He won't answer anyway,

Rosa. You know he never answers when he's in the fields. You'll just have to wait for him to call you back."

I mutter something halfway polite and hang up, my head pounding. Uncle Geno never gave me his cell number, insisting that nothing couldn't wait until he was out of the fields and back at the winery office.

Nothing *I* had to say, that is. Yet again proof I've been on the outside of the family business for years. Well, I have my own family business now. And I can't let Uncle Geno's bullshit ruin it.

I scroll through my phone list and stab at another number. It rings three times before the person on the other end picks up.

"Hey, Rosey Posey," Leo says. "What's up?"

I ignore my hated nickname and cut right to the chase. "Do you have any extra hail nets at Belmonte?"

Leo pauses for a minute. "Uh, I don't know. Why?"

"Because there's only a half dozen in the shed here at Caparelli, and those are unusable."

"Unusable?" His voice is cautious.

I close my eyes. "Big holes, clean rips down the center, the works."

He sucks in a breath. "Rosey."

"Look, I don't have time for a long discussion about all the ways Caparelli has been sabotaged over the past few weeks. The hailstorm is supposed to hit soon, and our equipment is missing or damaged. So if you or anyone at Belmonte cares even a tiny bit about Nonna's legacy, it would be awesome if we could get a little goddamn help over here."

"Of course I care," Leo shoots back, anger tingeing his voice. "But if you think we have anything to do with—"

I glance out the window, noting the dark clouds inching closer. "Forget it." I hang up and stand, needing to do something, anything, to get rid of this dread coursing through my veins.

A serious-enough hailstorm could completely devastate our crops, ruining any chance to have anything left to harvest. And it's almost on top of us.

I head to the mudroom, tug on my work boots, and pull my hair into a messy ponytail. I tuck work gloves into my pocket and stalk outside, squinting in what's left of the sun. The shed is closed again and the yard is empty, so I walk around to the front and start up the drive to the vineyard.

Jake and Emi are already there, spreading out a semi-repaired hail net over the vines closest to the road. There's another one at Jake's feet, and my heart sinks. Is that all we have?

I hear the rumble of a truck engine and turn, watching as Javi bypasses the parking area at the house altogether and pulls up right next to where Jake and Emi are working. I hurry to catch up.

He's already out of the cab of the truck and has the lift gate down, pulling himself up into the bed of the truck and sliding netting toward the edge of the bed. "Got the last ten," he says as he passes the nets to Jake and Emi.

I step forward for my share, letting out a little "oof" as the weight of two nets settles in my arms. I hear Jake snicker and shoot him a mock-glare.

It's a little thing, but for some reason, the tiny bit of teasing helps me settle. I stack my nets on top of the pile already started at the end of the row and turn to Jake, hands on my hips. "Okay, where do we start?"

He looks at the pile, then up at the long rows of grapevines. He's thinking what we're all thinking—not enough nets, not enough time. But that can't be helped, and at least it's something.

"Emi and Javi, why don't you take a few of the nets up to the Cab section, cover as much as you can. Rosa and I will stay down here and see how much we can protect of the Pinot grapes."

They nod and grab some of the nets, lugging them up the rows to the top right corner of the vineyard. Then they turn around to haul the rest of them into place.

Jake and I take a net and shake it out, stretching until we're sure nothing's folded over, that every inch of protection will cover our grapes through the impending storm. We start in opposite rows, lifting the net over the grapevines between us as we walk up the hill.

We're on our last net when I hear another engine on the road between Caparelli and the hockey player's fields. I glance down the row to see an unfamiliar truck parking behind Jake's and four men piling out of the cab.

"Wade! Thank God." Jake drops his edge of the net and strides down to the drive, sticking out his hand to shake Wade's, then pulling him in for a bro hug.

Wade shrugs. "Heard you were fucking up Rosa's fields, thought I'd bail you out." He laughs and shakes his head. "Kidding. You need nets, we had some extra, so once the guys and I were done with our vines we figured we'd come help you get set up before the hail hits."

"Shit." Jake lets out a breath. "You're a lifesaver, buddy. I'll even let you get away with your slander and lies. Just this once."

Wade grins and turns to his crew, telling them to pull their nets out of the back of the truck and then wait for Jake's directions.

We've got four teams working in different parts of the vineyard when I glance down the row to see an unfamiliar man heading across the drive from the edge of Jake's family's old vineyard.

I drop my side of the net and walk over to meet him, whoever he is. As I get closer, a few things stand out.

He's tall. Built. Good looking. And definitely a stranger.

"Can I help you?" I'm doing my best to be friendly, but I really don't have time for a social visit. We're working against the clock right now.

"Actually, that's what I was going to ask." At my look of confusion, he smiles a little awkwardly. "I'm Jansen Beck—just bought the place across the way." He hitches his thumb over his shoulder. "My foreman mentioned that it looked like you might be short on hail nets and workers, so I was going to offer you both."

"Are you kidding?" Jake comes up behind me, pulling his gloves off.

"Jake," I growl, elbowing him in the side. He lets out a little grunt.

Jansen's brow furrows. "Excuse me?"

"I was a total dick to you the other day, and you're still offering to help us out? You're a better person than I am," Jake says, holding out his hand to shake Jansen's. "Thank you for the offer. And sorry about my attitude."

The man shrugs. "Water under the bridge. I'd probably feel the same way if someone—well, anyway." He looks between the two of us. "I definitely overbought on hail nets, so I'll have my crew bring the extras over and help get them set up. We should be over in a few."

"Thanks so much," I say, tears pricking at the edges of my eyes. The relief from all this help, offered freely, is swamping me. "I'm Rosa, by the way."

"Nice to meet you, Rosa." He nods and jogs back to his

vineyard. I glance at Jake, who's looking pretty damn embarrassed.

"What the hell happened between you two?"

He shakes his head. "Remember I told you I met him the other day? He came over to introduce himself, I was an asshole, and now he's saving our butts. I owe him a hell of an apology."

I look at the clouds again, then back at the fields. We've probably got half an hour at best before the hail starts. But there are four more men headed across the fields carrying hail nets, and our crew, and Wade's, and for the first time since I saw the pitiful little stack of damaged nets in the shed, I feel a spark of hope.

Jake directs the new helpers toward another section of the vineyard, where we haven't managed to begin working yet, and the entire acreage buzzes with activity. When I survey the vines next, there are more netted than not, and I suck in a deep breath. We're not out of the danger zone yet, but I can see the light on the horizon.

Once more, a truck rumbles up the drive, pulling in behind Wade's. This time I recognize it, and the tears from earlier threaten to spill over.

Leo, Vittorio, and Gianni climb out of the truck, looking around awkwardly. Finally, V spots me and waves.

I hurry down the row to where they're standing. "Hey, guys," I say finally.

"What's up?"

Vittorio rolls his eyes. "Whatever. C'mere." He wraps his arms around me in a hug, and I really do start crying.

He steps back, his eyes wide with alarm. "Whoa, what's with the tears? Knock it off, Rosey!"

I laugh, my voice a little watery, and swipe at my cheeks. "Stronzo," I mutter, and he laughs so hard I think he's going to fall over.

"Never thought I'd hear a word like that out of your innocent little mouth," Vittorio says when he stops laughing. "Nonna would be appalled."

"Nonna would be thrilled that all of us can recognize at least one thing in Italian, even if it's just the word for *asshole*," Gianni counters.

I shake my head. "No, seriously, why are you here? Don't you have to take care of Belmonte's vines?"

"We've got a crew for that." Gianni's lips thin. "A very well-staffed crew. They're fine."

Leo waves a hand at the back of the truck. "After you called, I checked to see if we had any extra nets. There were—a few."

Gianni snorts. "More than a few. And most of them probably started out here."

"G," Leo says warningly, but Gianni just rolls his eyes.

"What? You know it's the truth." He looks at the people working all across the vineyard. "We came to offer our help—and the hail nets—but it looks like you've got it all under control."

"Actually, we could still use the help," Jake says, coming up behind me. "The hailstorm is likely to hit any minute. So if you're serious about that, we'd appreciate it. And thanks."

I nod. "Honestly, this means—everything." And I mean it. To know they've got my back—*our* backs—despite what Uncle Geno says? Priceless.

But we don't have time for chatting because the clouds are almost overhead, and the rumble of thunder in the distance startles all of us into action.

We work in teams of two, trudging up and down the rows of vines, placing the nets as quickly and carefully as we can. We want the vines protected without carelessness snapping off sections. There are just a couple of rows still uncovered when the hailstorm hits, sharp pellets of ice pummeling us as we redouble our efforts.

The hail is coming down hard as we finish, and I pull the back of my jacket up over my head. "Come down to the house!" I shout over the storm, gesturing at the big white building at the bottom of the drive. Wade and his crew pile into their truck and my cousins in theirs, while Jake offers Jansen and his employees a ride down the hill in his. I climb into the bed of Leo's truck with Emi and Javi, and we laugh in relief as the hail drums down on us. The weather is brutal, but the crops are protected.

At the house, I hop out of the truck bed and open the front door, not caring if people track water or mud into the place. Right now, all we want is someplace out of the storm.

Inside, I troop upstairs to the linen closet and haul out every towel on the shelves, bringing them down to the ridiculously large group gathered inside. Emi and Javi take them from me and pass them around while I hustle to the kitchen. It was a warm day until the storm hit, but we're all soaked to the bone, and a hot beverage sounds like heaven right about now. So I put on the kettle for hot water and start up the coffee maker.

"What can I do?"

I jump, startled by Jake's voice in my ear, and turn around. "Uh, maybe some snacks? I wasn't really prepared for a party."

His smile is lazy, a little amused. "Good thing you keep enough food around here to feed an army," he says.

And the thing is he's not wrong. But that's because he's here. Before Jake barreled his way into my vineyard and my home, the shelves would have been embarrassingly bare.

One more thing to thank Jake Wright for, I guess.

We pile up platters with cheese and crackers, fruit and veggies with fresh dip. Emi comes in and carries out a tray of mugs, while Javi follows with tea bags, packets of cocoa mix, and the full coffee pot. We put stuff down on the low coffee table and the desk in the office and, ridiculously, a box full of books I hadn't gotten around to emptying yet. Everyone digs in and keeps chatting in groups of two and three and four, Wade and Vittorio asking Javi about his plans after graduation and Leo showing Emi a new Brix measurer he bought this season that he apparently swears by.

After a minute or two, Jake walks over to where Gianni is lightheartedly grilling Jansen about some hockey game from a year or so ago. He holds his hand out to Jansen, who takes it with a tilt to his head. "Like I said earlier, I was a real jerk to you the other day. I'm sorry, for what it's worth. I shouldn't have taken it out on you."

Jansen shrugs. "It is what it is. I'm just glad we were able to help out." He gestures at his crew, sitting on the lower steps of the stairway to the second floor. "I've got a great team, which is mostly down to the fantastic crew your parents hired and trained over the years. So I owe you thanks as well. Or at least your family."

Jake nods. "I'm glad to hear it. Take Flight was something special."

For a moment, Jansen is quiet. "I hope it can be something special again someday as well."

Wade walks over then, wrapping an arm around Jake's shoulder. "And hey, now that Jake has signed on with Rosa and her sisters, we've got a Wright running a winery in Oak Creek Canyon again anyway."

"Oh, he's not staying," I blurt out before I can think better of it. My cheeks flame as every head in the room turns to look at me. Including Jake's.

Vittorio raises an eyebrow but doesn't say anything. Leo's eyes narrow. Wade just looks confused.

And Jake? I can't interpret Jake's expression to save my life.

"She's right," he finally says, breaking the tension in the room. "I'm just pitching in until Allegra and Bianca get back to Caparelli."

"Where are you headed after?" Wade takes a long sip of his coffee. "Italy again?"

Jake shrugs. "Not sure yet. I've got an offer to help set up a new winery in Washington state, near the Canadian border. But I haven't landed on anything."

And even though I've been preparing for this since the day he started, it still breaks my heart a little to hear that it's really going to happen.

"That's too bad," Jansen says slowly. "I would have loved to pick your brain sometime."

"Sorry to disappoint." Jake pours himself some more coffee and turns to Leo with a smile. "So tell me about this new Brix measurer. Is it really worth buying a new one?"

The conversations start flowing again, and I flit around the corners of the room, clearing away plates, freshening up mugs, switching out for wineglasses as the storm rages outside. The house is full and lively again, with people I've known and loved forever and people I've barely met. My heart is full, too, but it aches at the knowledge that as lovely as this is, it's just temporary. My cousins will go back to Uncle Geno and Belmonte, and Wade will take his crew back to his family vineyard. Jansen and his workers will return across the road, and Emi and Javi will finish out their internships before the new semester starts.

And Jake? He's just confirmed that he'll be gone, too. The house will be empty again.

And so will my heart.

Chapter 24

Jake

An hour or so later, the hailstorm finally ends, leaving behind an odd silence outside Caparelli's homestead. Inside, it's still a party atmosphere, and I'm finding myself caught up with feeling like part of it, part of a community I left behind so many years ago.

"So you actually just packed up and moved in here? Just like that?" Gianni is laughing so hard I think he's going to drop his wineglass. "Rosa must have pitched a fit."

"Hey," Rosa protests.

"To be fair, you sort of did," I respond.

"I can't believe you two are living in sin," Leo jokes.

I hold up a hand. "Separate rooms, thank you very much. This is a work arrangement."

And if it's leaning toward more than that? Nobody's business but our own.

The room is crowded but comfortable. Cozy in a way that makes me wish it wasn't temporary.

I've lived my life in blocks of "temporary" since high school. No roots, just wings that are all of a sudden ready to rest for a while. But with the folks living in San Luis Obispo and life in Oak Creek Canyon having moved on in the decade I've been gone, I don't know where I'm supposed to land.

I know where I want to be, who I want to be with. But I can't be the only one fighting for it.

I finish off my coffee and set the cup down on the windowsill, watching everyone chat and laugh, comfortable with each other. Both old friends and people I just met today.

Antonio, who's working for Jansen now after years with my parents, looks almost the same as he did a decade ago—maybe a little more weathered and a few more lines around his eyes, but the smile is one I remember well.

He's showing it off now, regaling Emi and Javi with tales of my juvenile delinquency as he grins for his audience. "And then, guess who I caught him with under the vines one afternoon when he was in high school?"

Uh-oh. Danger, Will Robinson.

"What Rosa and I got up to over a decade ago is nobody's business but ours," I say, trying to defuse the situation, but the hubbub gets even louder as the whole group decides to add their two cents to the conversation.

Rosa's cousins burst out laughing as she flies across the room to put a hand over my mouth, a bright pink flush on her cheeks. "That's enough of that story," she says over the noise. Then she points at Antonio. "That goes for you, too!"

"No, we want to hear more," Vittorio calls out. "I'm intrigued!"

"Rosey, were you a bad girl back in high school?" Leo fakes a shocked look. "And how did we not know this already?"

"None of your business!" She turns to point at Leo now. "And stop calling me Rosey!"

"Wait, why?" Vittorio says. "It's your nickname."

"I've hated it for years. Please, *please* call me Rosa."

"Sorry, Ros—Rosa."

"That's better." She huffs out a breath and looks around the room, daring anyone to contradict her.

Wade puts his arm around Jansen's shoulder and says, "Welcome to the madhouse, dude. Too late to back out now." Not gonna lie—he looks a little shell-shocked. And amused, too.

I mock-glare at Wade. "Way to throw us under the bus, buddy."

He laughs and shakes his head. "Whatever. You know it's true. Besides, working for your ex-girlfriend is bound to bring out the drama. No offense, Rosa."

Rosa rolls her eyes. "Never change, Wade."

Then sweet, innocent Emi pipes up, "You mean his ex-*wife*, right?"

Silence descends on the room like a thick blanket. I chance a look at Rosa, who's closing her eyes with a wince. Her hand drops away from my mouth, but neither of us say anything.

Emi looks at me. "Or was I wrong about the anniversary gift you gave her on our first day?"

Javier murmurs, "I don't think they wanted us to notice that."

"Um...sorry?"

Shit.

"Ex-wife?" Gianni finally says, his forehead crinkled in a frown. "What are you talking about?"

"When would you have gotten married? You broke up right after graduation," Wade adds.

"I—" Rosa is looking from person to person, her eyes wide with horror.

Yeah, this isn't the way I would have voted for this to go down, either.

Leo narrows his eyes at us. "Just what, exactly, have you two been getting up to this summer?"

Vittorio shrugs. "Well, they are living together," he says, his voice almost singsong.

"Living in the same location, not living *together* together," Rosa argues, but it gets swallowed up in the chatter of conversations whipping around the room.

"It's not like they could have gotten married and divorced since Jake got back," Gianni says, while Wade starts laughing and Jansen just looks around, baffled.

"Did I say something wrong?" Emi asks me quietly. "I'm so sorry."

I just shake my head. It's not her fault. It's not anybody's fault, really. It was bound to come out at some point.

This is Oak Creek Canyon, after all.

The doorbell rings, and Rosa's head whips around, staring at the entry. "What now," she mutters as she walks over to open the door.

Standing on the other side is her uncle Geno, his hand raised to knock on the door. Her aunt is standing behind him.

I start laughing along with Wade. This day just keeps getting more and more ridiculous.

Geno's hand drops as he stomps into the entryway, his face bright red and glowering. "What in the hell is going on here?"

Gianni raises his wineglass in his father's direction. "Welcome to the party, Dad."

Vittorio slaps his upper arm, almost making him drop the glass. "Shut up," he mutters.

Geno looks around, frowning at everyone in turn. Then he spies me, and the fury in his eyes almost makes me take a step back.

Almost.

"I thought I told you never to step foot on this property again," he growls, his hands clenched by his sides.

I'm not a kid anymore, so I stand my ground. "You did."

"Then what the hell are you doing here?"

I look over at Rosa, still standing by the open door. She glances at me, the look in her eyes both scared and determined. I tilt my head, and she gives me a tiny nod.

It's all the encouragement I need.

"I'm helping Rosa with the vineyard," I say. "I offered, she accepted, end of story."

"Like hell it is."

"I told you he was working here," Janet pipes up, but Geno ignores her.

"You need to leave," he tells me, but then Rosa steps forward.

"It's not your property anymore," she says, her voice thin and shaky. She clears her throat and starts again. "Jake is doing an amazing job helping me keep this vineyard running. I couldn't do it without him."

"You can't do it *with* him, either. Not without my own sons undermining me. Stealing resources from Belmonte." He whips his head around and narrows his eyes at his sons. "I'm not surprised Gianni was part of this, but Leo? I expected better from you."

Wow, Leo mouths, but Gianni jumps in.

"We only brought Rosa back the nets that should have stayed on this property anyway. They belong to Caparelli."

"They belong to *me!*" Geno roars, startling us all. "None of you have the right to take from me. From the family."

"Rosa *is* family," Vittorio protests, but Geno cuts him off with a sweeping motion of his hand.

"Enough." He looks around. "Who are all of these people? And why are they here?"

"Our friends and neighbors," I tell him. "They helped us out before the hailstorm hit. You're a little late if you want to join in."

"Don't you backtalk me."

I can't help it. I roll my eyes. "I'm not a teenager anymore, Geno."

"You're behaving like one. Both of you are."

Rosa closes the door behind them.

"Hi, Uncle Geno, Aunt Janet. Thanks for stopping by! Please, come on in." Her tone is dry as unbuttered toast, and I have to bite the inside of my cheek to keep from snorting out a laugh at her perfect sarcasm.

It's apparently lost on Geno, though, because he just gives her a pompous nod and marches over to stand in front of the window with his arms crossed.

Rosa closes her eyes for a moment. "Can I get you anything? Water? Coffee?"

Geno points a finger in my direction. "Tell him to go."

"Go where? I live here," I shoot back, but Rosa puts her hand on my arm and steps forward.

"Jake is helping me with Caparelli until Allegra and Bianca are back home. And frankly, the fact that he's staying in the house that Nonna left the three of us is really none of your business."

"It's my business if you're throwing away the family legacy on the boy who almost ruined your life!"

Geno's roar echoes through the downstairs, ringing in my ears and reminding me just how much he'd cowed Rosa—honestly, both of us—with his size and authority all those years ago.

Now, in front of a mostly unwilling audience, he just looks —ridiculous.

"Ruined my life?" Rosa looks incredulous. "How? By loving me? By marrying me?"

"You were a child!" He's moved in front of Rosa, looming over her, his face red with fury.

"Marrying you?" Janet is looking back and forth between the three of us, her expression puzzled. "You're married?"

Rosa takes a deep breath and lets it out. She glances at me, and I give a tiny shrug.

Her family, her choice how much to say.

"Yes. We got married ten years ago. When I was supposed to be on that high school graduation trip. We went to Vegas, and, well..." She hums the first few bars of "Here Comes the Bride."

It takes all my self-control to keep from laughing. I'm sure Rosa can see it on my face, too, because she bites down on her lower lip for just a second.

The rest of the room? That's a different story.

Emi and Javi are the most "in the know," just from that argument Rosa and I had in front of them on their first day, so this information doesn't surprise them. Rosa's cousins are looking back and forth from Geno to me, eyes wide, soaking up every salacious detail. Jansen, Wade, and their crews look like they'd rather be anywhere but in this crowded, crazy room.

Geno looks like he's about to stroke out right here on the hardwood floor. Janet can best be described as *horrified*.

"You got married? Way back then? And didn't tell anyone?" She turns slowly and stares at her husband. "You're not surprised. Why are you not surprised?"

He doesn't say anything, just stands there fuming. I jump in the gap, because I'm petty like that. "Oh, he already knew. He's known since the day we got back."

"What?" Janet's mouth drops open.

Geno glares at me. If looks could kill, I'd be a corpse right now.

"I handled it," he seethes through gritted teeth. "They got an annulment. Over and done." He glares at me again. "Until now."

"That doesn't mean you can keep something like that from me," she says, her voice wobbling a little.

Damn, I almost feel bad about that.

"There was a lot going on," he says defensively, and she straightens.

"That is no excuse, Geno." She glances at Rosa. "Apparently I've been kept out of the loop on a lot of things."

"Here's one more," Rosa says, talking to her aunt but staring at her uncle. "The annulment never happened. Jake and I are still married."

"No." Geno's bluster is finally quiet; I can barely hear his whispered response. "That can't be true."

"It is." Rosa takes a step closer to me, not quite touching but close enough her aunt and uncle both clock the move. "The paperwork was never filed. I verified it myself the other day."

"This ruins everything." Geno flings out his hand and points at me. "Don't you understand? He could take Caparelli from us!"

"What are you talking about?" Rosa gapes at him.

"He can claim ownership as your—" He swallows hard. "Your husband."

"I would never," I exclaim, but Rosa jumps to my defense anyway.

"You still don't get it, do you, Uncle Geno?" She shakes her head. "Jake is here helping me with Caparelli because he's a decent human being, not because he's trying to steal Caparelli away. Also, the only *us* he could take it from is me, Allegra, and Bianca, because you aren't part of it anymore. We are. Nonna left us Caparelli, and the three of us intend to make it something she would be proud of. So who I choose to hire or partner with or ask for help is *none of your business anymore.*"

Silence fills the room. I can hear the grandfather clock ticking in the corner, and every beat sounds like a rifle shot.

"Fine." Geno stomps to the door and flings it open, then turns back to look at us. The anger in his gaze is overpowering. "Go ahead and make your own mistakes. You always have, despite my best efforts. But when you lose Caparelli—and mark my words, you *will* lose Caparelli—don't come crawling back to Belmonte for help. I wash my hands of you." He shakes his head. "You, your sisters, whatever losers you decide to choose over your family. All of you."

He steps out the door onto the porch and heads to his truck, his shoulders a tight line. Janet scurries after him, tossing Rosa a tight-lipped glance as she leaves the house.

Everyone is silent and frozen as the rumble of Geno's truck fades away in the distance.

Then, the room leaps to life again.

"Welp, time for us to go," Gianni says, nudging his brothers and heading for the door. "Rosa, Jake, thanks for the hospitality."

"I expect all the details tomorrow," Wade murmurs to me in a low voice as he passes by, startling a muffled snort out of me.

The rest of the crowd files out in rapid succession, finally leaving the two of us alone.

Rosa and I stand there in silence until all we can see is the taillights of the departing vehicles as they turn at the bottom of the road.

"So." Rosa claps her hands together and smiles brightly. "That went well."

Then she sucks in a breath and spins around, heading for the stairs, but not before I can see the tears shining in her eyes.

Chapter 25

Rosa

"Rosa, wait."

I pause on the stairs, head still turned resolutely away, willing him to get it over with and let me go so I can cry in peace.

He touches my elbow, and it takes everything in me not to flinch away.

Not because I don't want him to touch me, but because I want it too much.

Like Uncle Geno said, I'd better get used to doing this on my own.

"Please." Jake's voice is low, rough, and I give in.

I turn, swiping under my eyes in a futile attempt to get rid of the evidence before he looks too closely.

It's a losing battle. His lips tighten, and he brushes his thumb across my cheekbone, finishing the job for me.

"He doesn't deserve your tears," he says fiercely, and I almost break down again.

Almost. Instead I suck in a deep breath, fist my hands on my hips, and look at him. "I know. But sometimes they just happen anyway."

His hand drops back down, and he tilts his head, looking at me. "You were magnificent, by the way."

"Why?" I laugh, the sound a little watery. "Because I basically told my uncle to fuck off? In front of an audience?"

"Well, that's part of it." He smiles and takes a step closer. "Mostly because for the first time, you claimed Caparelli with your whole heart. No hesitation. It was beautiful to see."

I heave in a breath and let it whoosh out, feeling the truth of his words. And in that moment, I realize—I'm proud of what I did, too.

I sit down on the bottom step of the stairs and look up at Jake. If it's a day for confronting the hard conversations, might as well go all in.

I ask the question that's been buzzing around in my head since he first told me we're still married. "Why?"

He looks down at me. "Why what?"

"Why didn't you turn in the paperwork?"

He shrugs. "You wouldn't talk to me."

The stiletto between my ribs twists just a little. "Uncle Geno..."

"The Rosa I knew wouldn't let Uncle Geno come between us." He sits next to me and bumps my shoulder with his. "When it came down to it, I wasn't ready to believe you wanted the annulment just because Geno said you did. I wanted to hear it from you."

"I believed him," I say in a small voice. "I believed you wanted the annulment, because he said you did. And I believed him when he said I owed it to the family, to Nonna, to do what was right. To make it right after everything I did wrong."

"Rosa." He puts a finger under my chin and turns my head

245

until I look him in the eye. "You've paid penance for this long enough. Yes, we were stupid kids. Yes, we shouldn't have lied. But in the long run, who did we really hurt except ourselves?"

"Nonna's heart attack..."

He interrupts. "Which would have happened whether you were home or not. You were eighteen, Rosa, and as far as I know you didn't have a medical license at the time."

I laugh through the tears I didn't even realize were falling again. "Still don't," I tell him.

"And she lived another nine and a half years," he reminds me. "So what's the real issue?"

I pause. "They needed me."

"Well, so did I."

I close my eyes. He's pressing at every painful memory, opening them up and shifting them just enough for me to realize I'd seen them from a different angle.

Maybe one that wasn't quite correct.

"I let down the family," I whisper. "I was foolish and reckless and thoughtless."

"You were eighteen and in love." His voice is flat. "At least *I* was in love. I assume you were as well."

"You know I was."

"And it makes me so damn angry to think of you cowering here in Oak Creek Canyon for the past ten years, feeling like you had to make up for...for what? For doing something for yourself for once?"

"I wasn't cowering," I mumble, but he keeps right on.

"All these years, I wondered what Geno had on you to make you do what he demanded. But now it makes sense. The biggest guilt trip in the history of the universe."

Was it? I felt guilty, of course. For running off and getting married so young, without family input or support. For being gone when Nonna had her heart attack. I'd always been her rock, the dependable grandchild. There for everything. But when she really needed me—when my sisters needed me, too—I was nowhere to be found.

And Uncle Geno was only looking out for me, right?

I think back, remembering how he encouraged me to go to community college *so we can keep an eye on you*. How I didn't need an internship away from home, since I'd be working for Belmonte anyway. How he piled on the menial busywork at Belmonte but never let me explore other options. And always, hovering over it all like the smoke from a wildfire in the hills, was the disapproval and disappointment.

I spent ten years trying to make it up to him, never quite reaching the mark.

But maybe that was the point.

Maybe the goal all along was to keep me in line, prevent me from leaving the fold.

Once Uncle Geno finished lecturing me that day about all the ways I'd failed the family, I believed I had no choice but to do what he said. My foolish, impulsive actions had harmed my sisters, my grandmother, my family. I had to make it right.

But by following Uncle Geno's orders, by falling into line, I hurt Jake.

And I hurt myself.

Hell, I spent the last ten years blaming myself—and Jake—for everything bad that happened since then. If I'd been less impulsive. If I'd thought things through.

But what would have changed? If I had been on the grad trip instead of eloping to Vegas, I would have been gone when everything happened anyway. Would it all have been my fault then, too?

Nonna still would have gotten sick. My sisters still would have been alone.

I still would have been an eighteen-year-old struggling with

Kate Davies

the weight of family obligations and expectations on my shoulders.

"I couldn't have prevented any of it from happening," I say, opening my eyes but not really seeing anything. "It wasn't my fault."

Jake pulls me into a rough hug, wrapping his arms around me and pulling me close. "That's what I've been trying to tell you, sweetheart," he murmurs into my ear.

I shiver as his breath brushes my earlobe. His warmth surrounds me, chasing away the ice inside. I pull back and press a kiss to his cheek. "Thank you," I whisper.

"No thanks necessary," he says, his large hand stroking my back in soothing circles. "This was probably a long time coming."

Ten years and two weeks, to be exact. And while I'm sitting here on the stairs making peace with what was done to me back then, I haven't yet made amends for what I did to Jake.

"I should have talked to you." I look down. "I was a coward, and you didn't deserve that."

"No, I didn't."

I can't quite hold back my flinch.

"I'm not going to lie to you, Rosa, and I won't sugarcoat it. I didn't deserve that." He pauses. "But neither did you."

The tears are flowing steadily now, and I brush them away impatiently. "Be honest—I deserved it a little bit."

"No." He pulls back and takes both my hands in his. "You didn't. No matter how much your overactive sense of responsibility tries to pin it on you."

I hiccup a laugh, then sigh again. "I've felt guilty for a really long time now."

"Well, it's time to stop." Then he slants a look at me. "Unless you're feeling guilty for breaking my heart. That'd be okay."

248

"Yours wasn't the only one," I say quietly. There's a long pause. "I really am sorry."

"So am I." At my questioning look, he adds, "For running away. For *staying* away. The fact that we didn't have this conversation sometime in the past ten years is as much my fault as it is yours. Even if I didn't recognize that until recently."

"God, we're a pair of fools, aren't we?"

"I won't tell if you don't," he says.

I laugh a little. "Good to know."

We sit quietly on the steps, both of us lost in our own thoughts for a little while. Then something else occurs to me. "Okay, I get why you didn't file the annulment back then. But why not anytime since? Didn't it..." I swallow, clear my throat. "Tie you down?"

He shrugs and looks down. "Well. I haven't been a saint."

"It's okay," I tell him, and it's the truth. I don't feel betrayed or cheated on or anything. Our marriage has just been on paper for the past ten years.

"But." He turns and looks me in the eye. "The truth is I never met anyone else I wanted to take that step with."

That is...a lot. I blow out a breath, then another thought occurs to me.

"What if *I* had met someone I wanted to *take that step with*?" I glare at him. "I could have been a bigamist!"

His cheeks color. "I, uh, may have been keeping tabs? From a distance?" At my raised eyebrow, he clarifies. "My mom likes to talk. Especially about the neighbors, including my 'darling ex-girlfriend,'" he says, making air quotes. "If you had gotten even slightly serious about anyone, I would have made sure you were free and clear. I promise."

I nod. "Thank you."

We sit quietly for another moment, then he sighs and leans

back, elbows on the step behind us. "I'm glad we finally talked about it," he says. "It's nice to get some closure, you know?"

I swallow, hard, the reminder of his limited time left in Oak Creek Canyon like a cold, wet towel dropping onto my head. "Yeah," I chirp. "Very nice."

He squeezes my shoulder and stands, starting to gather up the remnants of our impromptu post-hailstorm party.

Suddenly, a wave of exhaustion sweeps over me, and I lean back on the stairs, my eyes closing.

His voice comes from across the room. "You doing okay, sweetheart?"

My heart clenches in my chest. I don't know how to answer that.

Finally, I just hum a noncommittal answer and push myself up off the step. "Tired," I mumble as I help him collect the dishes and carry them into the kitchen.

He nods, putting the mugs in the sink. "Long day."

When the room is set to rights—sort of—we head to the stairs once more, Jake locking the front door as he walks by. We're quiet, but it's not awkward.

I could get used to this.

I know I shouldn't.

When we reach the landing, we both turn in the direction of my room. I stop, placing a hand on his chest. "Jake, I don't think—"

"Just to sleep." He places his hand over mine, linking our fingers together. He lifts it to his mouth and presses a gentle kiss to my knuckles. "I'd just like to hold you tonight, if that's okay."

I nod, afraid if I open my mouth I'll start to cry. Again. Hand in hand, we walk down the hall. When we get to my room I reach for the light switch with my free hand, but Jake shakes his head. "The moon's enough light for me," he says.

He's not wrong. The sky is clear now, the storm clouds having disappeared over the past several hours, and bright beams of moonlight filter in through the curtains behind my bed. I strip off my clothes, pulling on the sleep set from under my pillow as Jake goes to brush his teeth. He kisses my forehead, his breath minty fresh, as we trade places.

When I'm done in the bathroom, I return to my room to find Jake under the covers, a hint of bare chest showing. A pulse of heat arrows through me, but exhaustion wins out. I crawl under the covers with him, snuggling into his side, his arm wrapping around me.

"Sleep well, Mrs. Wright," he whispers, and I pinch his side. He laughs softly and wraps me up in his arms.

"You, too, Mr. Martinelli."

He presses a kiss to my shoulder and chuckles. "Touché," he says.

I close my eyes and fall into a deep, dreamless sleep.

I WAKE UP EARLY, THE SUN STARTING TO PEEK THROUGH the curtains. I'm warm and cozy and wrapped up in my comforter like a weighted blanket.

Except it's not a weighted blanket. It's Jake, one arm slung over my waist, his knee tucked between my legs. I'm the little spoon, and everywhere he touches me, I'm on fire.

I have a vague memory of being wrapped up like this the night we made love, but when I woke up that morning, Jake was already gone, working in the fields early.

Today he's still here.

His breathing is slow and steady, the warm puffs of his

breath against the back of my neck sending a shiver down my spine. I move a little, experimentally, and he sighs in his sleep, tugging me closer. I feel relaxed. Protected.

Cherished.

My body wants to snuggle in closer, but my mind is ringing alarm bells at high volume. I try to pull away again, but he just wraps his arm around my waist a little tighter. My ass snugs up against him, his morning wood noticeable.

I'm torn. On the one hand, the more time I spend with Jake, the more likely my heart will be broken. Again.

On the other hand, would it really be so wrong to enjoy what little time we do have together before he leaves? Again?

I chew on my lip, trying to decide what to do. Stay? Go? Fake a head injury and pretend I have no idea how we ended up here?

"Stop thinking so loudly," Jake grumbles against my shoulder, one hand tugging me closer. "It's too early for ethical dilemmas."

My breath hitches. "Why do you assume I'm having an ethical dilemma?"

He presses a kiss to my shoulder. "You forget I know you better than anyone. You live for ethical dilemmas."

He's not wrong, but at the same time, he's not totally right, either. "Knew me," I correct him.

"Hmm?"

"You *knew* me better than anyone. But that was ten years ago. I'm not the same girl I was then."

"You're not a girl at all." His broad palm strokes down my side, coming to rest on my hip. "You're a woman. And I, for one, am damn glad about that."

My lips curve into a smile, my eyes closed. "You're not half bad yourself," I tease.

"Gee, thanks," he deadpans, but his voice is fond.

I snuggle back into his embrace, enjoying being the little spoon. I can feel his erection between my ass cheeks, and I bite my lip to hold back a moan.

Yeah, he's going to leave. But right now, he's here. And I'm here. And we're technically still married, so...

Why not enjoy the time we have, while we have it?

For so long, I've lived my life doing for others. Now I'd like to do something for me.

Hand trembling, I roll over and press my palm against his cheek. "Jake."

His eyes sharpen. He places his hand over mine and turns his head to kiss my palm. "Rosa." His eyes are shining in the early-morning light, and my heart squeezes.

"Yes." It's an unspoken question, but I'm answering it anyway. *Yes, Jake. Yes, I want you.*

Yes.

Screw my alarm bells. I've got limited time with this man, so I might as well make the most of it.

I don't even care about our combined morning breath or the sheet lines I'm sure I have on my face or the doubts that keep tiptoeing into my brain.

Our hands drop away from his face, and we lie there, facing each other. I turn my palm in his and lace our fingers together.

His eyes heat, and his free hand slides up my back, tangling in the hair at the base of my neck.

He leans down and kisses me, and I...

I kiss him back.

Chapter 26

Jake

There's no finesse in this kiss, no delicacy. No, it's all teeth and tongue and clashing mouths, stealing my breath and my willpower at the same moment. I grip the back of Rosa's head and hold her close, licking into her mouth on a groan.

And she's right there with me, nipping my lower lip, then soothing it with her tongue. With almost superhuman effort, I wrench my mouth away from hers, breathing hard. She whimpers, then starts planting little kisses across my jaw and down my throat.

Rosa throws off the covers and wriggles out of her teeny tank top, pulling it over her head and dropping it next to the bed. Her panties follow. Then she gestures to my boxer briefs, the only thing I slept in last night. "Come on, catch up," she says, her voice a low murmur.

I shove them off in one swift move, my cock springing free as I strip. I toss them somewhere in the vicinity of the bedroom door and reach for her again.

Rosa rolls to her side, one hand reaching out to wrap around my cock. I shudder as she strokes it slowly, root to tip. She hums and strokes it again.

"Keep doing that and I won't last," I warn her. My body's already on fire, ready to explode.

She leans forward and licks around the tip. "Really? Do tell."

I circle her wrist with my fingers and slowly, deliberately, pull her hand away. Much as I'm enjoying the experience, I don't want it to be over before it really even begins. Her lips purse together in a tiny pout, but that changes to a grin as I sling one leg over her body until I'm hovering over her. I lean down and kiss her. She surges up, pressing into the kiss like that's all she needs.

Yeah, I kinda feel the same way.

Slowly, I lower myself so we're skin to skin, my arms bracketing her head, my legs between hers. I roll my hips, my cock sliding deliciously between her slick folds. She moans and wraps her legs around my hips, bringing us into even more perfect alignment.

If this is a fever dream, I never want to wake up.

She slides one hand down my spine, pressing gently on the small of my back. I take the hint and roll my hips again and again, until I break away and roll to the side, breathing heavily.

"If we're gonna keep this up, I need a condom," I tell her.

She nods and stretches over to the nightstand, taking a packet out of the box in the drawer. She hands it to me, and I roll it down my length, then lower myself back between her thighs.

We both groan as my cock nudges her opening. She wraps her legs around my waist, and I slide inside her. My movements are slow, unhurried, and she rolls her hips in time with mine.

I can feel my orgasm growing like a wave deep in the ocean,

building and building until I crash against her shore. She clings to my shoulders as we ride the cresting surf together.

I roll to the side, taking my weight off her, and pull her into my embrace.

If this is all we get before I leave, I want to make the most of it.

Long moments later, she mumbles into my neck, "We probably need to get up."

"I'm going to pretend you didn't say that. At least for the next five minutes."

I feel her smile against my shoulder. "I can give you five minutes."

What I want to say is *I want more than five minutes.* But I don't.

Because harvest is coming, and with it, a finish line that I can see growing closer every day. And the more I lean into the rhythm of being with Rosa, the more it's going to destroy me when I have to walk away.

Chapter 27

Rosa

E mi and Javi are both hard at work in the vineyard by the time Jake and I make an appearance, but I can't bring myself to care. The four of us remove the hail nets and fold them up, stacking them at the end of the rows of vines. We'll have to sort them out later—Wade's, Jansen's, Belmonte's, ours —but for now, our focus is on clearing the vineyard and inspecting the crops for damage.

I'm not as well-versed in identifying problems as Jake and the interns, so I hang back as they trek through the rows, lifting leaves, peering at the clusters of grapes. Javi takes notes as Jake points out areas for further inspection, and by noon everyone seems to be breathing easier. I pull Jake aside and ask him for his honest opinion.

"Not perfect," he says, "but pretty damn close. We were able to save most of the crops, and the little damage we did take on should reverse itself by next season."

I can feel my knees start to go weak, but I take a breath and force myself to stay standing. "Thank God," I breathe.

The outcome could have been disastrous, I know. If it wasn't for Jake, our ragtag crew, and the generosity of friends and family, we could have lost an entire season's worth of grapes. All our hard work, financial strain, and dreams—down the drain in one bad weather pattern. And helped along with a dash of sabotage.

I head to the house a few minutes earlier than the other three, promising them a quick lunch before they dive back into the work. As I putter around the kitchen, I glance at the metal sign on the wall that Jake gave me just two short weeks ago.

Somehow it's become my focal point, my guide for rebuilding this long-neglected winery. Bring it back to what it used to be, take it forward to what it could become.

The combination of past and potential has taken hold of me, and I don't want to let go.

And somehow I know I'm not just thinking about Caparelli.

I can't run from the truth anymore. When the harvest comes, I want Jake to be there. I want him by my side and in my bed. Our past, our present, and our potential.

But ten years ago, I let him leave. And now I don't know how to ask him to stay.

Once lunch is over, Jake gives Emi and Javier instructions for the rest of the afternoon. As they head out, he adds, "Rosa and I are going to return the hail nets, so when you're done, go ahead and go home for the night. Good work today."

I wait until the back door closes, then say, "We are?"

He leans over and kisses me, a brief hard smack of the lips. "Yup. No time like the present."

Well, okay then. I resist the urge to press my fingertips to my lips, still tingling from that kiss.

Jake drives us up the hill to the vineyard in his truck, and we load the stacks of nets into the back. I start moving the final bunch when he stops me with a hand on my arm. "Your cousins said those nets were originally from Caparelli."

I nod. "Some of them, but not all. And I refuse to give Uncle Geno a single thing to hold over my head anymore."

He doesn't smile, exactly, but the expression on his face tells me he knows the subtext of what I just said.

There's something powerful about being *seen*, I realize, and I didn't know how much I missed that until Jake came back into my life.

We wave goodbye to Emi and Javier and make the short drive around to the front of Jansen's property. Jake offloads the hail nets while I chat with the foreman, Antonio, thanking him again for the crew's help yesterday.

"Neighbors help neighbors," he says simply, tugging his hat a little lower against the blazing sun. "Turned out to be a pretty good evening after all that. Except for the business at the end."

I blush and try to figure out a way to change the subject.

"All done," Jake says, shoving his hands into his pockets as he joins us. "Let us know if there's any way we can repay the favor."

"Will do," Antonio replies and turns to go. Then he stops and calls over his shoulder, "Hey, forgot to mention this yester-day, but you don't happen to have a night crew, do you?"

Jake and I look at each other, confused. "No," I say. "Why?"

He shrugs. "Oh, Pedro said he saw someone in your vines a few times over the past couple weeks. He likes to walk later in the evening, when it's not so hot. He thought the guy worked for you, then realized he didn't see him yesterday when we were setting up the hail nets."

My heart starts beating faster. "Do you think he could identify whoever it was? If possible?"

"Suppose so. I'll ask him."

"And if anyone sees something like that again, let us know, okay?" Jake adds.

We thank him again and head to the truck. Once we're in the cab, I turn to Jake. "That was promising."

"Yep." He backs up the truck and turns it around, heading into town. "Let's drop these off at Wade's before we head over to Belmonte."

I nod, not particularly anxious to be around my uncle again so soon after last night's blowup. Maybe if we stall long enough, he won't be there when we bring the nets back.

A quick detour to Wade's, though, isn't enough to put off the inevitable, and far too soon we're turning onto the long road to Belmonte.

I realize it's been weeks since I've been here. And isn't it funny how these weeks at Caparelli with Jake have felt more like home to me than the place I lived and worked at for most of my adult life? I lean my head on the window and watch the scenery pass by, the long straight rows of vines climbing the hillsides on either side of the road to the family home.

Here and there I can see workers in the fields, so many of them, and a tiny rush of sadness overtakes me as I wish I could provide Caparelli with the same support. Then I look at Jake and think of Javi and Emi back on our land doing the same work on a smaller scale, and I know I'm doing my best. *We're* doing *our* best.

Nonna would be proud.

Jake pulls into one of the parking spaces to the side of the winery building, gravel crunching under his tires. He turns off the truck, and we both sit there for a moment, watching the buzz of activity all around us. It's late in the afternoon, and workers are putting away their equipment, chatting with each other, piling into their own vehicles to head home for the evening. I see my cousins, working alongside the crew, and I feel a pang of loss at what I never really had here. I was never part of the team.

Maybe that's what Nonna saw; maybe she knew my sisters and I would always be on the outskirts of a Belmonte/Caparelli combination that Geno ran. Maybe she knew we needed something just for us.

Geno walks around the edge of the barn, and I feel my body stiffen. Without speaking, Jake puts his hand on my knee and squeezes gently.

Maybe he knows what I need, too.

My gaze flicks over to the man Geno is talking to, and for a moment I can't breathe.

Then I gasp. "Holy *shit*."

Chapter 28

Jake

"What?" I turn my head to stare at Rosa, not sure what's making her swear so unexpectedly. I follow her gaze out the windshield and see her looking not at her uncle but at the man he's talking to.

I've never seen him before in my life.

"Who's that?" I ask, but she's already scrambling to undo her seat belt and jumping out of the truck.

"Damien?" she calls out, and both heads turn to look at her.

Geno looks as pissed off as he did last night. The other guy?

Looks guilty as hell.

"Who's Damien?" I mutter to myself as I follow behind her. She comes to a stop in front of the two, her hands on her hips, radiating all the fierce anger her five-foot-something frame can muster.

Not gonna lie—if I was one of those guys, I'd be a little scared of her.

"I thought you moved to the coast," she snaps, and I finally get with the program.

This is the guy who quit right before I showed up. The one who abandoned his job to open a surf shop.

Not a lot of surfing happening at Belmonte, though. So what the hell is he doing here?

"I, uh, changed my mind," the guy says, sounding just about as dim as he looks. Doesn't surprise me, with the way he left Caparelli—the crops half-dead from lack of water, the place barely tended to.

She turns her fury onto her uncle. "And why in the world would you hire this loser? He's incompetent!"

"Hey!" Surfer Boy says, but both Geno and Rosa ignore him.

Geno rolls his eyes and turns away. "Who I hire has nothing to do with you," he snaps.

Rosa looks over at Damien again. "How long have you worked here?"

He doesn't answer.

Leo walks up. "What's going on?" he asks, looking at all four of us in turn.

Don't ask me, man. I have no idea.

Rosa turns to her cousin. "How long has this guy worked here?"

"All summer," he replies, while Geno barrels into the conversation, trying to drown him out.

All summer.

Things start to click.

"So he's been working for you since what, May? Late April?" I ask, my eyes narrowing.

Leo nods. "Not the most dependable, but Dad insisted we keep him on."

"I am standing *right here*," the guy protests.

"Since late April, huh?" Rosa is talking to Leo but doesn't take her eyes off Damien. "Including the first couple weeks of June, right? When he was—theoretically, at least—working for me?"

"Wait, what?" Leo's head snaps in Damien's direction. "Why were you working two jobs? No wonder you didn't show up half the time back then." He looks at Geno. "I wanted to fire him, remember? And you wouldn't let me."

Geno looms over Leo, his eyes narrowed to slits. "You don't know what you're talking about. I suggest you stop right now."

"Nah, I think you're on the right track, Leo. Don't stop now." I clap him on the shoulder. "Doing great."

"What in the hell is going on?" Leo throws his hands into the air.

"See, if I'm reading this situation right, Damien here didn't have two jobs. Well, he was getting two paychecks, but..." I glance at the guy. "You were never really working for Rosa, were you?"

He glowers at me but says nothing.

Rosa steps forward. "What, were you *spying* on me for my uncle? Is that it?"

"How dare you," Geno snarls.

"Or maybe," I add, "it wasn't just spying. Maybe he was finding ways to make life difficult for you."

Geno's mouth snaps shut.

Rosa nods firmly. "The sabotage."

"What sabotage?" Geno and Leo say at the same time.

"Oh, come on," I scoff. "The water being cut off? The missing pest traps? The damaged hail nets? All the complaints to try to shut Caparelli down?"

Leo's hands are tight fists next to his body. He takes a step toward Geno. "You're trying to get Caparelli shut down?"

"Of course not!" Geno waves a dismissive hand at Rosa and

me. "Don't listen to them. They've held a grudge against me for ten years!"

"No, Uncle Geno, that's not what's going on," Rosa says. "All I want is a logical explanation for why Damien is here, on your staff, when he said he was leaving town a month ago. And why he was being paid by you when he was also working for me."

Geno clenches his jaw, a muscle jumping.

Leo takes a step toward Rosa. "You really think your place was being sabotaged?"

She looks at me, then turns back and nods. "We don't think it was being sabotaged. We're sure of it. So sure, in fact, that we've reported it to the police."

Damien starts to step to the side, clearly looking for an escape, so I pivot until I'm right next to him. I clamp a hand on his shoulder. "You don't have anywhere you need to be, do you?"

He slumps, looking at Geno, who turns away with a look of disgust on his face.

Gianni comes out of the house, probably pulled outside by our not-so-quiet argument. "What the hell is going on out here?" He looks at Geno. "Dad?"

The man says nothing, just stands there looking furious.

Leo says, "Someone's been sabotaging Caparelli. Rosa and Jake think it's this guy." He waves a dismissive hand at Damien.

"What? Why would someone sabotage Caparelli?" Gianni shakes his head. "I don't get it."

"See, if the vines die or get damaged in a hailstorm or we get shut down by the authorities over some bullshit made-up complaint, we won't be able to survive the season. And your father can swoop in and take it away from us." Rosa's eyes fill with tears, and she swipes furiously at them. "Whatever it takes, right?"

"I don't want the vines dead," Geno yells. "I just want them *back!*"

Silence follows his statement. I glance around and realize that everyone is looking at us. And I mean everyone. Workers, Aunt Janet, Vittorio.

Geno whirls around, stabbing a finger at Damien. "And *you!* I asked you to make it *difficult*, not damaged!"

"How else was I supposed to get her to give up?" Damien argues. "Even when I was working there, she kept at it, no matter what. I had to pretend to leave the area just to have a shot at screwing things up enough to break her down."

"Well, it didn't work, did it? She's still at it, thanks to this asshole," Geno growls, waving a hand at me. "And you *never* should have messed with the vineyard itself. Those vines are too precious to sabotage!"

"But not me, right, Uncle Geno?" Rosa's voice is quiet but steady. She takes a step back. "I want you to understand one thing: No matter what happens, my sisters and I will *never* give Caparelli back to you. We would sell it first."

"That's not what I meant," he snaps, but I've had enough. I pull out my phone and a business card and start dialing.

"What are you doing?" Geno asks me.

"Calling the cops." He grabs for my phone, but I move out of reach. I look over at Leo and ask, "Can you make sure Damien doesn't try to take off? I think Deputy Romero might want to have a word with him."

Leo nods, his mouth a thin line.

"You're calling the police?" Janet has a hand over her mouth.

"Of course." I shrug. "We're talking about property damage, false complaints, theft...the list goes on. If Geno is telling the truth and Damien here was going rogue, he's got nothing to worry about." I stop and correct myself. "Well, very little to worry about."

Rosa tugs at my hand, and I look down. "We forgot something," she says.

I tilt my head.

She turns to her cousins. "The hail nets are in the back of the truck. The extra ones, not the nets that belonged to Caparelli. Those, we're keeping."

She lifts our linked hands, smiles quietly, and leads the way back to my truck. She lowers the tailgate, the guys offload the nets, and I finally get Deputy Romero on the line.

The card he gave me came in handy after all.

Damien tries once again to sneak off, but Leo and Gianni each take a shoulder and seat him on the bumper of my truck, holding him there for the imminent arrival of Romero. Geno and Janet are arguing, some of the workers are surreptitiously snapping photos—probably for social media posts, and Rosa?

Rosa lifts up on her tiptoes and kisses me on the cheek.

"What was that for?" I murmur.

"That's for everything you've done this summer," she whispers back.

Then the deputy's truck rumbles up the drive, and we don't talk again for another two hours.

THE SKY IS FULLY DARK WHEN WE STEP INSIDE THE HOUSE, stomachs grumbling. "We should have stopped for dinner," I whine, leaning against the wall right next to the door.

"Don't be a baby," Rosa teases as she locks the door and turns on the light. "Have a bowl of cereal."

I follow her to the kitchen. "How'd you know that's my favorite?"

She taps her forehead. "Intuition. Also, we're both too exhausted to make a full meal."

"True enough."

We scarf down some cereal and fruit, and wash the dishes together, our hips and shoulders and hands bumping together as we move around each other in the small space. It feels cozy and peaceful and right.

Then Rosa turns off the light in the kitchen, and I double-check the locks on the front and back doors, and we head upstairs to bed.

Without having to say anything, we both turn left at the top of the stairs, and I join her in what's starting to feel like our room. This is dangerous, I know, but I can't bring myself to go back to my own room on the other side of the house. We take turns in the bathroom, and when I come back into the room, Rosa is in bed, in her little pajama set, the moonlight streaming down on the curves and valleys of her body under the covers.

For a moment, I imagine a lifetime of nights like this, where I slip under the covers with her after a long day and she curls into my side instinctively, her head on my bare chest, her arm around my waist.

I press a kiss to her forehead, and she hums sleepily in my arms. Her hand at my waist slides down to cup me, and I arch into her touch.

I can't help myself. I want all the memories I can take with me when I go.

Chapter 29

Rosa

I t's late in the morning when I finally wake up. Jake is gone, of course—probably out in the fields working.

It feels almost decadent, lounging in bed until—I check my phone, plugged in on the nightstand—a quarter to nine.

After the excitement and stress of the past couple days, I clearly needed the extra rest.

Yawning, I wander downstairs to the kitchen and pour myself a mug of coffee, doctoring it with half-and-half and a teaspoon of sugar. I grab an apple out of the fridge and sit at the table, scrolling through my phone while I eat.

It takes me way too long to notice the note on the kitchen table.

Meet me under the oak tree, it says in Jake's rough scrawl.

I flash back to all the other notes like this he's left for me over the years. Tucked into a jacket pocket, left in my locker at school, hidden under a barrel in the wine cave like a scavenger hunt with my favorite prize at the end of it.

My heartbeat picks up, and I hurry out the door, wondering what Jake is up to now.

I pass Emi and Javier in the vineyard, and they call out a cheery hello as I walk by.

The sun is hot overhead, and I wish I'd thought to wear a hat. Or sunglasses. I squint down the road, shading my eyes with my hand.

Jansen's place is abuzz, workers striding up and down the rows of vines, and I wave at a couple of people I recognize from the other night. I keep walking, and the big tree on the edge of the property comes into view.

He's sitting there, under the broad branches, a smile on his gorgeous, familiar face. All the other times we've met here flash through my mind—as children ready to play after schoolwork was done for the day, as friends heading off to the next summer party by the river, as boyfriend and girlfriend eager to spend every stolen moment together.

The day he proposed.

The day he came back—and helped me save Caparelli.

I hope, with everything in me, that this will be a happy memory, too.

He lifts a hand and waves me over. "Have a seat," he offers, patting the ground next to him.

I sit. "Is Jansen going to boot our asses for trespassing?"

"Nah." He plucks a blade of grass and twirls it between his fingers. "I got permission."

"Good call." I squint at him. "So what's going on?"

"I have something for you." He reaches over and pulls a box toward himself, then lifts out a stack of papers and hands them to me.

I glance down, and my heart drops.

They're our annulment papers.

"I don't understand." My hands are shaking.

He turns slightly so his whole body is facing me. "Rosa, for years I've hated your uncle for making your decisions for you. For forcing you to sign the annulment papers, for keeping you under his thumb, telling you what to do. Your choice, your autonomy, was taken away."

I nod, as much to encourage him to keep talking as it is to show that I'm listening.

"And last night, as I held you in bed, I realized I'm just as bad as he is."

"Jake, no—"

He holds his hand up. "Yes, I am. He took your choice away when he made you agree to the annulment. I took your choice away when I didn't file the papers without even discussing it with you. I kept you tied to me, legally, without your knowledge or your consent."

I stare at him, barely blinking.

"In all of this, you've been left out of the conversation. I'm done doing that, Rosa. Whatever happens now is all up to you."

"What do you mean?"

He pushes to his feet and starts pacing. "I mean if you want to file the papers, go ahead. If you want me to leave, I'm gone. But if you want me to stay..." He shoves a hand through his hair. "I'll stay, Rosa. I'll stay forever."

"Jake," I breathe. I'm trembling for a different reason now. "What—what are you saying?"

He holds out his hand, and I take it, rising to my feet. He's close enough I can smell the clean scent of him. I'm dizzy with it.

"I love you, Rosa. I always have, and I always will. But I want you to have the freedom to make this decision. For you. For us. It's your turn to choose."

"My turn."

"And if you want to take it slow, think about it, I can move into town."

Every cell in my body protests at that idea. "And the job offer?"

"I called Tomás this morning to tell him I wasn't available."

"You turned it down?"

He gives me a look that feels like a *duh* and shrugs. "Oak Creek Canyon is home, Rosa. I don't want to keep running. Whether or not we're together."

The sound of *that* is like a punch in the gut.

"And I also met up with Jansen to see if he'd be interested in hiring me as a consultant. After harvest, of course."

"Is...is he?"

Jake nods. "I figure that's something I'd be good at, whether it's full time or just a side hustle."

"You would." I bump my shoulder into his biceps. "So which would you rather do?"

"Well, if I'm working with you here, at Caparelli, it would have to be a side hustle. But ultimately, it's all up to you." He turns and faces me, still holding my hand. "So what do you say?"

It feels like all of Oak Creek Canyon is holding its breath right now.

All I can see, feel, touch is Jake.

Making this choice? It's scary. It's overwhelming.

It's the easiest thing I've ever done.

"I choose you," I say, stepping forward and wrapping my arms around him. "I choose us, Jake. I want you to stay."

He lets out a long, shaky breath, his arms tightening around my waist. "Thank God," he groans, his voice muffled.

We stand there for long moments, wrapped up in each other, until a distant shout from one of Jansen's crew startles us apart. Then we both laugh.

"So, what now?" Jake says. "I can still move out, you know. Take things slow."

"Slow?" I arch a brow at him.

"Ask you out on dates. Woo you." He grins. "I want to woo the shit out of you, Rosa."

"As delightful as that sounds," I tell him wryly, "we've spent the first ten years of our marriage apart. The farthest you're moving is into my bedroom, mister."

"Well, in that case..." Jake leans over and pulls something else out of the box. He hands me a black velvet pouch. "This is yours as well."

Hands shaking, I loosen the drawstring and tip the opening over my palm. A necklace tumbles out, with a rose pendant on it.

And nestled next to the rose is my wedding ring.

"Jake," I breathe, tears brimming.

"You're not supposed to cry," he says, panic rising in his eyes.

I wrap my arms around his neck and laugh damply. "Good tears," I tell him. "Definitely good tears."

I can't believe he saved them, all these years.

"I love you," I tell him finally. The words have been ready to break free for a while now, and it's a relief to let them out into the world. "I love you so much, husband."

"I like the sound of that. I love you, too. Wife." Jake kisses me, and I lose myself in the soft, deep, delicious sensation.

It's different this time. As we pull apart, I try to figure out why.

Then it hits me. That undertone of worry and uncertainty is gone. All that's left is the love, the joy, and the bone-deep knowledge that we're in this together.

I hand the necklace to him and lift my hair out of the way as he places it around my neck.

Maybe sometime soon the wedding band will be back on my finger, but for right now, it's exactly where it should be.

I take his hand and thread our fingers together, tugging him toward the house. "Come on, husband. Let's go burn these annulment papers."

"Whatever you say, sweetheart," he says, pressing a kiss to the back of my hand. "But I do have to get back to work eventually."

As we pass by our vines, I wave at Emi and Javi, and Emi grins when she spots our linked hands.

I glance at Jake. "I think our crew can hold down the fort for at least a little while."

It's not like everything is magically solved. We'll need to come clean with the rest of our families and friends, work on improving our communication skills, get to know each other again on a deeper level.

Treat Sasha to a spa day as a thank-you for encouraging me to keep the door to my wounded heart open a tiny bit. Just in case.

Tell Allegra and Bianca—and deal with the fallout when they realize literally everyone else knew before they did.

Fix the mess with the IRS before they come knocking with an audit.

I think I'll leave that one to Jake.

But overall?

I couldn't be happier.

Back at the house, we don't actually do anything with the annulment papers. Instead I tug him into my—our—bedroom and push him onto the bed. I climb on after and straddle him, my palms cupping his gorgeous, bearded face. We kiss and kiss, his hands gripping my ass and my blood pounding in my veins.

I break the kiss and move off of him, stripping as I go. He's naked in record time as well.

He springs forward and tackles me back into the pillows, pressing kisses to my neck and collarbone. I giggle at his sudden playfulness and the way his beard tickles my sensitive skin. His wide palm rests on my stomach, and I groan as it slides up and covers my breast.

His other hand slips between my thighs and teases me with gentle, tantalizing strokes. In no time at all, I'm ready.

Or maybe I've been ready all along—and just too stubborn to realize it.

I break the kiss and fumble in the drawer of my nightstand, pulling a condom out of the rapidly depleting box.

Then he rolls it on and pulls me close, and I smile and welcome him home.

THE END

...THANKS SO MUCH FOR SPENDING TIME WITH JAKE AND Rosa. I hope you enjoyed reading their story as much as I enjoyed writing it! Want more content? Sign up for my newsletter and get an exclusive bonus scene!

AND FOR MORE POUR DECISIONS, PICK UP KELLY Jamieson's Gone With The Wine and PG Forte's Que Sera, Syrah!

 Created with Vellum

Acknowledgments

They say it takes a village, and my village is populated with so many wonderful, supportive people. First, thank you to Kelly and PG. This book literally wouldn't exist without your creativity, enthusiasm, and support. I'm so glad we brainstormed this idea so many years ago—and then followed through! I'd write with you two again any time.

Thanks go to my first and longest-running beta reader, Maia. I appreciate you more than you could possibly know.

There were several winemaking professionals who patiently answered my questions and helped me figure my way around a (fictional) vineyard and winery. Thank you to Kim Roberts of Westport Winery, Brett Cummings, of Warr-King Wines, and most especially viticulturist Rodolpho Callado. Any mistakes in the book are one hundred percent mine.

Thanks to my local romance author crew—Rachel Grant, Kris Kennedy, Serena Bell—for the beta reads, the patience, the tapas, and the laughs. I couldn't have done it without you.

And finally, thanks to my wonderful family, for the years of support, encouragement, and cheerleading. (Shoutout to Emily for the fantastic playlist—you're hired for every book from here on out.) I love you all!

About the Author

From food to fiction, Kate likes things spicy! Award-winning, bestselling contemporary romance author Kate Davies writes books featuring strong, sexy men and women finding their happily ever afters. She enjoys traveling, reading, trying new recipes, and spending time with family and friends. Kate lives in the Pacific Northwest with her husband.

Also by Kate Davies

Seattle Nights

Taking the Cake

Strip Tease

Challenging Carter

Girls Most Likely To...

Most Likely To Succeed

Cutest Couple

Life of the Party

Royals and Rebels

Lessons in Love

Lessons in Trust

Standalone

Hooked

Hallowed Love

Home for Christmas

Going for Broke

www.ingramcontent.com/pod-product-compliance
Lightning Source LLC
Chambersburg PA
CBHW050146120726
47903CB00002B/510